Killing Alma

Published by Dennis Martin Carey

A CIP catalogue record for this book is
available from the British Library.

ISBN 978-0-9931943-5-1

Mum

Chapter 1

The end.

That's what I think it is.

Above my head, the hole in the roof of my house, the rumble of burning timber, the crack-and-pop of flames caught in a lake wind.

The punctured tyre is there, staring down from its fractured axle like a twisted eye weighing me in final judgement.

A yellow flame gives an exploratory lick through the roof's rip. Ribbons of smoke in the blue-sky gap are ghosted away by the breeze.

"Like in Dexter McEvoy's storybooks, Alma." I talk as if she were here, watching, waiting for my last breath. "The end of *my* story."

Alma is silent, the voice in my head hushed since I took my seat.

I draw on a cigarette. The light-headedness of nicotine-in-lung. I'll miss that when I'm gone.

A cough tries to punch its way out. I reign it in and mushroom a narrow cone of smoke into the moted air.

"The way Dexter read it, Alma." My voice grates like footsteps in gravel. "The…end. Heartbeat pause. His eyes rising from the page as he closed the book. 'What you think of that, Thomas?'"

But Alma knew all this. I'd told her all about Dexter McEvoy.

The cough comes. I wretch forward in the chair. My lungs crush empty, their ravaged surfaces sticky with the stain of a million smokes.

I wait for the in-breath. The wreckage, the draughty destruction of the house—my house, my home—blurs in watery eyes. I gasp the air and my lungs prise apart, the pain like peeling skin. It burns like a bastard.

I settle, wheezing, and search for a place to quench my cigarette. I crush it on the dust-covered arm of the chair, reckless, the black crescent of burnt varnish of no consequence. I'd suffer for that if Alma was here.

A rend of roof felt falls spinning, slaps to the ground.

Heat overhead, uncomfortable now.

Diesel fumes, sharp, acidic, sear my nostrils.

It won't be long.

Smoke descends, whirls around me.

I shut my eyes, wait for the explosion.

Slabs of iron expand and yawn. It sounds distant. Fatigue confusing me, or my blood-filled ear playing tricks?

The eruption doesn't come, but another memory does in its stead—I'm cramming thoughts in. "We were happy, Alma. A while, anyway." In the early days. Ephemeral love, driven out by strife and misfortune and disloyalty. My disloyalty.

Not like in a story, no. "In books, Alma, everything must make sense." Dexter told me that. In life, reality occurs, nothing has to make sense. Real life is messy.

The heat. I think I smell burning hair.

The tormented squeal of twisting timber.

A chimney stone drops through the rupture. It smashes by my chair. The charred pieces are lost in the debris.

Heavy metals, radiating heat, shift into view.

The house groans under the weighty movement.

My shoulders hunch in reflex, preparing to take on the burden.

A slide of slate tiles, one after the other, rapidly, hurl themselves through the gap, shatter by my sandals. Shards prick the stretched skin of my swollen feet.

The ceiling drops. The end. I catch hold of a breath.

A shroud of embers, soot, roof-dirt my age, descends around me.

I hiccup a cough, blink away the dust.

I am still alive. And my heart beats steadily in my chest. I'm numbed by it all.

The busted tyre is inches from my face. It revolves, stops, carousels back a quarter-turn with an anxious whine. It stares intently with its lug-holed pupil. Smoke seeps from the rubber like incense from a priest's funeral thurible.

What I did was wrong. It was all wrong. All my fault.

A flame is born on the cushion of Matty's chair. I'll miss Matty. John Kavanaugh not so much, no. Wait until Kavanaugh sees what I have done.

The flame ignites memories of my baby girl. I didn't want to think about Noleen. Not now. Was what happened to Noleen my fault, too?

I'm caught unawares, thought I was beyond emotion. It climbs from the pit of my stomach, girdling my chest like a cooper's hoop, the iron grip of it constricting my ribs. On up, around my throat, choking off my breath.

Guilt. I'm overwhelmed by guilt, as if I've been dropped into a barrel of shame.

I wish I could go back, change everything, make things right.

I tilt my head at the tickle of a tear. It crests a cheekbone, gathers dust in a surge of remorse. More tears come, hiccupping blubs and thick, racking sobs. The guilt overflows, spills down my face in streaks.

I can't speak. But I have to speak. Before I die. Before the end. I owe her that much.

"I'm sorry, Alma." I inhale hot air. "I am truly sorry."

Lighted embers drip around me. Shadows flicker through the smoke. Flames roar.

The fuel will catch, and it will be done.

I'm exhausted.

Autumn. A good season to die.

I'm ready now, ready for the end.

"Tommy?" A woman's voice, calling. "Tommy. What in the name a fuck?"

Chapter 2

It should have been the end. It was what Alma would have wanted. It was what I deserved.

But the world went on with autumn, my heart went on with its beating, and my story continued for another while. Only stories in books make sense, follow a plan. Remember? In life, not so much.

It was, however, the start of the end.

It's what brought me here, to this bed.

But I should go back. Back further. Tell what brought me *there*. Tell my story. It's what my friend, Dexter McEvoy, would expect.

Chapter 3

It was the sight of an unfamiliar vehicle in the village that roused me from my idle wistfulness. The size of it, the glisten of the paintwork, the distinct stately grille. Rare to see a car so big drive down a track so small.

The previous day had been hot, the sun at midday directly above our heads casting short shadows. That day was grey, a cold bite in the breeze, a day for tea.

The car halted beside my front yard.

I put down the pot, reached over the sink, pulled back the bottom net curtain. A broken cuff button tapped the glass as I rubbed a circle clean with a sleeve of my jacket.

The head and shoulders of a stranger in a peaked cap backed up to open a rear door. He stood to attention, like a Garda Síochána tending the Taoiseach outside the Steward's Lodge up in Dublin. He didn't salute.

There was something odd about the way the door opened.

It had been a good few years, but I immediately recognised the man who climbed out of the car. Had it been twenty years?

With recognition, came a prickling rush of adrenaline. My hand shook when I brought the cigarette to my lips.

His hair was thinner but still a creditable shade of straw, and swept back over the ears like folded wings. How old would he be? He carried only a little more timber, and he moved like his father. Can you inherit an injury limp?

What did the multi-millionaire from Manchester, want with me?

He checked his phone—he'd be lucky to have reception—and pulled his coat collar up around his neck. He accepted something from the driver, and walked towards the kitchen door, picking steps between the inquisitive geese that crowded the yard.

The house an embarrassing shambles, and he was approaching my door.

The heart in me raced. I had a headful of questions. Did he know about me calling on his wife, Rhiannon, in London? Was Rhiannon over here with him? Or, was he simply here to pay his respects?

He knocked on the door. It was not the metallic knock of an iron piece of door furniture in the style of a goose in flight, I had yet to repair that, but the jaunty bare-knuckle rap of a confident man's fist.

I hesitated, cast around me at the chaos, considered not answering.

He knocked again, impatient in the cold.

I quenched the cigarette in the sink and shuffled towards the door, cringing at the pain in my feet. I paused at the kitchen table to lean and rest.

What if I didn't let him in?

That was the moment. I can nail it down to that precise moment. The commencement of my story's final act. It's remarkable how one seemingly insignificant decision can determine so much.

You see, I half hoped he'd go away, get back in his expensive car and leave. But it was only half a hope, nought-point-five as my friend, Matt Darcy, might say.

The other half was the hope of news of Rhiannon. A pathetic, longing hope, yet it was a stubborn curiosity. Did he carry a message about her? My head spun in desperate confusion.

Only the first half-hope was likely, yet the curious half won.

I swallowed the shame of the clutter, reached for the latch, pulled the door open.

John Kavanaugh beamed a smile of porcelain-white teeth and threw an arm wide. "And, sure here he is. Mister Cassidy himself." The greeting was more extravagant than our relationship warranted. "Been a while, Tommy. Too feckin long, I'm thinkin."

The accent was polished, anglicised, yet more old-Mayo than any accent I heard from those who lived here their entire lives. He stole away the h's that went after t's and put them after s's. It gave s's the hiss of the sea running ashore on sand. He pronounced it, *Mishter*, the sibilance a deliberate ingratiation.

"Thought I'd stop by to see my old friend." *T'ought I'd shtop by.*

I didn't recall him ever being a friend.

"Keepin well, you are?"

"Hello, John," I said.

He wore a fur coat, sheepskin, calf length, cloaked over his suit and hanging off his shoulders like an oversized opera cape. It looked like the shed hide of a mammoth beast.

"I'm fecken froze." He leaned towards me on thin legs, as though braced. "Can I come in?" His nose was pointed, beak-like. His hair was a uniform blonde, too uniform for it not to be the work of a costly Manchester coiffeuse. Parallel comb tracks ran through its rigid slickness like a busy rail junction. He looked like a lanky bird, but furry and with an over-extravagant crown.

I held my ground at the door and reassessed my options. He didn't seem angry with me.

He lost patience with my silence. "Can you spare five minutes, Tommy?" *Shpare*. "I've a tiny little proposition for you." His narrow neck moved inside the studded white collar of his red pinstripe shirt without touching material. "I think you'll very much like what I have to say."

He leaned back, threw a glance up the field, and unveiled a litre bottle of whiskey from the folds of the fur coat.

He was the brother-in-law of my dead wife, and he was bearing a gift. It would have been churlish to deny him entry.

*

I poured John Kavanaugh tea, the pot unsteady in my grip.

He rubbed his hands and warmed them at the fire, bent as though about to dive forehead-first into the flames.

Flaps of fur brushed charred turf mould back and forth over the granite hearth. Alma's hearth. She wanted a hearth and mantle in granite. They were bigger than what I would have chosen, but their hulking, sharp-edged, stony greyness provided the blend of bulky extravagance and traditional sturdiness that Alma desired. It was a finishing touch, her contribution to the work she insisted be done on the kitchen.

"Would you prefer whiskey?" I asked.

"No, thank you. That's for you, Tommy. A present from John Kavanaugh." If he knew about me contacting Rhiannon, he didn't show it.

I stirred in milk.

"To keep the chill from old bones," he said. "You need something over here." He laughed. A hollow laugh, it too lacking any warmth. "Can you believe the weather? Was yesterday the summer? One bloody day?"

He accepted his tea standing up. Gold cufflinks peeked from the sleeve of his suit jacket when he reached for the drink.

Heat from the fire lifted a chemical smell of dry-cleaning solvent from his coat's pelt.

John Kavanaugh looked healthy, all-in-all. The hair, the orange skin, the bleached teeth. A monied, expensively groomed type of healthy. He carried an air of procured youthfulness.

I wondered how he could spend all that money on himself yet, somehow, still manage to look cheap.

There was a smear of goose shit on the turn-up of his trouser.

"Grand car," I said, for the want of something to say.

"It's a Rolls-Royce, Tommy."

"Is it?" I glanced at the window to look suitably impressed.

"A Rolls-Royce Phantom."

I widened my eyes. "A phantom?"

"Available in over forty thousand colours, and the paint's put on by a bloody robot." He laughed again.

Forty thousand colours and he chose gold. So predictable.

He was going to tell me how much it cost. The man who abandoned his wife and children to hardship and struggle was going to tell me how much he spent on a Rolls-Royce Phantom.

"You'll never guess the price, Tommy."

Here we go. "Heap of money, I bet."

"I won't say, but I'd near to feck-all change from a million."

"Euros?"

"Pounds, Tommy. English pounds. I'd need to hire a two-tonne pickup if I was to pay for it in euros. Not working out to be worth much at all, are they? This country was ripped off when they brought in the euro. Expensive coming home nowadays. Prices have gone up to hell."

He'd left for England almost as soon as he could walk, but he still referred to Ireland as 'home'. "The savage loves his native shore." Daddy used to say that to me.

"A heap of money, all right." I turned to the draining board, spooned sugar into my tea.

"Get nothing for a million these days, Tommy."

I regretted allowing him in, though I was curious about his proposition.

"Now it's the kilometers," he said. "They'll be some scam to rip you off with the kilometers as well, just you watch."

I stared out at the gold Rolls-Royce Phantom and wondered what a million pounds sterling would amount to in euros at the current exchange rate. The spoon chinked in my chipped cup. "That your driver?" I asked.

"My chauffeur," he said. "Who'd have thought it, Tommy? The old fella would shite himself if he were still here to see me now."

His father would not have liked the colour of the car.

"Will he take a cup of tea?"

"Mark doesn't drink tea, Tommy. A funny story. When he was a lad, he worked for British Gas digging holes in Manchester. Apprentice to an Irish gas fitter. Didn't yer man have Mark making the tea every five minutes. 'Make the tay, Mark?' That's all he got out of your man. Went on for three years. 'Mark, go an make the tay?' Didn't all the tea-making put Mark off tea for life."

“Is that right?” It wasn’t that funny a story. Was it rude of me not to turn around and face him?

“Won’t touch a drop since.”

A rush of doubt and suspicion pricked at my nerves. Something wasn’t right. John Kavanaugh was drinking tea from a stained mug telling me stories about his chauffeur. I’d given up hope of any news about Rhiannon. I wondered what his proposition might be.

Mark stood sentinel by the gold Rolls-Royce and gazed around the village. His chest swelled as he inhaled the view. He looked smart in his uniform.

Kavanaugh’s greasy-window reflection surveyed the kitchen. He shook his head at the disarray, at the blackened-plaster seam of damp fungal growth that ran from the door to the corner, at the dust layered on the empty shelves.

He swayed his body at the unwashed crockery that littered the table like abandoned coracles on a lake and hopped himself clear of the turf burns in the hearthrug beneath his feet.

It was astounding how things could deteriorate so quickly. Alma buried three whole weeks and I was already living in squalor.

He spotted the stain on his turn-up, “Feck’s sake”, and reached to wipe it with a handkerchief.

I absently stirred another spoon of sugar into my tea. It would be too sweet to drink now. I dearly wanted to ask after Rhiannon, prompt him for news, any news, but I thought better of it. I coughed into a fist and waited.

“Listen, Tommy. My condolences about Alma.” About time he mentioned her. “I heard it happened here in the house.”

His words stabbed me. I gripped the drainer, plunged the wet spoon into the sugar bowl, shovelled more sugar into my tea. Dug again with the spoon. Brown blotches spread in the bowl. Alma would be shouting at me by now about the lumps. Tea spilled from the cup with the vigour of my clumsy stirring.

“Tommy, you all right?”

I turned and faced Kavanaugh. “I explained everything to the hospital.”

Kavanaugh raised his free hand in submission. "No, listen, sorry. I didn't mean..." He shook his head, tittered nervously. "No, no, Tommy. I don't care what happened. I mean, I do care, obviously. Of course I care. But I didn't mean anything. God, no. I was only..."

It calmed me to watch him squirm.

"Not at all," he said. "She was a lovely woman, sure enough. One of the best. I just…" He stepped further away from the fireplace. "No, God. That's not why I'm here."

I believed him. He hadn't called to learn the truth about what happened to Alma.

"No, we wanted to be back for the funeral," he said. "When we heard. But you know how it is. Work and the kids and everything."

The kids and everything? I knew for a fact it wasn't his children who kept him from attending Alma's funeral. Rhiannon had confirmed that.

"I understand," I said, with a forgiving smile.

"Sorry for your troubles, Tommy." There was little solace or compassion in his words and less in his face.

I smiled in acknowledgement. "Of course."

He made as if to extend a hand, then didn't, rubbed the back of his neck instead, fidgeting like a man who all of a sudden wanted to be elsewhere. "Look it," he said, his hand back in the refuge of a pocket. "I'll be in town tomorrow night. Will you be in yourself?" Another porcelain smile. "I'd like the two of us have a quiet pint together."

A quiet pint in town with John Kavanaugh, the multi-millionaire from Manchester? It was a swift change of tack.

"We'll do that, we will?" he said. "Raise a glass to Alma."

I scratched at my stubbled chin. It seemed I'd have to meet him for a drink if I was to learn why he came to see me.

"I need to be off, Tommy." He scanned the walls and the mantelpiece for a clock. Disappointed, he wedged his cup into a space on the table and jerked an arm. The rich sheen of a heavy gold watch slid from under the sleeve and crashed into his thumb. He gave a final glance back at the hearth. "Tell you what I'll do," he said. "I'll get you picked up in the Royce. No need you to worry about transport. We'll have a drink for Alma, and I'll run through my proposition."

The proposition, yes. The visit was only about his proposition. I checked on the car.

Outside on the lane, Matt Darcy, half man, half bicycle, peddled towards the house from the direction of Mulligan's bridge. He pulled back on the brakes and squealed to a halt behind the Rolls-Royce. A conversation started up between him and Mark. Matty lay over the handlebars in a coquettish manner, rested his chin in the palm of a hand. His head bobbed when he spoke.

I cleared my throat and smiled.

Alma wouldn't have minded a spin in a Rolls-Royce but would have taken issue knowing it belonged to John Kavanaugh. Her last journey to town was in a lorry, on the way to the hospital. My last journey into town was for her funeral, a few days later.

Matty was off the bicycle, wheeling it around the Rolls-Royce, peering and pointing. He was interrogating Mark with a barrage of questions, nodding intently at the answers.

Matty was flirting with the chauffeur.

Mark took steps to squeeze himself between Matty and the Phantom for fear Matty would scratch the car with a brake lever.

I decided I would meet John Kavanaugh in town, find out about his proposition. Plus, I'd never ridden in a Rolls-Royce.

Outside, Matty allowed himself to get tangled up in the pedals. He took his bicycle everywhere, he knew how to wheel it without getting tangled in the pedals.

Mark held the bike upright while Matty freed himself. Matty thanked him with a pat on the arm. They shared a laugh.

I turned to face John Kavanaugh. "That'll be grand, John."

"Settled, then."

I noticed he hadn't touched the tea, and wondered what it was, other than the money, that Rhiannon ever saw in him.

Chapter 4

I got to know Rhiannon Harkin during the summer of 1984, well before the country was bothered by euros or kilometers. At the time, I earned decent-enough money at the Owencas Electricity Generating Station, but across Ireland, it was a period of recession and emigration and crippling unemployment. Yet, in the swelter of Buckley's Dance Hall, none of those things bothered Rhiannon Harkin.

The venue was low-domed with corrugated iron walls and chemical toilets. The music resounded off the roof. An ex-priest sold Buckley's soft drinks from the boot of a car backed up to the fire exit. Lads patrolled the dance floor's perimeter with expectant faces and traded drunken advances with cautious girls.

I never patrolled, too old for that carry-on. A few dances, if I was lucky, and I usually left on my own.

If I'm honest—and I say this only to provide context – though never the most assured with women, I wasn't the ugliest yoke on the street corner. I understand a mother's praise holds limited currency in this regard, but when I was young my mammy would wrap me in her arms and whisper, "You're the handsomest boy in Ireland," before kissing my face until it glistened with her affection. She later took to calling me her Montgomery Clift after I took her to watch *A Place in the Sun* in a draughty cinema house in Gortcastle in celebration of my first wage packet. Something about the hair and the eyebrows, apparently. Clift's character in the film decided to kill off his wife so that he could marry a more exciting lady played by Elizabeth Taylor.

Any contact I did have with women was usually initiated by the woman. So it was with Rhiannon Harkin.

"You look like a man at a dance who's lookin to get off with someone specific, but she hasn't yet turned up." She trapped me in the stare of her violet eyes. Before I could escape, she stepped close, body bumping body, her head next to mine, and whispered over my shoulder. "Will I do until she arrives?"

I'd noticed her dancing. I could feel her heat against me. "No," I said.

Her cheek glanced mine as she stepped away.

I missed her immediately. "I mean no, I wasn't looking for someone specific."

She smiled like a film star. "So are you goin to ask me to dance? Or would you rather carry on drinkin your red lemonade?"

The members of a touring five-piece from Coventry in England called Seldom Sober were shouting into microphones. The floor heaved with people. If it wasn't for the two-finger shove in the spine from Matt Darcy as he relieved me of my plastic cup, I'd have opted for the red lemonade.

She was too young. And too beautiful. The men crowded around the exits like hesitant unpenned cattle knew it, the women casting I-want-to-look-like-that glances as they danced around their handbags knew it, the handsome accordion player fronting the band knew it.

And she knew it. I could see it in her walk as I followed her like a reluctant uncle to the middle of the floor. I half expected her to abandon me and the whole dance hall to erupt laughing and pointing in some callous elaborate hoax.

She didn't abandon me. She said, "You dance well, Tommy Cassidy."

I was never more grateful for my mother's tuition. "Thank you."

Chapter 5

"You look like shite," Matt Darcy said.

I had taken to drinking heavily. I smoked too many cigarettes, swallowed too many tablets. I had a progressive disease that had turned the simple act of drawing breath into a wrestle with my ribcage. I knew I looked like shite, but I didn't want Matt Darcy reminding me. I struck back low. "I'm only after burying my wife."

Matty didn't flinch. "And you'll end up beside her the way you're at." He spoke like this because he cared. It was typical of Matt Darcy to care. He sat in his usual seat, the other side of the fire, and hung his cap off the end of the chair's arm.

Outside, the crush of stone under the tyres was louder than the hum of the engine as the Rolls-Royce Phantom pulled away from the house.

"How're things?" he said.

"Grand."

Matty didn't look convinced. "That cough?"

"The doctor was out at me."

"And?"

"It's grand."

"I doubt–"

"Leave it, Matty." I shrugged an ache from my arm. Mountain rain had worked its way into my bones, no summer long enough to dry me out.

Matty sat back in the chair. He had a tired face, dimpled at the cheeks and square of jaw yet it never lost the hollow-temple, skull-clinging look of the weary athlete.

Matt Darcy was my friend, probably my truest friend. He was kept from my house for months, but when Alma died he was back at my side, being a friend.

I smiled. "Should you be riding a bike with your own ailment?"

Matty's features creased in question.

"How did you get on?" I said. "At the hospital."

He pinched the flab at his throat, his face a picture of sudden worry. "Fine, yeah."

"You want to tell me?" I said.

"If you want to know."

"Up to you. I understand if it's delicate."

"Too private, ya mean?"

"I understand if you think that."

"I didn't come in to talk about me and my ailment."

I said nothing. He was aching to tell me.

He glanced at the window. "What did Kavanaugh want?"

I lifted my eyebrows, waited.

Matty gave in. "Let me tell you about the hospital firstly."

"Grand."

"Ya remember the initial visit, ya do?" he said. "When yer man stuck the camera up?"

"The exploratory visit."

"You make it sound like preparation for a land survey. It was an initial investigation. Well, this was a new doctor."

I took a cigarette from the packet. Matty didn't smoke.

"When he had the camera up," Matty said, "he asked me if the tumour had been marked."

"Who did?"

"The second doctor."

"Marked?"

"I told him it had, with a tattoo.'"

I blew out the match. "What type of tattoo?"

"It's not a bloody Celtic cross or a shamrock! It's just a mark. He marked the bloody thing. He called it a tattoo."

"The first doctor?"

"Right. But listen. When he put the camera up there."

"Who?"

"Up me."

"I meant, who put the camera up?"

"The second doctor. Listen to me."

I flicked the match into the fire. "I'm listening."

"I said, and I wish I hadn't. I said, about the tattoo."

I nodded for Matty to continue.

"I told him he was the first person I'd shown it off to.'"

"Why?"

"What do ya mean, 'why'? Did you expect I'd be goin around town lettin people take a peek up my anus?"

"No."

"Why would I go around town doin that?"

"No. I meant why did you wish you hadn't said that?"

"Because he started laughin."

"I have you now."

"I mean really laughin."

"Shaking laughing?"

"Correct."

"And he was holding the camera?"

"That's right." Matty half-raised himself off the seat as though easing the memory of the discomfort.

"It was uncomfortable?"

"And unprofessional."

"So how did you get on?"

"I told him to stop the laughin."

"No, the results. Of the examination."

"It'll be weeks. Or months. He cut a bit away to be sent off." Matty settled back in his chair, stared into the fire. "Results in a few months." He ran a thumb around the end of his wide chin.

I could nearly hear the churn of his troubled mind. "Try not to worry, Matty."

"I'm not." He rubbed his hand back and forth along the leg of a trouser.

"Are you worried?"

"Yeah. A bit."

"Are you thinking about arranging the wake?"

Matty barked out a laugh. "The livin wake?"

"Yeah."

"Fuck off, Tommy."

The bowel cancer scare was a recent development. Matty first mentioned it on the day of Alma's funeral.

"Only the good die young, Matty. Isn't that what they say?"

"I'm neither young nor good." Matty shoved his spectacles back up his nose.

He wasn't young, neither of us was, but he was good. The best man I'd ever met.

"I'll be fine," he said.

"You better be."

"Anyhow," he said, wide-eyed, moving the conversation on. "What did that phallus want?"

"You mean John Kavanaugh?"

"Has he lost weight?"

"Gained it. A bit. I thought."

"Streak a piss like the father."

"A drink in town. Brought me that." I swung my chin at the bottle of whiskey on the drainer.

Matty made as if to check his watch, but he didn't wear a watch. "Unopened, I see. Too early, or have ya gone off Jamieson?"

I didn't react.

"Surprised it's lasted this long, is all."

He was goading me. I rose above it. "I was saving it until you called."

He scoffed.

The humour of his visit hadn't lasted long. It was the way of things, lately. We were back to his interfering ways.

"Will you pour two measures or shall I wait until you leave?"

"What if I take it away with me?" he said.

I'd kill him stone dead before I'd allow him to do that. "Matty, just–"

"All right, so." Resigned, he drew his hands up onto the arms of the chair. "Glasses?"

"I've cups."

Matt Darcy pushed himself up, stepped over to the sink in his too-big Wellington boots. His rickety body creaked and groaned as he turned and twisted in his search through cupboards.

A sportsman in his youth, and well into his thirties, Matty paid for those athletic endeavours in breaks and sprains and torn ligaments. His elderly frame remained slim, but he carried excess weight around his midriff, the belly, according to Matty, a genetic gift from his father.

"An ominous sign, Tommy." He blew dust from a cup. "You've sunk to the depths of alcoholic depravity when you start drinkin your whiskey from a cup." He poured a generous measure, handed it to me. "You're drinkin with the Devil when you sup whiskey from a vessel that's meant to take tea. You realise that, don't you?"

It was rhetorical. I'd been drinking with the Devil ever since I buried Alma. I knew about the Devil, and Matty knew I knew about the Devil. I flicked my cigarette stub into the hell-heat of the turf fire. It flared before being consumed in eternal damnation.

Matty peered into a mug from the drainer. "Holy God." He stirred its contents with a finger, emptied it into the sink, ran the mug under the tap for half a minute, shook it dry. He resumed his seat. "You've not told me why," he said, his voice raised a pitch by the swallow of whiskey.

"Why what?" I delved pockets for another smoke.

"I'm not askin why the first sip a whiskey should burn the bloody neck of a man." He grimaced at the mug. Matty didn't drink. Not really. Not like me. His face tilted in a conspiratorial smile. "Nor why it is I'm attracted to younger men in caps and uniforms who know a thing or two about expensive cars." His thin eyebrows ascended over the frame of his spectacles, stretching his features.

"I saw you," I said. "Outside. Is he queer?"

"Potentially. But why does John Kavanaugh want to take *you* for a drink in town? And, more to the point, why is he tryin to soften you up with bottles a Jamieson?"

I lit a cigarette, filled my lungs. "Something about a proposition."

"I knew it!" Matty was giddy, buoyed by the whiskey, perhaps. "When I saw the Roller outside the house I knew from the bridge it was John Kavanaugh. The Manchester multi-millionaire wants to buy the place off you, don't he? Not happy owning the big house beyont, and the half-a-Mayo of land that goes with it. He now wants your plot as well."

"He calls it a Royce."

"Who does, what?"

"The Roller. John Kavanaugh calls it a Royce."

"He can go and ride the wheel a my bike. The father was the same, a proper bollix. It's not good to speak ill of the dead but that gimp of a limp he effected? Like this." Matty rose. "And nothing wrong with him." Matty sat down again.

Old John Kavanaugh, young John Kavanaugh's father, was hostile territory for Matty. He was about to denigrate old John Kavanaugh, not without cause, but I'd heard it all before.

"The man was full of hate. Hated tinkers, hated gays, hated the disabled, and he especially hated disabled gay tinkers." Matty's cheeks were florid from whiskey and sudden fury. "And he was a sorry excuse for a footballer."

"Young John didn't say anything about buying the place." I said and left my drink down on the hearth. A stain of blood on the granite lay beneath the cup like a misshapen coaster. An innate respect for the dead made me move the cup.

"Be more like it if he gave a few pound to his wife," Matty said.

I sat up.

"Are they still married?" Matty said. "There's talk he's taken up with another woman in Manchester."

I reached for my drink and took a gulp. It was only talk, and talk had a way of being wrong.

"Did you not think to ask after Rhiannon?" Matty said. "Would've been tricky, all right, I suppose. Awkward, like."

I didn't respond, the burn of the whiskey a welcome distraction. Matty had no reason to mention Rhiannon. Flirting with an eligible chauffeur was one thing, flirting with delicate talk about Rhiannon was another thing altogether. I waited for the conversation to veer back onto steadier ground.

In the uneasy silence, a bubble of air, trapped for millennia, hissed out of a hot sod of turf like a dry fart.

Matty grimaced as the whiskey tore at him again. "His name's Mark." He nodded at the window. "Tidy lookin in his cap."

I relaxed my shoulders, relieved, warmed by amber flames on the outside, by amber whiskey on the inside. "Anyhow," I said, "it's not for sale."

"Ya say that, but ya don't know what he's offering, yet."

"Hasn't offered anything."

"I'll value it."

"It's not for sale."

"What would ya hope for?"

The whiskey brought a comfort, numbed the pain in my lungs. I whispered, "Where would we go?", and threw most of my cigarette into the fire.

Matty pursed and stretched pliable lips, pushed his spectacles up on his nose, sat forward in his seat. He pointed with a finger of the hand that held his cup. "You'd be set for life. You could go anywhere ya wanted."

There was nowhere I could go. I wouldn't leave Duncarrick, and I wouldn't leave Alma. Not now. I'd miss the few ornaments of hers I had left, the smell of her black dresses hung in the wardrobe, our conversations in which she'd chastise me about my drinking. I didn't want to leave.

Matty's mind had also set off on a journey, a journey whose bends and contours were reflected in the transformations of his flexile face. His features settled. A single eyebrow arched up his forehead. "Would ya get a million for it?"

I almost choked on a swallow of phlegm.

"Ah, no," he said. "I'm coddin."

"Well, don't."

"Ya wouldn't get that much, no. Ya might if it was up in Phoenix Park. Prices are flyin in Dublin, according to the papers."

I reached for another cigarette while Matty rambled.

"Wouldn't get that sort a money in this village. Arsehole a Mayo."

Matty was wrong about the village being the arsehole of Mayo. He liked to disparage the village, and County Mayo, and, when he had enough drink taken, the whole of Ireland. For a man that made a living selling it, he held a strong dislike for the land.

"You go right up to the castle, you do?" Matty wrinkled and stretched his nose. The spectacles bobbed. "Down to the road…" An absent whisper to himself. "Over as far as the maren." He was surveying the land in his head and plotted its outline in the air with a warped finger. "To the children's rest."

I could hear the geospatial reckonings click in his brain, a brilliantly facile mathematical-engine of a brain, its whirring cogs no worse for being lubricated by a few sups of whiskey.

"Thirty-nine and three-quarter acres," he said, triumphant. "Give or take a quarter acre. And subject to a cadastral survey."

I was always amazed when he reminded me that he was able to do that. It made me wonder if Matty still submitted mathematical conundrums to the local newspaper. 'The quickest way to add up all the numbers from 1 to 100', that sort of thing.

He noticed me admiring him. "Impressive, isn't it? You'd have more if it wasn't all piled up in a heap."

My land wasn't flat, far from it. It climbed steeply from behind the house to what Daddy christened 'The Rise'. Flat for a hundred strides or so and up again at an angle vicious enough to rip the lungs from the youngest shepherd. Up and up as far as 'Castle Mound'. But it wasn't a mound, it was a mountain. My mountain. Daddy farmed mountain sheep. When I was able for the chest-heaving climb, so did I.

"One hundred and twenty-five thousand euro," Matty said, and winked. "Including the house. Everything."

"What's the exchange rate from pounds to euros?"

The country was in the process of converting its road signs from miles to kilometers. While I refused to acknowledge the inevitable metrification of all things numerical, Matty had equipped himself with a rapid conversion he could do in his head. The euro currency system, introduced several years earlier, caused consternation throughout the country, but Matty was perfectly at ease with its monetary conversions. My arithmetic had gone with my Irish, and anyway, Matty helped me through every year of number at school, so oughtn't I keep him sharp?

"Pound or Punt?"

"English."

"Are you thinkin England?" he said. "Stick a handful of earth into yer bag and off? Where'd ya go in England?"

I gave a phlegmy laugh. "John Kavanaugh's Rolls-Royce. He reckons it cost nearly a million pounds sterling."

"And you believe him?"

"Why wouldn't I?"

"When the words came out of his mouth, did they smell of bullshit?" He straightened his back. Hairs that sprung from his nostrils stirred as he inflated himself ready for the calculation. He shut his eyes when he spoke. "Mornin papers quote one point four nine to the pound, makin a million worth one and a half. Subtract a percent." The eyes opened. "Fourteen hundred and ninety. Thousand, that is."

"Fourteen hundred and ninety thousand euro?" Muscles in my stomach clenched and folded me forward. I coughed into a palm. "For a car?"

Matty swallowed the rest of his whiskey. His neat ears flushed red. "If ya sell up, you'll probably have enough money to buy the woman with the stickin-back wings that sits on the bonnet." He flicked a hand at me.

I smiled for Matty, and wondered at the absurd, squandering stupidity of John Kavanaugh and his taking up with a new woman in Manchester.

Chapter 6

"Here."

"What time is it?"

"Look around you, see the clocks."

"You sure?"

"Of what?"

"Are you sure this is what we want?"

"Swallow them down."

"What about you?"

"Lie back your head."

"Was that too many?"

"We agreed. I'll take care of it. Just rest now."

Chapter 7

A few days after the dance with Rhiannon Harkin, I called into Buckley's Bar and Lounge in town. I'd been on the mountain after work and had the dog with me. I sent it over to the wall where it lay contented, looking back at me with loyal eyes.

I was listening to Buckley tell me of a friend of his who was heading away to America and had a car to sell, when Rhiannon strolled into the pub with five or six friends. She wore a summer dress, her arms bare.

"He's after a quick sale," Buckley said. "Reckon he'd let it go soft, for cash."

Lisa-Marie Gavin served Rhiannon's crowd their drinks, laughing and swearing and joking across the counter.

I wondered if Rhiannon was going out of her way to avoid making eye contact with me.

The group settled around the pool table and started up a competition. Rhiannon's playing partner was a tall lad with fair hair. Handsome, in a boyish way. Fit-looking. I guessed the same age as Rhiannon. He held a toothpick in his teeth that he moved to the side of his mouth when he bent to play a shot.

I had no idea what the toothpick was about.

Rhiannon and the lad shared a cue. He placed his hand over hers when he took it from her, allowed his hand to linger on her back when he returned it. Growing in confidence, he moved behind her when she took her next shot and pressed himself against her.

She turned and stamped the end of the pool cue down on the toe of his runner.

"Only a couple of years old and goes well," Buckley said. "Looked after as far as I can see." Buckley liked to play the dealmaker, encouraging trade in the town like a one-man Ministry for Public Enterprise. "Think it'd suit you, is all."

*

I drained my glass and was about to leave when I heard, "Would you like to buy me a drink, Tommy Cassidy?"

It was Rhiannon. If she had offered to buy me a drink, I was insecure enough to have found it patronising, as though she felt sorry for the old man drinking on his own and felt obliged to invite me to join her little party of youngsters. Me buying her a drink felt as though she was joining my company.

"I would," I said.

She ordered a pint. She hadn't the shape of a woman who drank pints. "That your dog?" she said.

"I'm leaving him out this round. Drank enough for one night, and he's work in the morning."

She smiled, like a film star, turned a bar stool and perched herself upon it.

A couple of her friends came over to say good night. The lad with the toothpick wasn't among them.

Rhiannon and I drank until Buckley decided he wanted to go to bed and he closed the bar.

"Will I send him over to you, I will?" Buckley said, lifting our empty glasses and wiping the counter.

"I wouldn't mind taking a look at it," I said.

Outside, Rhiannon and I paused in the yellow glow of the pub sign.

I jammed my hands in my pockets. "I'll say goodnight, so." I hoped she'd walk off before she saw me mounting my bicycle. "Buckley will soon be in his boxers, going around switching lights off."

She laughed. "God, imagine it." She bent and ran her hand the length of the dog's back, her fingers kneading the spine.

I'm sure the dog squirmed in appreciation.

It was the nearest I ever came to feeling jealous of a dog.

She paid no heed to the bicycle and watched as the dog and I set off for Duncarrick in the dark. She called after me, "We should meet up, Tommy Cassidy."

I raised a hand in acknowledgement, and tried hard not to lose my balance.

Chapter 8

The village that forgot the time.

Duncarrick is positioned on the western seaboard of Ireland, two miles from the Atlantic Ocean as the crow flies. It sits in the hollow of Cloonta Beg—Cloonta pronounced *Clooncha*, but everyone knows that—the first mountain to pierce the clouds that roll in from the sea, the first line of defence for the whole of Ireland from the full force of invading, land-bound Atlantic storms.

The mountain wraps itself around the village, cradling it in its lap, hiding it away from strangers.

Streams and rivers slalom off the mountain in winter roars and summer trickles to feed the lake. The freshwater lake, in turn, overflows into two tributaries that take what the lake doesn't need on the next stage of a journey back to the open sea.

The majority of Duncarrick slopes. The snaking tracks connecting its houses climb and fall between staked banks raised from dug ditches, the stakes grey and twisted with age and connected, intermittently, by slack stretches of rust-eaten wire dotted with catches of windswept wool.

The curtilage Daddy inherited, and that he bequeathed to me, sits on the northern edge of the village. It's sloping acres scythe a curving, narrow course up the north-western shoulder of Cloonta Beg as far as Castle Mound. A rumour persists that a castle stood on the land above mine four hundred years ago. Apart from giving the village a name, 'the fort on a rock', I had come across no evidence of a castle.

The soil is typical of hereabouts, sitting on a stony layer of peat and barely deep enough to yield a meagre crop of potato. With care, it's good pasture. Without care, a field will overrun with nettles between spring and autumn, and purple-headed thistle and mayweed that can grow as high as the old stone walls in the summer.

The house I grew up in was also typical: a low, lime-washed building of three rooms, a plank door at the back, and a shine of light from a small window over the kitchen sink. Daddy had it roofed with black slate tiles following a fire that ripped through the thatch the summer before I started school.

The village is remote, six miles from any place that could call itself a town, twelve miles from the nearest hospital.

It's the type of place writers and poets might visit for literary inspiration, where artists and photographers might pause to capture breath-taking vistas, or where musicians might discover a melody in the wind that blows in from the sea to sculpt the landscape. None come, it's too remote.

At a time when mobile telephone companies boasted of achieving 90% population coverage, we were stuck firmly in the 10%. Many corners of the village are still unburdened by signal.

Duncarrick is not famous for being the last place in Ireland to get electricity.

The Rural Electrification of Ireland began in 1946. Officially, it ended in 1978 with the celebratory fanfare of a switch-on in a remote mountain location in County Kerry. Unofficially, it ended here, three months later.

The village dignitaries, by that I mean Parish Priest, undertaker and publican, registered the village with the Electricity Supply Board a day after the mandatory deadline. The village passed unnoticed in the consequential administrative oversight. The resulting red-faces hushed through a late electrification, the power relayed along hastily erected tarred poles, without upsetting the celebrations that were already in the planning for Kerry.

RTÉ, Raidió Teilifís Éireann, broadcast a radio documentary about Duncarrick a decade later. A researcher unearthed the truth about the electrification fiasco and they sent a reporter. They called the satire *The Village that Forgot the Time*, and the edited broadcast unsubtly attempted to portray us as a community of bogtrotters and Neolithic culchies.

"In this remote and forgotten part of County Mayo," the narrator said in his rolling, radio-presenter voice, "crime is more a perception than a reality. The statistics speak for themselves. Burglaries, zero. Car crimes, zero. Missing donkeys, one. It makes you yearn for the Ireland of yesteryear. There is no Garda Station. In fact, Garda Síochána bother to visit just twice a year, and one of them is just a pass-through on the way to the fair in town."

We do have roads, and cars, and lorries, and buses twice a week, but RTÉ ripped the arse out of it by riding the presenter in on an open-topped jaunting cart. You could hear the horse's clop-clopping coming through on the radio, and, in nature-inspired retribution, the torrential rain hammering down on the presenter's microphone.

There was an advantage to infrequent visits from the Guards: we got away with murder.

Chapter 9

I remember it being a long, hot Sunday in July. Rhiannon Harkin and I had, by then, met up a few times. A couple of pints—Rhiannon enjoyed her pints—in Buckley's. One Saturday-night dance. But the day I want to tell you about was definitely a long, hot Sunday in July.

I picked her up in the car I'd bought from Buckley's America-bound friend. I admit I was pleased to show it off to Rhiannon.

We walked a way across fields and sat at the edge of a river on warm grass, our bare feet revived in the water's cool flow.

Ask any local man about Rhiannon Harkin and most would describe her as haughty, with a head full of notions. Though young, she was beautiful enough for men to take an interest and have an opinion. The detached air was dismissed as a symptom of a belief that her surroundings were somehow unworthy of her presence.

It was convenient for men to describe Rhiannon Harkin that way. It made her less intimidating. I thought she had spirit.

She liked to talk. "You're more my sister's age. You should be stepping out with her."

Her statement startled me. There was an age between us, sure enough. I wondered if she was starting to regret ever having asked me to dance.

I tried to brush off her youthful rebuke. "I think my mother and father might have *stepped out*."

"If it was you and Alma instead of you and me, you'd be stepping out." She didn't want to let this thing go.

"Your sister Alma's lovely enough. Maybe it is her I should be dating." That quietened her. "But, it's you I met at the dance, and it's you I choose to have my babies." I blushed, couldn't help it. As soon as I said it, I blushed. What was happening to me?

Rhiannon Harkin screamed and kicked her legs and made the river water furious and white. "Fuck sake, Tommy Cassidy, listen to yourself!"

I understood her alarm. A month together, and I was already talking of babies. "You've my trousers soaked."

I wanted to take it back, the baby comment, but I left it out there. It was the truth, maybe. How I felt, at times. I was knocking on, not the oldest bachelor in town but almost, and there I was, on a date with Rhiannon Harkin, a decade and a half younger.

"It's *definitely* my sister you should be talkin to," she said. "If it's babies yer after, Alma's yer man." She smiled, let her head loll back, beautiful, her film star pose. "I don't intend ever havin the kids," she said. "Three years of shitty nappies, sleep deprivation and breast feedin?"

"They can be a job of work, all right." I was still trying to get a grip of myself.

"No thanks. My independence is worth too much to allow babies to shackle me."

"You're not one for children, so?" I said.

"Amn't I miles too young?"

Nineteen. That's how old Rhiannon told me she was.

There was an uncertainty to dating, especially someone so young. But there I was, nearly thirty-four years of age and I was going on dates. With a nineteen-year-old. I was too old to be wasting time going on nervous dates with young girls.

Would it be old-fashioned of me to admit I'd have been a little more comfortable if she was at least a year older? Twenty. Twenty would be grand. Safer, anyhow, in some manner. Ironically, I couldn't see our little friendship lasting until she reached twenty.

"Problem with kids," she said, "for me, anyway, is I resent how children are used in a patriarchal ideology of female control."

I remembered she was still at college or university or someplace. "I'm not even sure I know what that means."

"Really?"

"Female control?"

"Well, in a patriarchal ideology, it's acknowledged that it's men who really benefit from having children."

"Grand."

"Yet they make out it's the women who want them."

"I see." I recalled hearing that she won a scholarly prize for some talk she did.

"For men, having children means an increase in social status, a continuation of their genetic imprint, an heir to inherit, even promotion at work. Don't laugh, I'm serious."

I was smiling because I was nervous. I didn't know what else to do. "I'm listening. Go on." She was an enjoyable listen, sure enough.

She hadn't finished. "And meanwhile, it's the woman who does all the bloody work. It's true, though. The woman carries the bloody thing, goes through all the joys of childbirth, and it's the woman who does the rearing. All at little or no cost to the man. Yet, for some reason, men still like to live under the illusion that they're doing women an enormous favour when they finally agree to plant a baby in their bellies."

Plant a baby?

"I've too much respect for my perineum to have babies." She was incorrigible. "Would you risk your perineum to have a baby?"

I wasn't entirely sure I had a perineum, so I ignored the question. "Sounds like you've thought it through."

She lit up her face with the broadest of smiles. "I'm messin with you. I'm sorry."

"I don't mind." I genuinely didn't.

"It's college," she said. "Shauna McGarret."

Her being at college was another gauge of the years between us. "Shauna McGarret?"

"My professor. She's brilliant. A breath of fresh air."

I changed the subject. "Why isn't Alma married? She must be late twenties?"

"There you go. That social pressure Professor McGarret talks about. Social pressure to get married and the social pressure to have children. Have you heard of the so-called *biological urge*?"

"I'm not totally ignorant."

"It's men who created women's biological urge. Did ya know that?" She thrust her chin out, challenging me. She had a gracile jaw, slender, the skin perfect. "There's no such thing as a biological urge to have a child, just social pressure."

"We're animals," I said. "Like sheep." I was more comfortable talking about sheep. "Of course there's an urge to have offspring." I patted my pockets for cigarettes, exaggerating the effort to look busy, fished a packet out into the sun and lit up.

Rhiannon recognised the diversion. "Enough feminist talk for today?"

"I envy you your education. It's impressive."

"Really?"

"Yes, really."

She watched the water caress her ankles. "Thank you."

"Would help if what you said made sense, but."

"Ah, okay," she said. "Proper funny."

"No, I'm joking. Not about it being funny, about it not making sense, I mean. Does that make sense?"

She chuckled. "Yeah, perfect."

"It is impressive. My mother used to tell me education is no heavy weight to carry."

"You mean it don't you?"

"Mean what?"

"That you're impressed."

"I am," I said.

She threw a stalk of grass into the river as if firing a dart. "Right." She propped herself up on a rigid arm. "You asked, so. Eight years between us to the day. Alma and me. We share a birth date." She paused to let me appreciate the coincidence.

"To the day?"

"Which means that even on my birthday she has to have a share of the attention." Her tone had soured.

"Come on," I said. "I'm sure it's not too bad."

She brightened again, the gloom lifted as quickly as it had descended. "Saint Alma hits twenty-eight next birthday. Not as old as you, though, I believe. Is that right?"

"Okay. So first you bombard me with *feminism*, now you've moved onto *ageism. Young* lady. Twenty-eight's a lot older than me."

"Is in me arse. How much older are you than Alma? Tell me."

"A full year."

"A full year? And a few more bloated ones besides, I reckon. I worked out you're in your thirties."

"Maybe."

She threw herself back on the grass. Her giggle sounded like trickling water. "I knew it."

I was curious. "Why Saint Alma?"

"Saint Alma?"

"You called her Saint Alma."

"I did." She propped herself up on her elbows and straightened a leg out of the water. She wore a delicate silver anklet. Her foot looked tiny, perfectly proportioned. Each toenail was painted a different colour: teal, orange, pink, orange again but darker and with a glitter, electric blue. Imagine a mad rainbow. Water dribbled from her slim ankle as though she was sprinkling a little of her beauty into the river.

"Because, because, because," she said. "Because everyone thinks that about her. Holier than Saint Brigid, for Christ's sake. So, I call her Saint Alma. But she's not a saint. Far from it." She fell silent, worked her foot side to side as though assessing her paintwork. "If you looked it up, the name Alma even means 'all good'. Saint All Good. She was destined to be everyone's saint since the day she popped out of Mammy."

I raised a foot out of the water and held it next to hers. Misshapen toes, bleached of colour by the chill of the river, horned and fractured brown nails. A constricted vein, that would become varicose in a few years, ran back and forth along the length of my shinbone like a meandering blue rivulet. I felt old next to her.

"Never had a drink in her life," Rhiannon said. "I don't believe she's ever been out with a man. She used to work in the lace factory, but something happened there and now she spends all her time around the house, looking after Mammy. It's a pity. She's still not a bad-looking woman, but...Anyway, she chose her own life and it's up to her."

"How is your mother?"

Mae Harkin, Rhiannon's mother, was one of two people in a black and white photograph on display alongside obsolete turfing equipment in the foyer of the power station. The man shaking her hand in the picture, a grinning Minister for Transport and Power with oiled hair, had just cut the ribbon. It was 1956, and Mayo had a newly opened power station.

More men paused in the foyer to admire the photograph of Mae Harkin than did to appreciate the antique turfing equipment.

Mae took ill and retired from work a couple of years after I started working there. Sometime in the last year, she was admitted to the hospital. The woman from Human Resources was full of talk about her in the work's cafeteria. "A mental ward, apparently. The men always did think her insanely beautiful." A few around the table laughed at that. A woman who worked in Accounts said, "Her eldest daughter, Alma, visits her every day."

"Mammy's still in hospital," Rhiannon said. "Alma wants her home, but I think she should stay where she is until they get the medication right and straighten her head out. She's safer in hospital."

"Alma still in at her every day?"

"How did you know about that?"

"Someone at work mentioned it."

"They still talk about Mammy at the power station?"

"Why wouldn't they, isn't she a legend?"

"That's nice, I suppose."

I watched Rhiannon roll that thought around her head as she bit the red from her bottom lip.

"Yeah, every day," she said, at last. "Alma. She gets the bus or a lift in in the morning, comes home when the bell rings for the end of visiting."

"She sounds like a good person."

"See, you're at it now." Rhiannon sat up. "Everyone thinks she's a *good bloody person*." Both feet were back in the water.

"Sounds like she is."

"You didn't grow up with her, but." She became sullen, swiped curls off her forehead. "Not as good as everyone thinks." Rhiannon was jealous.

"I heard she virtually raised you?"

"Fuck that. She'll not be my role model! I'm not like her. She can hang around the house as long as she wants, but I refuse to be stuck here for the rest of my life."

"If you say so."

"And you can stop with the patronising. I told you before that I want out of here. I want England. I want London. I'm off as soon as my course ends. See a bit of the world. I want to go where no-one knows my name, where there're things to do and places to go twenty-four hours a day. Rain and midges, that's all that's here. I need to breathe some pollution."

It was another thing that set us apart. I was content where I was. The thought of leaving Duncarrick, never mind Ireland, tied my stomach in a griping knot. And here was Rhiannon, mad to be away from it. "You can be a fierce one," I said.

That smile again. "Part of my charm." She relaxed back on the grass, stretched her arms over her head. Her summer dress, the same one she wore playing pool with the young lad, rode up her thighs. Such long legs, pale in the sun's light. "Mammy's been mad for as long as I can remember," she said. "She lost a child after me. Not been right since that, really."

I shuddered at the thought of losing a child.

"Held down her job for a good while, she did, but she wasn't in half the time. I'd say they only tolerated it because she was there at the beginning. Do ya know she was the first woman to work at the power station?"

"Her picture's in the foyer to commemorate that."

"She was only twenty-one. And gorgeous."

"It's a good picture."

"You know, she's been ill so long I can barely remember my real mammy." Her feet stirred circles in the water. Muscles in her legs rippled the curve of her thighs. "Alma stepped in, took on the role. Helped in her way, I suppose…But no, that's not for me. I couldn't do it. I refuse to do it."

"You would if you had to."

"Will *you* take me to England?"

I took a deep nasal breath. No good would come of me going to England. I had plans, and England was not part of them. "I wouldn't be one for–"

"None of the lads my age have the balls to go any place." She raised an arm, played her fingers on the nape of my neck.

My shoulders hunched. I was naturally uncomfortable with public shows of affection. I preferred physical contact to be private.

"They all boast about shippin out," she said. "But dance night in Buckley's on a Saturday is the true height of their aspirations. That and the ride with some biddy in the back of a car before heading home."

"Come on with that."

She sensed my embarrassment, was brazen enough to exploit it. "Or, becoming a country and Irish singer and getting more rides." Rhiannon laughed as she spoke, stroked my neck as though massaging it to sleep.

I twisted my head to scan the fields, reminded myself we were out in the remotest patch of the whole of Ireland—there was no-one for miles—and allowed her to continue.

"Or," she said. "The more ambitious want to play for Manchester United and be ridin a different woman every night. As if that's going to bloody happen."

"They're not all like that," I said, passively. "And they'll be away from here soon enough."

She laughed, recalled her hand, sat up. “For a lad aged between eighteen and twenty-one, the urge to have sex is greater than the urge to eat. Did ya know that?”

“Professor McGarret, again?”

“But you’re not like that.”

“Like my food too much.” I was too bloody old. Is that what she was referring to?

“It’s not a criticism,” she said. “Absolutely no need to get defensive. It’s…It’s just nice to be with a fella and not be constantly mauled like some fuckin sex doll just out the box.”

It was my turn to laugh, but not with sarcasm, more as a release of nervous intimidation.

“And you’ve your own car.”

“I have now, yeah.”

“Austin.”

“Yeah. An Austin eleven hundred.”

“Ooo, I say. An Austin eleven hundred.” She made her voice whoop. “That’s nice.” She smiled, squinting against the sun, her face lit up by its rays, mocking me, yet still lovely. “For most lads, Tommy Cassidy, it’s all about the shaggin, and they’re not half as handsome as you.”

The sun suddenly felt very warm.

In a movement that had me reaching to save her, she pushed herself off the bank and into the river. She turned assuredly, the sun behind her, with no regard for the chill of the water or the rocks and stones that cobbled the riverbed. “Come on in.”

“I won’t, thanks.”

The hem of her cotton dress caught in the river’s gentle rush and stuck to her thighs like transparent tissue.

“You haven’t answered my question,” she said.

I could no longer remember her question, I couldn’t remember anything, she was dazzling in the sunlight.

“Will you take me to England?”

England. That was it. I couldn’t take her to England. “You’re not getting back into the car until that dress dries.”

“Are you worried about it?”

“England?”

"The wet dress."

"No." The wet dress looked great. "I mean yes. I'm worried about the car seat."

She tilted her head, swayed her body in and out of the sun in a blurry, seductive manner. "You do realise, Tommy Cassidy, that we're out here all on our ownsome."

"And what of it?" I tried to remain calm.

"With not another soul for miles."

"I doubt there'd be many this far out, no."

"Have you ever done it out in the open?"

She was nineteen years old. I wanted to swallow, but she was staring right at me. I could feel the sweat push out of me. "Depends on what you mean."

"Fancy pluckin a feather from the goose?"

I knew what I hoped she meant, but I couldn't be sure. Was that what the youngsters were calling it? It was an exquisite yet terrifying moment of anticipation.

She wasn't one to waste time waiting for a response. "But if you're worried about the dress…" She crossed her arms and reached down for the hem. In a liquid flourish, she straightened and peeled the dress over her head. In slight hesitation, she held it against her body, cast her eye up and down the riverbank.

She relaxed, giggled, and threw the dress over me.

The wet hem was cool on my face. The dress smelled of citrus, oranges maybe, an intoxicating smell of youthfulness. I swept it away and raised a hand to my forehead to block the glare.

Apart from a pair of knickers, she was naked, full-breasted perfection. The narrow bands of the pants rose high on the curve of her hips to form a thin V. The colour matched one of her toenails. She played with her hair, black and shiny as wet peat, and splayed it out with her fingers, creating a corona of curls.

I swear to Christ I could not breathe. I dare not blink.

She waded to the bank and bent towards me.

"What are you doing?" I knew well what she was doing.

She eased me back with a hand on my chest and grappled with the buckle of my belt.

"Someone might see us."

"No-one'll see us." Rhiannon Harkin, nineteen years old and the world's most beautiful woman, was naked over me, and she was undoing my trousers.

I flicked the cigarette into the river and sucked in the slight bulge of belly.

Chapter 10

Alma had no sympathy for any sickness brought on by drink.

My head was over the wok. My stomach heaved in a dry retch. Can you vomit out a respiratory disease? Nothing came.

Alma was in my head. "May God help you."

I knew God wouldn't help. I'd known that for some time.

Alma's wok was a remnant of her attempt to convert us to a vegetarian diet. For about half a year we ate undercooked stir-fried vegetables mixed with limp bean sprouts and sticky, black soy sauce. I was concerned the village would get to hear that a man who bred sheep had turned vegetarian.

I searched for clues as to how long I had slept. No clock on the dressing table, and I didn't have a watch.

When Alma died, I removed all her clocks from the house and, in a fit of rage, buried them beneath the hazel tree that grew un-pollarded at the top of the first field. All two hundred and thirty-two of them.

A corner of light from the bedroom window spotted Alma's statue of *The Last Supper*. The delicate work was a representation of the painting by the Spaniard, Juan de Juanes. Matt Darcy bought it as a ninth wedding anniversary gift for Alma and me.

When we unwrapped Matty's present, I told Alma we were lucky we didn't get a ceramic electrical insulator. "I can see why you'd be jealous," she said to me. "At least Matty has a crumb of refinement." She loved what she called 'the movement' of the figures, the disciples gathered in adoring denial around Jesus, having just heard the news that their master is about to be betrayed.

I only saw stillness but took an interest and told Alma the Judas figure was my favourite, clutching his money pouch and robed in yellow, the ancient colour of envy and deceit. Judas sat with his back to us, hiding his face, conscience-stricken. I suggested he was the only one sensible enough to have a seat on the near side of the table, where it was less crowded. Alma didn't laugh, but said, "May God forgive the ignorant philistine, Tom Cassidy."

Jesus now basked in the window's sunlight, the shadow of his raised hand darkening St Peter's upturned face. Thanks to the reliable tilt and turn of the earth, the shadow told me it was one o'clock, as near as damn it. I'd slept for thirteen hours.

I rose from the bed, staggered into the kitchen on wooden joints, and in my own steady time emptied the wok, rekindled the fire with an unread newspaper across the opening to draw a draught, made sweet tea, smoked a cigarette, and searched the drawers for tablets and Alma's red address book.

The Devil blast John Kavanaugh and his trip into town.

I was still drunk when I settled by the fire, glad to get the weight off unsteady legs.

"It was a middling night, Alma," I said, my croaked voice a whisper so as not to aggravate the throb in my head.

Alma didn't reply.

"The Rolls-Royce Phantom is the extended wheelbase model with a seven litre, V-twelve engine. Four hundred and fifty-five horsepower."

Alma didn't share my enthusiasm for engines and machinery. Since she died, I could talk about them without censorship.

"Yellow leather seats, the colour of Judas's robes. And the back doors open the wrong way."

Mark, the chauffeur, called them 'suicide doors'. I questioned why anyone who could afford to travel in the back of a Rolls-Royce Phantom would even consider doing away with themselves.

"Mark seems nice enough," I told Alma. "Insisted I didn't smoke in the car." I added, as an afterthought, "Matty likes him."

When I entered Buckley's, John Kavanaugh was already there, a double whiskey waiting for me on the counter. Lisa-Marie Gavin had waited until I arrived, for fear the head would die on Buckley's awful beer, and within seconds had a pint sat up beside it.

"Lisa-Marie is grand," I said, and I sipped at the sweet tea. "Though still swears like a navvy."

Alma wouldn't like the swearing, especially from a woman.

I hadn't seen Lisa-Marie since Alma's wake.

"She offered to come over and do some washing. I declined. Said we were grand enough. She's too busy, anyway."

John Kavanaugh suggested him and I move into the quiet alcove in Buckley's, where the acting crowd usually sat.

"There's a new woman in charge now, Alma. Appeared in some soap opera on R.T.E. They weren't there of course, not on a Wednesday. Just the two of us, me and Kavanaugh."

Ryan Matthews was outside Buckley's when I went out for a smoke. He passed on his condolences and apologised for having to rush off to England and miss Alma's funeral. He told me he had to pick up a trailer from a bloke someplace in Northamptonshire. He held back tears when he recalled rushing Alma and me into the hospital. Queer to see a man that big cry.

"Ryan said he was sorry my job in London didn't work out. I thought he'd go on about the accident but he didn't. Maybe James Taylor hasn't mentioned it to Ryan. I wonder how the poor lad is?"

Alma and I had argued about the accident in London. It was the reason I had to return to Duncarrick. She thought it was my fault, that I did it deliberately. Alma thought everything that went wrong was my fault.

I paid Ryan Matthews the money I owed him. He'd forgot about it, then didn't want to take it. I insisted. Other than that, I didn't have to put my hand in my pocket all night.

Lisa-Marie ferried drinks to us. John Kavanaugh clutched her fingers for longer than necessary every time he pressed a fresh twenty-euro note into her hand. I had a vague memory of an altercation between the two of them.

"She's probably worn out," I said to Alma. "Told me she works in Costcutter all day, in Buckley's all night. And she's started breeding cattle. Buying weanling heifers like there will never again be a weanling heifer to buy. Why wouldn't she get cranky? John Kavanaugh was decent, Alma. I think he has changed, to be fair."

My face reddened in a flush of embarrassment when I remembered I asked John Kavanaugh about Rhiannon. I must have been drunk. I was drunk.

"John said Rhiannon was well."

He must have been just as drunk. He told me they all lived in Manchester. She might have moved. He made no mention of them having split up, nor of him having another woman. Not that he would to me, I dare say. If what he said was true, Rhiannon and John Kavanaugh were back together, raising their family. A good thing, I suppose.

"The boys are teenagers now I bet."

Late in the evening, Kavanaugh explained his proposition to me. I wasn't keen at first. After a few more whiskies, we shook hands on it.

I don't remember what time we left Buckley's.

It came to me then, the altercation, John Kavanaugh making a drunken grab for Lisa-Marie as we staggered to the door. Lisa-Marie slapped his face.

A real voice, not Alma's, "Tommy? You up?"

I ended my conversation with Alma.

The latch rattled and the kitchen door swung open.

"Look at the state a you." Matt Darcy stood with one hand on the doorframe, bent over. A Wellington boot rested across a knee. He scraped goose shit off the sole with a stick.

I coughed into a hand, wiped it on a trouser leg.

"Are ya goin to repair this door knocker?" Matty said.

"Asks the man who never used it."

He crossed the kitchen, oversized Wellington boots jolloping over the linoleum. He paused to take a concerned deep breath at the table littered with newspapers, cups filled with crushed cigarette butts, letters, and dirty crockery. "Eighty percent a bacteria in a house," he said, "can be found on dirty plates."

More words of advice from Matt Darcy.

He weighed the kettle. "Have ya eaten?"

"Not able."

"I've sausages." He struck a match. "Knew you'd be hangin out yer arse." The gas popped, and blue flames hissed and stretched out beneath the kettle. "Must eat. Have ya any lard?"

My stomach churned.

Matty contorted his face as he wrestled a reluctant packet of crushed sausages from his jacket pocket. "Has Gilhooly called in to see you, yet?"

The sour taste that bloomed at the back of my throat made me wince. I swallowed back the bile. "Gilhooly?"

"Michael Gilhooly. The guard."

"I know him."

"He's Inspector Michael Gilhooly now."

"Why would he call to see me?"

"Just thought he'd call. He's been askin about Alma, God rest her soul."

A flush of adrenaline made my ribs tighten. I rubbed clammy palms over the wooden arm of the chair. "Asking who?"

Matty shrugged. "I don't know, me and a few others. Goin round like a big bear with a briar up its arse. Intimidatin people with his eyes and his uniform."

Palpitations inflamed the pain in my head. "What was he asking?" I cast a look of anger at the fireplace. If I was more able, I'd have dragged my chair away from the heat.

"Asked me when I saw her last."

"What did you say?"

Matty creased his forehead in query. "I told the truth. Hardly at all in the last while before her accident. The lard? Where have ya the lard?" He pushed his spectacles back up his nose, wrenched open the oven door.

I hadn't seen Michael Gilhooly since his daughter's christening. She must be coming on eight or nine years old, now. I wondered if she ever wore the silver bracelet Alma wrapped for her. Baby Delores. We had her name engraved on its outer surface.

I'd heard that since that time, Gilhooly was promoted out of Sligo, only to be promoted into Mayo a few years later. He now held territorial jurisdiction over Duncarrick.

He'd made a success of *his* career. I'd also heard he had become a contrary bastard.

"No bother," Matty announced to the open oven. "There's dry fat in the pan." He lifted the frying pan to his nose, then clattered it down on the hob.

The crack and moan of the warming kettle echoed in my ears, the pain in my head flaring at the cacophony of Matty's cooking.

"There's a bit a the animal about Gilhooly, don't ya think?"

I didn't answer. To be honest, I was surprised it took the guards so long to start their investigating. I was beginning to think they wouldn't bother.

"Somethin wolf-like about the man," Matty said. "If, indeed, he is a man. Wouldn't let him near a field a my sheep for fear he'd slaughter the lot a them. He's the sort of creature that if a tribe a Maasai speared him to death on the Kenyan savannah, they'd dance round a fire to celebrate. Eyes're too small for a wolf, but. You can't beat a rope a sausages. Is it only this shitey seeded bread ya have?"

*

Matty handed me the saucer of food.

I nibbled buttered bread and overcooked sausages under a shroud of smoke that hovered over us like a greasy storm cloud. "This is tasty," I lied.

Matty chomped his food, oblivious to the fog. "A sausage is the best cure known to man for a hangover."

I wanted to ask about Inspector Gilhooly.

Matty forked more sausage into his mouth. "So, what did he want?"

"I was going to ask you the same."

"How do you mean?"

"Inspector Gilhooly."

"I don't mean Gilhooly." Matty spluttered food when he spoke. "I mean the Manchester multi-millionaire. What did Kavanaugh want?"

"I was about to tell Alma," I said.

Matty stopped chewing, pressed his knees together. He stared into the fire.

I was still drunk and drowsy. I didn't usually talk like that in front of Matty; it made him uncomfortable. "He was decent," I said

Matty resumed his chewing. "My arse."

"Very decent."

"I bet he was." He took a bite from a folded slice of bread. "Doesn't know the meanin of the word. Was I right about him wantin to buy you out?"

Of course Matty was right.

"How did you know?"

"Because he's a bollix!" Matty spat bread into his lap. "Wouldn't pierce that bastard with a pitchfork for fear a the stench that came out of him." He wrenched his face as he swallowed. "No offence, but I can read John Kavanaugh like a book."

"You're grand."

"I know the way the Kavanaughs operate. I know what he's up to." He paused and waited for me to ask a question.

I didn't.

He stopped waiting. "God rest her soul, but Alma's not dead five minutes and that bollockstone is over in Manchester thinkin you'll be wantin to sell up and move away. Thinks he'll get this pace for a good price. He thinks you'll want away from the memories, leave it all behind ya. He thinks you'll sell up for half nothin. The rabid-dog's bollix."

I gave a weak smile. Matty had turned against the idea of me selling the farm. I didn't want him to crush my excitement. For the first time in a long time, I thought something good was happening. It would be an opportunity for me to right a few wrongs. And Christ knows there had been plenty of wrongs.

Matty cleared the lump in his throat with a wash of tea. "How much?" he said.

"Told me not to say anything. To anyone. Mentioned you by name."

"I bet. The arse-wipe."

"A hundred and fifty."

Matty's mouth gaped. The rounded end of a burnt sausage peeked over the front of his bottom denture. More money than he had calculated. Twenty-five thousand euros more.

I read conflict in the rapid blinking of his magnified eyes.

"Including the house?" he asked.

I barked out a cough. More coughs came, each more painful than the last. I folded forward. My poor lungs.

"Don't die now," Matty said. "You're about to be rich."

"Not including the house," I wheezed, and wiped water from my eyes.

"Is the doctor doing anythin with that cough? It's with you a while."

"I stay in the house." I cleared my throat. "Long as I like."

Matty resumed chewing and talked, words and food spilling from his mouth. "The house is worth almost thirty. If I deduct the house, it'll give…as a fraction…" His eyes widened. He stopped chewing. "Why would John Kavanaugh pay ya near sixty percent over the odds?"

"I know." I sucked air through rattly airways. I could feel a smile stretch my face despite the pain in my chest. "I hadn't your numbers, Matty." Breathe. "But I knew it was a good price." Air and euphoria made me lightheaded.

"It's *too* good."

"He seems changed, Matty."

"He's up to somethin."

"Seems a decent man, to be fair."

"He's like the father!" A splash of tea slopped onto Matty's trousers.

Matty and I started at the Owencas Electricity Generating Station in the early 1980s. We spent four years of our life working the late shift together. If anyone asked, we said we maintained the two Babcock and Wilcox boilers that produced over two hundred thousand pounds of steam pressure per hour to drive turbo-alternators. But it was more of a cleaning job, shovelling out barrowfuls of ash to keep the boilers at peak efficiency. John Kavanaugh's father—also called John, so you're clear—worked with us. Matty and old John Kavanaugh didn't get on, Matty having to put up with a steady stream of malevolent, homophobic workplace abuse. "It's banter, only," was the reassurance Matty received. There came a time when they were both in the running for a promotion, but when old John Kavanaugh accused Matty of stealing an antique ceramic electrical insulator from an archive display in the foyer, Matty was threatened with dismissal. John Kavanaugh got the foreman post.

It was to be old John Kavanaugh's first of many steps up the promotion ladder and into the well-paid, rarefied atmosphere of senior corporate management.

But that wasn't the only reason Matt Darcy resented old John Kavanaugh.

I cleared my throat. "Said he'd work in some kind of sweetener for me. Some extra euros for a few drinks for myself, is how he put it."

Matty placed his cup and plate on the hearth. "Some kind a sweetener?" His face looked like he'd just bitten into a wormwood beetle, something bitter and alive that was hiding in his sausage. "John Kavanaugh?"

He wiped his tea-damp trousers with a hand. "I don't like it, Tommy. He's a rogue. He's not clever enough to end up with a gold, feckin Roycer-Roller under his backside by doin deals that are decent. He's a schemer. A whoreson jackass. A lecherous villain."

Matty's insults had become sixteenth-century English, almost Shakespearean. I chose not to interrupt him.

He continued, “John Kavanaugh would only do a deal if he was tearin the arse out a ya. He’s an exploiter. ‘John Kavanaugh First’, that’s his slogan. Well that approach only works for so long.”

“Seems to be doing well out of it,” I said.

“Exploitin people?”

“Told me he’s selling a load of houses in Manchester.”

“It’s short-term exploitation, by the son and heir of a rabid mongrel dog.”

“Have you ever read any plays by William Shakespeare?”

“It’s all about him.” Matty was finger-wagging. “What about those that’s left? The people who work for him. What will they do when he’s impoverished everyone?”

Tilting at windmills, that’s what Matty was doing, like Don Quixote—I was familiar with that story—and I disagreed.

“I’m only telling you what he offered.” I supped sweet tea while Matty rooted to clear the last bits of sausage and beetle from around his teeth with his tongue.

“Has he had it valued?” Matty asked.

“Said we need to do it. But said it was irrelevant. More a formality. Whatever, he’s offered me a hundred and fifty thousand. We shook hands on it.”

“Get it valued anyway. I might have underestimated.” The last sentence lacked conviction, Matty didn’t believe it, he was too cussed to accept he might be wrong, and too obstinate to change his mind. “They’ve all these electro-optical scanning stations these days. Half an arc-second accuracy.”

I focussed on my sausage sandwich, but I had no appetite.

“They can tell how much land ya have to within a square inch.” He held up a hand, thumb and forefinger exactly one inch apart.

“I know what an inch looks like, Matty. John Kavanaugh is sending a valuer around tomorrow.”

“Who’s he sendin?”

I hadn’t intended to tell Matty about the valuer, but it was too late. “Gorman, from Castlebar.”

"Gorman? James bloody Gorman? James Gorman and John Kavanaugh? You're gettin into bed with a right pair a pissers."

"It'll be grand. The money's guaranteed. We drank to it."

"That scut Gorman wouldn't recognise an electro-optical scanning station if one toppled from its tripod and hit him in the testicles."

"John Kavanaugh guaranteed me the money," I repeated. "He's changed, Matty. He was decent all night with the drink. He even asked after you and your artificial knee."

Matty sucked his teeth and glared into the fire. His head twitched. At first, I thought he was wrestling with the possibility that he made a mistake on his valuation of the land, but his hands clenched into tight fists and cords appeared in his narrow neck. He slopped more of his tea when he picked up the cup. "I can't believe you're goin along with this."

His tone was a mix of disappointment, warning and threat. That was how Matty could be. He liked to interfere. I should have ended it there, sent him away, but I knew from experience that it's not easy to throw a friend out of your house.

"You're blinded by the money," he said. "John Kavanaugh is flashin notes in front a yer nose and he's leadin you a dance."

Matty was jealous.

The pain in my skull throbbed. "Are you jealous?"

Matty was indignant. "I'm not jealous." He pushed back his glasses and glared at me to show he wasn't jealous. "He'll make an eejit of ya, despite all the books you've listened to."

Matty had flaws. He was exhibiting one of them.

"Matty, I have no-one to leave it to. We've no chil–" I had to stop. The words came up on me by surprise. I choked them back. I was still drunk, but that made it all the more painful. We had a child. Noleen. Our daughter. Born in the January of the year of the big snow, three and a half years ago.

I swallowed the thought and wheezed in air. "I'll not get an opportunity like this again." My voice was a half whisper. "It's the side of a mountain, Matty. A mountain I can't climb anymore." I dragged air into my lungs, but it felt as if I was trying to breathe underwater and drowning. “The money might do someone some good.” I wanted Matty to leave.

“Someone some good?” Matty spat the words out. “Someone some good?” The same again but louder.

“That’s enough, Matty.”

“Who? Who do you want to do good?”

I didn’t want to get into that with Matty. Not then, maybe not ever.

Matty put his tea on the floor, removed his top denture and worked a seed free with a fingernail. He sucked his finger, replaced his teeth. “Ya just see euro signs.” He was angry, shouting.

Tension in my forehead spread to my jaw. I didn’t want to fall out with Matty again, but his insinuations vexed me. He had no idea what I intended to do with the money.

He raised an arm to introduce his vision of me. “Ya just see yourself sittin up on a bar stool in Buckley’s with a trouser-full a cash for the rest a yer life.”

I tried to lighten the mood. “Might take a cruise.” I wanted to resolve this conflict amicably.

“A cruise? A fine one to be takin cruises.” The distraction launched Matty into a familiar monologue, one born out of his own guilt and frustration. “Four hundred poor souls, on half minimum wage, havin to double-up on jobs to keep their families back home fed?” Matty had cruised, thought he knew how they operated. He was going to tell me about the guitarist.

“Like the guitarist,” I prompted.

“The bloody guitarist was one, yeah. Up all hours playin in the cabaret. First thing next mornin the same fella’s fryin omelettes for ya on a two-ring hob in the corner of the dining room.”

“And the porthole,” I said. This was easy.

“Yes. That afternoon the poor bastard’s slung over the side a the ship in a boson’s chair paintin the portholes.”

“Painting the glass?” I had used the same childish interruption before. I was determined to keep this light.

"Don't start that. I'm serious. Ya know damn well what I mean. Corporate exploitation is what it is. It's what Kavanaugh would do. Is doing. To you. I bet ya he's got people imported from Eastern Europe and the former territories of the British Empire on his building sites over in Manchester. Workin like skivvies on shite money."

Matty had brought the conversation around to John Kavanaugh again. The jealousy was eating him.

I gave it one more try. "Like the Maasai are exploited?"

He looked me in the face, his own face creased with uncertainty. "Yes, like the Maasai."

Wracked with guilt about the slightest indulgence of his own, Matty tended to disparage anyone who considered enjoying the same 'misdemeanour'. The safari was a famous example. Unburdened with the reluctance I have for moving away and exploring, he went on a safari a few years back. A real one. Yes, Matty on safari, in Kenya, I swear to Christ.

"You saw elephants," I said.

"I know what I saw."

"And lions. The Maasai Mara, was it?" I was annoyed with him, but I didn't want to fall out.

"I saw a lot a things."

"But you don't think others should have the same opportunity?"

He had boasted of seeing elephants and lions, cheetahs and giraffes and even a rhinoceros and her calf, wild, in their natural surroundings. When he came home he wrote to the Kenyan Cabinet Secretary for Tourism in Nairobi, demanding that sight-seeing safaris be outlawed with immediate effect to protect the animals and preserve their habitat.

It was typical of him having taken part in a safari himself, to then want to close them all down.

Matty blew out between pursed lips, shook his head. "I know what you're doing. Alma, God rest her, wouldn't allow you to go ahead with the sale. Not to him. Not after the way he's treated Rhiannon. You know he has another woman in Manchester?"

"That's only talk," I said. "You know nothing."

"That's where you're wrong," Matty said. "I know he has a child by her."

I knew about the child too, but it was too late to admit that to Matty. I felt the pulse of my palpitating heart in my throat.

Matty looked me in the eye. "A girl. Only a year old. The man has children all over the country."

I didn't want Matty using Alma and Rhiannon, or even this woman and child in Manchester, against me.

"It's greed, Tommy Cassidy, pure greed. And I'll tell ya now, it'll end badly."

I eased my jaw apart to relieve the clench of my teeth. I gave him one last chance to withdraw, to pull back from his accusation, a way out. "You can advise me on the best cruises."

"You sit there, breathing like a cycle tyre with a fast puncture, and the greed is blindin ya. Greed is your new wife."

Blood rose in my face. I had enough of his begrudgery. I sucked in air. "Have you finished?"

Matty glanced down at his plate, knowing well I wasn't referring to his food. He hadn't finished. "John Kavanaugh, and his money, and his asking about my artificial knee, could never, for all I care, fuck off enough." He bared his teeth. "You're a dope, Tommy. A drunken dope. Since Alma died, Jesus man, I don't think you've been a day sober. What are you hidin from? What are you guilty of? What really happened to Alma, Tommy?"

A redness rose from his neck, filled the hollow cheeks. He knew he had gone too far. A vein at his temple throbbed livid against his skull.

It was time for this discussion to end.

I swallowed loudly. "If you have, you can go."

He leaned forward in his chair, extended an open hand out towards me. There was tremble on his chin. He looked lost, like a cade lamb abandoned by its ewe, like he was begging. "Let me be here when Gorman comes around. I know land."

I didn't want a jealous, redundant auctioneer fouling up our arrangement. "Mind yourself on the road, Matty."

He stood up, glared down at me, his magnified eyes filling his spectacles. Light from the fire caught a tiny fracture in the bottom corner of one of the lenses, made it glimmer. "I don't think you're interested in goin on a cruise."

"Not in the slightest."

He stood over me, paunched and ruddy-faced, and huffed his chest. He looked small, as though planted in the oversized Wellington boots, two feeble sapling trunks in baggy trousers. He had more to say, was debating in his own mind whether to say it.

I cut him off. "Matty."

A hand darted up to sit his spectacles back on the bridge of his nose. "I'm takin back the rest a the sausages."

Chapter 11

Rhiannon Harkin was a whirlwind, a rushing, spinning human vortex that consumed all that got close to her and whirled them into the air. For a while, I was intoxicated on the excitement, the mad, youthful passion of it all.

Every outing with Rhiannon turned into an adventure, often an adventure with risks, and often those risks were carnal in nature.

I developed a new swagger in my step, began to feel worthy of this beautiful, younger woman, that I deserved her, even.

She favoured short skirts when we went out for the night. I spent money on clothes, took to dressing younger, all pale-blue blazers and collarless pastel T-shirts, like the fellas out of *Miami Vice* on the television.

I was proud of her, enjoyed being in her company, enjoyed showing her off. I thought her clever, bold and amusing. We became a regular item at Buckley's Dance Hall on the outskirts of town, and though the venue was in no way salubrious, Rhiannon shone brighter than the glitterball and made it look like Las Vegas.

She spent money I didn't think she had and bought me a pair of cowboy boots the colour of a west Mayo sunset, with pull straps, and stitched detail on the sides that looked, according to Matt Darcy, "Like two sheep shaggin in a patch of cabbage."

I almost bought myself a matching leather jacket with metal studs and tassels and the wings of an eagle spread across the shoulders. Fortunately, before Matt Darcy caught me wearing it, the sane part of my brain convinced me I looked a proper gobdaw. I left the jacket on a chair in the changing room and crept out of the shop like a sneak-thief.

Rhiannon Harkin was beautiful and glamorous. And for a while, a little of that glamour rubbed off on me. If I was Montgomery Clift, I'd found my Elizabeth Taylor.

Now and again, I'd near have to kick my own shins to make sure that what was happening to me was real. More than once I wrestled with the morality of dating a woman so young.

I'll admit I found it hard to keep up. I had nearly fifteen years on her for Christ's sake, and when not with her, I was working at the power station or busy establishing the farm.

I was under no illusions. She wanted to try out an older man, and I was lucky enough to be the older man she chose to try out. I'd do for her, for the time being, and I was shallow and insecure enough to be grand with that. Why wouldn't I be? What could possibly go wrong?

I remember it as a time of tremendous excitement. I was excited that plans for the farm were coming together, in a place and among people I knew, and I was excited to have a spirited, beautiful young woman riding around in my new car.

I knew it wouldn't last. I knew it couldn't last. Our ambitions differed too greatly. Yet that time with Rhiannon was probably the most fulfilling few months of my life. For the first time in my life I was energised with a force of purpose that made me feel damn near indestructible. My memories of that early time with Rhiannon are among my happiest, fondest memories.

Rhiannon ruined it all when she said she was falling in love with me.

*

We were in Buckley's Bar and Lounge, in town. Rhiannon wanted to pay for our two pints, but I insisted, told her she could buy the next round.

A small group of lads crowded the corner of the bar, beneath the television, filling it with raucous, taunting laughter and a blended aroma of cheap aftershaves that would strip paint from the bonnet of a tractor. I could tell they had drink taken, and a couple of them were brave enough to nudge elbows and give Rhiannon the once-over leer.

She suggested we sit in the alcove, an area partitioned off from the main bar area, as secluded and intimate as Buckley's Bar and Lounge had to offer.

One of the lads threw a hopeful 'hello there' smirk across the bar at Rhiannon, and I was pleased when she kept on with her long-legged, film star strut and didn't look over.

Two children of a bloke who worked in the power station cannoned balls around the pool table. I dropped four coins on the top rail, above the chute. "A few games on me."

"Thank you, Mister Cassidy."

"You're grand. Tell your dad I was asking after him."

"Look at Mister Generous," Rhiannon said.

A meeting was coming to a close in the alcove. A dozen or so loud and animated people in flamboyant hats and voluminous scarves talked over each other excitedly, shaking hands and hugging.

Bernadette Joyce was chairing. "You're a worthless lout, Tomás O'Caiside." Her words of long ago, my name in Irish form, ran through my head, as they did whenever I caught sight of my old school teacher. She'd bawl them as she brought the chalk-stained rule whipping down on my knuckles. "A lout is bad enough, but you're a worthless one." I remembered the sting of the rule, along with the sniggers of the other children.

I wanted to retreat. An inner chill lifted hair on the back of my neck. I glanced at Rhiannon self-consciously and shrugged it away.

"All right, all right, calm yourselves," Mrs Joyce told the meeting, swatting at the chaos with a light hand. "Calm yourselves, this needs doing properly." Mrs Joyce waited for order. "So, ladies and gentlemen, boys and girls, the inaugural meeting of the West Coast Performers, the first amateur dramatics group west of Castlebar, is now closed. Let's make theatre!"

The meeting erupted again.

"See you all at first rehearsal," she said above the melee. "And Siobhán, be sure and get your father to come along. The role of Old Mahon is made for him. Tell him I said he must do it."

As the West Coast Performers dispersed, Rhiannon and I sidestepped our way past tables into the alcove to take up the bench seat.

I mouthed a greeting to familiar faces as their second glances bounced between me and Rhiannon. "Missus Joyce, how are you?"

She looked up from gathering her meeting papers, glanced at Rhiannon. "Well, well, well. If it's not Tomás O'Caiside." Her brow wrinkled as she cast an eye over my attire. Her pursed-lip scowl said, 'You should be ashamed of yourself.'

I fastened the buttons on my blazer.

Rhiannon said, "Hello, Bernadette."

"Hello, Ríonann, my dear." Mrs Joyce's face said, 'What on earth are you doing with him?'

"Are you well, Missus Joyce?"

"Fine, Tomás. Fine." Mrs Joyce became all business with her papers. "We just had a very productive meeting, so I'm fine. Amateur dramatics, Tomás. Of any interest to you? Maybe not. But Ríonann, the stage would suit you. I'll be in touch with your mother to raise it. How is your mother?"

"Coming out of hospital soon."

"Very good, very good. Your sister will look after her." Mrs Joyce rapped the table twice with the edge of her papers. "Now." She glanced again at us both, raised her chin in the air. I could see her sifting through old school registers in her head, trying to work out how old Rhiannon was. She gave a resigned sigh. "I think I'll leave you to it. Have a good evening."

I waited until Mrs Joyce had left the alcove before I sat down. "On first-name terms with my old school teacher, I see."

Rhiannon was giggling. "The only woman I know that has all the men she ever taught still shakin in their shoes."

"She was a vicious dragon."

"Ah, don't. She's a friend of Mammy's." Rhiannon was still laughing at me. "Though I heard she was *firm*, all right."

"Punched me once."

Rhiannon yelped. “What? No!” She laughed hard and rocked back on the bench seat, raising her thighs.

“I’m serious,” I said. “I was up on Cloonta Beg mount with sheep. Near where they put the television mast.”

“When you should’ve been in school?”

“Pissing rain. And yeah, I should’ve been in school the same day. My father was always keeping me off school to work the sheep. Didn’t Missus Joyce see me from the schoolroom window.”

“I’d say she’d be annoyed by that, all right.”

“She called me out to the front of the class the next day.”

“And?”

“She boxed me across the mouth.”

Rhiannon slapped a hand to her face in mock horror. “No!”

“Swear to Christ.” I turned my chin to show Rhiannon a scar that wasn’t there.

“Stop it.”

I tried my best Mrs Joyce voice. “All you’ll end up good for, Tomás O'Caiside, is chasing sheep around a hill.”

Rhiannon could barely talk. “That’s proper funny.”

“Still wouldn’t like to cross her,” I said.

Rhiannon wiped a tear from beneath an eye with a knuckle. “Jesus, I’d love to have seen that.”

“I’d never be calling her by her first name, for sure.”

“Ah, don’t.” She rubbed her leg against mine. “Poor little you.”

“Probably did me no harm, do you think?”

“Mindin sheep?”

“The punch in the gob from teacher.”

“Enough. Stop it.” Rhiannon blinked damp eyelashes. “You’ve me makeup fecked.”

“Boys must always respect their teachers. Them’s the rules.”

She recovered her composure. “I understand she suffered no bullshit did Missus Joyce. Or sheep-shit either, in your case.” Rhiannon chuckled again—that smile. “I think you’re different to other boys.”

Boys. She made me feel like a boy. "Good thing or bad thing?" I thought about Mrs Joyce and her disapproving look.

Rhiannon crossed her legs, sat forward, perched her perfect chin on the back of a hand. Her perfume was vanilla, floral, spicy. "A good thing. You're a man for a start, not a boy." Her big eyes were glassy, moist, her stare intent. "And you're a bit fuckin gorgeous. I hadn't realised before that half the bloody women in town are after you. Even the married ones."

The burn of a blush grew out of the top of my collarless T-shirt.

She said, "I'm wrecked fightin the bitches off."

I wondered what the women in town thought about me wandering around with a woman Rhiannon's age. "If that were anywhere near true," I said, "I know which half Missus Joyce would be cheering for." I swigged my pint. It was sour.

"God," she said. "Your face. The beer taste that bad?"

"Its tastes of…hopelessness."

She giggled.

"With an undertone of despair."

Rhiannon laughed, lifted an arm around my shoulders.

I stretched my neck, checked who might see us.

"You can have mine, so."

No-one was looking our way. "I don't even want mine," I said.

"Come here," she said, and inched closer. "When are you goin to whisk me off to London?"

I wasn't expecting that. "I'm not so sure I'm going to London."

She smiled. A forgiving smile, as if I had made some mistake. "What's to keep you here?"

"Other than work, you mean?"

"At the power station? What is it you do, shovel soot?" It came across as non-judgemental, but I couldn't be sure. "Come on," she said. "There are loads of jobs in London. I've checked. Place is full of jobs. Better jobs. Better opportunities."

I was relieved when she took back her arm.

It wasn't just the power station job that kept me in Duncarrick. I considered talking Rhiannon through how I was extending the family cottage—spare bedroom and a wider kitchen—how I was investing my money in sheep, and how, thanks to the E.E.C., farming was on the up. I was poised, ready to take advantage.

Then there was the fear. The fear of leaving.

I tried to catch Buckley's eye to complain about the beer. He was busy trying to operate the remote control for the television while serving more of his shitty beer to the young lads sitting up at the counter. Liverpool was playing Dinamo Bucuresti in a European Cup quarter-final soccer match on the flickering screen.

My mundane plans would not be of any interest to Rhiannon. Her attentions were far removed from agricultural property development and animal husbandry and the unmitigated hard graft and financial responsibilities that both involved. I doubted the commitment to such an enterprise of a girl who bothered to paint her toenails five different colours and shop around for a pair of sunset-red cowboy boots.

"London sounds exciting, all right." I took the glass to my lips, hoping the bite of the first sip had dulled my taste buds.

"We'd do well in London," she said. "You and I. Both of us together. We make a great team."

My throat tightened around the swallow of beer. It nearly choked me.

Buckley was still fumbling with the controls, his old bald-headed face dour, trying to stop the picture from scrolling upwards. A few of the lads were ribbing him.

"Fierce expensive, them decent aerials, Mister Buckley, are they?"

"Ones that work, you mean?" another said.

"I thought horizontal hold was a four-five-one formation."

Buckley wasn't perturbed. He jabbed the remote at the television. "Calm down, now. The lot a ye."

I left my pint down on the table, and she watched me light up a cigarette, staring and smiling as though it was the most remarkable ritual she had ever witnessed.

The lads at the bar grew impatient, struck up an out-of-key rendition of *You'll Never Walk Alone*. There was shoving, a punch on an arm. One took a lighter to another's Liverpool scarf.

Buckley had to call it to a halt. "Any more of that and ye'll be put out on your arses."

The ruckus dissolved into laughter.

"Toxic machismo," Rhiannon said, her face a scowl of contracted brows.

"What is?"

"Them is." She jutted her chin at the counter. "Like rutting stags, they are. Except they're at it all year round."

An old fella in a greasy cap shielded himself with his walking stick as he shuffled past the lads, fearful his pint would be knocked from his uncertain grip.

"Look at poor Michael," Rhiannon said. "He's terrified they'll set his mac alight."

"They're only having a laugh. I was the same myself, once."

"Can ya not smell it?"

"Michael can't help the smell," I said. "He's problems with a bag he wears."

"Not Michael. Them bucks at the counter. The whirlpool of aggressive hormones off them. Shauna McGarret reckons it's one reason they end up killin themselves. Competitive, toxic machismo."

My mouth gaped. Patriarchal ideology, social pressures, the propensity of young men to do themselves in: Professor Shauna McGarret had an opinion on the lot. "Easy on," I said. "None of them lads would think of doing that."

"You'd be surprised. They're a vulnerable bunch of angry, competing stags."

"How do you know that? They're having a drink, watching a soccer match. It's what lads do."

"Anyhow," she said, the intent stare back in her eyes. "I doubt you were ever an arsehole like them."

"Oh, now *you'd* be surprised."

Michael wobbled clear with his pint, found refuge by the pool table, propped against it for support. The children paused their playing, waited for him to shuffle on.

Shouts at the bar. The drag and scrape of bar stools across the floor as the lads drew back from the wash of a toppled pint of beer.

"Right," Buckley hollered, striding towards them, armed with a dishcloth. "Telly's going off."

I readied myself to go to Buckley's assistance, to help quell any rising aggression.

"Ah, no. Sorry." Muffled guffaws from the lads. "Jases we're sorry, Mister Buckley."

"Sit," Rhiannon said. "Buckley can cope. Though he's treating them so much like feckin children, he'll put them up to bed next."

Buckley mopped up the spill. "Lift that glass!"

The television remained on.

"See what I mean?" Rhiannon said. "Young men are such pricks." She leaned against me, placed a hand on the inside of my leg and massaged the muscle.

I drew my knees together, glanced around to see who might be watching, coughed. "The big fella." I jutted my head in the general direction of the bar. "Red soccer shirt. He can be awkward enough in drink."

"Conway." Rhiannon knew the lad. "He was a prick at school."

At school. A reminder that this woman feeling the inside of my thigh was little more than just out of school.

Her captured hand worked its way towards my crotch.

"Rhiannon." I checked again to see if anyone was watching. I half expected the father of the children playing pool to walk in on us. "Not here."

"Then leave the drinks. Let's go someplace we can pluck the goose."

"Jesus." I shook my head, huffed. "We've full pints."

"I'm falling in love with you, Tommy Cassidy."

"Don't!"

She was unsure if I meant 'Don't fall in love with me' or 'Don't grope me in Buckley's', but pulled her hand away just in case. She frowned in the general direction of the lads at the bar. Her shoulders slumped.

Even in all the make-up, she looked young. Young, beautiful, and a little forlorn.

Chapter 12

When Matt Darcy stomped out of my house, the remains of the string of raw sausages bulging through the clench of his angry fingers, I remained slumped in the chair and gazed into the open fire, only the flames for company.

My breath wheezed and whistled.

Charred turf popped and crackled.

A leaky tap dripped water into the sink.

My breathing had got worse, no wonder Matty mentioned it, and my condition would only deteriorate. "We've bronchodilators that'll relax the muscles in your lungs," the doctor had told me. "They'll widen your airways." His brow furrowed in obligatory compassion. "But if you really want to help yourself…Well, Tommy, I suppose you know what you have to do."

I hadn't long left.

The flicker of the flames was a comfort, and along with the bit of food and the alcohol still in my system, weighed heavily on my eyelids. A weary apathy seeped into my bones.

I lit a cigarette, filled my lungs with smoke. I hadn't the breath to blow out the match, so I shook it to death.

'My way or no way', that was how it was with Matty. Always happy to give advice—*too* happy to give advice—he had a tendency to forget that advice was just that, *advice*: an opinion, a recommendation, offered as a guide. Not an instruction, not an order.

I regretted the argument, but even Alma would agree Matty could be awkward, and his advice often came across as a command, a mandate. There's a difference between advising and controlling. Matty forgot that sometimes.

He was jealous of the little bit of money coming my way from John Kavanaugh—correction, the lot of money—with no regard for what I might use it for. Matty only thought in numbers.

The turf glowed. I sheltered in the comfort of its peaty aroma and counted my misfortunes. A troubled marriage. Noleen's death and the subsequent lack of children. The failed farm. Rhiannon. Everything.

It was all my fault. I knew that.

There was a time when I thought I could make a better job of the farm than Daddy had. But Alma and I were only married when Europe decided there was something wrong with a grant system that encouraged mountains of excess butter, storage warehouses of lamb and beef, and silos of unwanted wheat.

I lost the job at the power station just as E.E.C. grants started to dwindle.

"If ya want to get something bad enough," Daddy used to say, "you've to work for it. And sometimes, Thomas, the workin's more of a reward than the gettin." Mammy would scoff when he came out with that one.

I was as unsuccessful as Alma told me I would be.

My recent turn of fate was the one thing, the only positive thing, that prevented my melancholy from becoming humiliation. I needed to remain strong. A plan was forming. A final gesture before it was too late. My chance to right some of the wrongs.

The cigarette grew hot on my fingers, its tail of ash long and leaning. I flicked it into the fire.

I was due some good fortune, and John Kavanaugh had provided it.

Turf tumbled in on itself, its soft rumble disturbing my reverie.

I was determined. Matt Darcy wouldn't get in my way. Alma wasn't here to ridicule.

John Kavanaugh. Of all people. I smiled at the irony. My smile grew into a yawn.

The fire died to embers, and in the quiet of the miserly light of the kitchen, the tap released a lonely drip into the sink. It was the last thing I heard before sleep took me and the dreams returned.

Chapter 13

"Have we enough?"

"We have plenty."

"Do you know what you're doing? The doctor–"

"What about the doctor?"

"I don't know. Should we ask the doctor?"

"We don't need the doctor."

"No. It's just…It's hard to remember sometimes."

"That's what we want."

"Yes…I'm sorry."

"A drop of tea. Wash them down."

Chapter 14

Following the discussion with Rhiannon in Buckley's, I asked around half-heartedly about opportunities in London. A bloke in town told me Tate and Lyle, the sugar refiners, were recruiting at their factory in the East End.

Matt Darcy helped me complete the single-sided application form. He was sweating from an eight-mile training run when we sat down at the table. "Is this it?"

"That's all they sent, yeah."

"Are you goin to sell up?" Matty knew enough about me to fill in the boxes without asking me any questions. "What about all you've spent on the farm? You're only just gettin goin."

"I'm exploring options."

"That young one turnin yer head, Tommy?"

I barked out a dismissive laugh. "If I didn't know you so well, I'd say you were jealous, Matty."

"No. Get stuck in. Fair play to ya."

"Not jealous?"

"Just lookin out for you I am."

"A *little* jealous?"

"Just fuckin be careful is all."

"I'm grand. Sorry."

"Okay," he said. "It's good yer grand. I'm leavin, too."

"Leaving Ireland?"

"Old John Kavanaugh."

I barked out a laugh. "You're leaving John Kavanaugh?"

"Yeah."

"I didn't know you two had such a relationship."

"Fuck off. The power station. I'm leaving the power station. Goin out on me own." A bead of sweat fell from his chin, splashed the bottom of the form.

"I thought you were sacked?"

"I wasn't sacked. Though that little incident with the ceramic thing, the electrical insulator, has forced the issue.

Bastard Kavanaugh, sure ya couldn't work under him. Who'd want to take orders from a bully?"

"What will you do?"

"Auctioneering. I'm meeting a fella tomorrow."

"Don't you need qualifications or something?"

"Scrawl yer name here. Just a head for figures. It's easy money. Get in touch if yer sellin. You can be me first client."

Matty had the head for figures, but I was unsure how easy the money would be.

My signature faltered, bogged when it reached the damp spot on the paper.

Matty wrote the address for Tate and Lyle on the front of the envelope.

The envelope sat in the glove compartment of the car for almost a week before I threw it away. I told Matt Darcy I wouldn't be his first client.

*

I broke the news to Rhiannon on a trip up to Dublin to see a reunion show of the original line-up of the Irish folk band, Sláinte.

Reservations I had about the journey away from Duncarrick were set aside when Rhiannon insisted we stop for a contorting bout of back-seat sex in a field off the Ballaghaderreen-to-Tibohine road. When we got back underway, we wound the windows down and drove through a sweaty summer heat that would wilt metal.

Rhiannon seemed her talkative self, shouting above the din of rushing air, full of opinions on the concert. "That Stephen Moor. He looks like a bearded potato."

"Hold on," I said. "He also sings like an angel."

Rhiannon sang a line from one of his songs. She had a good voice. Laughter and songs in the roaring draughts of the open windows.

We were somewhere clear of Mullingar when she brought up the subject of London. We wound up the windows and I told her that I would not be going to London. I explained that if she was insistent, if she was sure that was what she wanted to do, she would have to go without me.

I thought it only right that she knew. I was being honest with her, and with myself.

An argument erupted.

She accused me of dumping her for someone else. That's the word she used, 'dumping', as if we were a couple of school kids falling out in the playground. The next thing, she didn't want to go to the show at all. "Stop the car," she said.

I tried to calm her. I explained my plans for the farm, though she'd heard them before, and I told her straight that I understood her reservations about taking on such a life. It wouldn't be easy. "London isn't part of my plans," I said. "And you've made it clear that farming isn't part of yours."

"It's not," she yelled. "There's no way I'm staying here to raise fuckin sheep."

"I understand that," I said. "It's bloody hard work."

"But there's a complication."

"What complication?"

Rhiannon was reluctant to explain her 'complication'. When she did, I nearly killed us both.

*

It was the worst concert I had ever attended. The four musicians seemed delighted to be back together, but I didn't listen and found myself hoping the notoriously heavy drinkers got stupid drunk in the interval, started fighting, smashed each other's instruments, and never played together again.

Rhiannon must have felt the same. On the way across the potholed car park, I asked her if she enjoyed Sláinte.

"Fuck Sláinte. And fuck you."

She wanted to stay the night in Dublin on her own, get the train down in the morning. There was no way in hell I'd leave her in Dublin to find her own way home.

Chapter 15

I'll tell you something about Matt Darcy. At nine years of age, Matt Darcy could leap a five-bar gate from a standing start. Not a notable achievement for, let us say, someone twice that age and six-foot tall, but young Matty was diminutive. The gate stood a full inch and a half higher than him. I'd stand and watch, smoking a hand-rolled cigarette, and be amazed at his athleticism.

Never tall, hard work made him lean, and a competitive fire in his belly forced him to challenge his own physical ability at every opportunity. Apart from leaping field gates at will, he ran the eighteen-mile perimeter of the lake in a village-record time, and led a light-weight but well-drilled tug-o-war team to victory at the Town Fair for six consecutive years.

As we grew up, no physical or sporting endeavour seemed beyond my friend, Matt Darcy.

Take the football, for example. Many people are *good* at football. Fewer are *very good.* Others, like me, are better at watching, and fishing the ball from the stream that runs alongside the playing field. Few have the perfect synthesis of strength and endurance, of guile and agility, of confidence and determination to be *sublimely good.*

These are the individuals who play their sport with a divinity gifted to them by no less a footballing coach than God himself. At least, that was Matt Darcy's explanation for his remarkable prowess on the football field.

"I'm to Gaelic football what Georgie Best is to soccer, Tommy." Adding with a wink, "Not as fond of the girls, but."

Modesty never burdened the young Matt Darcy.

He did excel in the football. He'd tell anyone who'd listen that he made the pitch, aged only fifteen, when Mayo beat Leitrim in the 1967 Connaught Senior Football Championship at Tuam Stadium in Galway. It was true, he did make the pitch, but only after the final whistle, during the celebratory crowd invasion.

Following that, he wrote letters to the Gaelic Athletic Association calling for fences around pitches to protect players. A precocious arrogance and not yet old enough to legally smoke.

Within two years, he was a regular member of the Mayo county Gaelic football squad. Before long, extraordinary speed and agility enabled him to dominate the centre field in every match he played.

Near the middle of the 1970s, Matty missed out on a Connaught Championship final due to an injured shoulder. He was devastated, and Mayo lost to Sligo without him.

A fallow decade followed with Matty in and out of the Mayo squad, plagued by the weakened shoulder. It wasn't until the second half of the 1980s that his opportunity came again. The shoulder was holding up well and Mayo's fortunes were improved by Matty's regular appearances. In 1987, Mayo was slated to meet Galway in the provincial Connaught Final.

Matty and the team were in phenomenal form. Now in his mid-thirties, it was generally accepted by everyone who followed the sport that this was to be Matty's final chance at footballing glory.

A month before the final, the Mayo team embarked on a brief promotional tour of the county, playing short exhibition matches in small-town locations. They wanted everyone to know they were back, with the best centre-half-forward the county had ever seen.

In deference to Matty's wishes, they came here to Duncarrick. We put up a team. Three other villages gathered teams together for the privilege of playing against the heroes of the Mayo squad. Old John Kavanaugh captained our team.

The day of the incident followed a night of heavy rain.

*

A keen, early-morning sun lifted dampness from the grass, Its warmth helped give the event a festive feel. An event committee had organised a tug-of-war that no-one signed up for, and a turf-cutting demonstration, and a man with a beard to show how difficult it was to cut wool from wriggling sheep with rusty hand clippers.

Having Matt Darcy, our local hero, in the Mayo team of all-stars heightened the excitement.

The only thing missing were sticks with county-coloured balloons tied to them.

Expectations were high.

I felt low.

Matty excused himself from signing autographs for the children of people he went to school with and jogged over to me, his face lopsided with smiles. "Hey, misery guts," he said. "Cheer up, ya sour bastard." He was togged out in the green and red, his well-muscled legs pale as limewash. "Get over her. It's been months."

I scanned the field in reflex, hoping beyond hope to see Rhiannon Harkin strolling towards me from the road.

"She wasn't right for you, Tommy."

"Will you shut up, to fuck," I said.

Matty spoke the truth, of course he did. I knew that, yet I couldn't rid myself of the raw hollowness I felt without her.

"Old John Kavanaugh's putting out a team," I said.

Matty scoffed. "Ya seen who's in it? Them lads wouldn't know a football if one hit them in the testicles."

"Be careful is all. It's slippy out there and they've not a clue what they're at."

"I know ya miss her, Tommy. Just be careful, *you*."

What did he think I was going to do?

"Listen," Matty said. "We're after an extra kitman for the big match. I can get you in if ya want to be part of the adventure."

"I don't know much about–"

"You can fold a bloody shirt, sure? Come on. You can travel down in the team bus."

"The team has a bus?"

"Buckley's lending us his school bus for the Connaught Final, yeah."

I gave the field another scan. Two young girls in flowery dresses held hands and chewed on sugar sandwiches as they stood staring at the bent-over man clipping sheep. The turf cutters were propped on the long shafts of their strap socket sleáns, talking and laughing and not doing much cutting of turf. A group of lads made running hand passes with the football Matty had just written his name across. Old men with walking sticks gathered on the side-line of a deserted and, for the day that was in it, hallowed playing pitch. Women stretched out plaid wool blankets on the damp grass, their camp for the day. But there was no sign of Rhiannon.

She was far away in England and, I was sure, not thinking about me.

I paid for Rhiannon to go to England a few days after our argument in the car, and I had not heard from her since. It had been a couple of months but seemed like a small lifetime. It had been a final goodbye, the ending of our relationship, but a message of some sort wouldn't have hurt her. If only to let me know she was all right. I still carried the regret of not talking her out of leaving.

Buckley, seemingly unburdened by regrets, had the stocked freezer from his grocery shop put on the back of a cart and had it set up in the corner of the field. The clatter from the petrol-driven generator was a clarion call for children to pester parents for ice cream.

Why not be the Mayo team's kitman? I knew a few of the players, and if I could travel as far as Dublin with Rhiannon, I could cope with a journey to Castlebar with Matty. It might do me good. "All right, so."

"You'll be fine," Matty said. "You can be my boot man."

"I'm not polishing your boots."

"Less work than your cowpunchers."

I no longer wore the red boots Rhiannon bought me. "Fuck off, Matty. You're annoying me now."

*

The plan was for each member of the Mayo squad to play in one of four games against the local teams. The matches were billed as friendly, six-a-side kick-a-bouts of fifteen minutes each, opportunities to showcase the abilities of the squad players. Everyone enjoyed the thrill of it all, and as the matches progressed, even I felt lifted, buoyed by the skills and natural competitive rivalry.

Capitalising on the novelty of the occasion, Buckley sold ice lollies to lines of children at inflated prices.

"Aren't they eleven pence cheaper back in the shop, Mister Buckley?"

"Who sent you over? Yer father, was it? Was it? Tell him I've a pitch fee to recover. Now, pay up or put that back in the fridge and step aside the queue."

I wasn't aware of any pitch fee.

Matt Darcy's team of six was rostered to play in the final game, a suitable climax to the event here in Duncarrick.

By the time Matty's team took to the field, Buckley was winding the generator lead around a shirt-sleeved arm. In addition to the ice lollies, he had sold out of biscuits, warm red lemonade that had no time to cool in the freezer, all the sweets from the shop, and loaves of bread and packets of wholemeal flour. He had cleared out the grocery shop. Business boomed for Mr Buckley.

Matty's team was matched against old John Kavanaugh and his team of notorious thugs and rogues. When the Mayo head coach got wind of the calibre and reputation of the home side, he tried to cancel the game.

The crowd got restless. Derisive calls of "Spoilsport" and "Big shot" were heard around the field.

The coach relented.

It must have been the final minute. We had witnessed a quarter of an hour of mayhem, boots and fists flying with indiscriminate abandon. The head coach had paced the sideline screaming obscenities and was held back from running on-field on three occasions by Mayo team officials.

The crowd, in the end, was anxious for it to stop. The game had lost any entertainment value and had descended into chaos. There was growing concern that the six Mayo players might be killed just before the big match with Galway.

Matt Darcy rose into the air, instinct forbidding him to hold back, at full stretch for a high ball that even he would be unlikely to hold on to. Incredibly, like a man in possession of an extra finger, he gathered the ball one-handed and drew it to his chest.

Before Matty landed, John Kavanaugh skidded in from behind, feet first, roaring some terrible roar. He was intent on injury; there was no other explanation.

The crack of bone echoed off the clubhouse wall, crossed the open field, and sailed on out over the lake.

People raised hands to their cheeks and spun away.

A woman screamed.

Everyone there heard the multiple fracture of Mayo's chances in the forthcoming Provincial Connaught Final against Galway.

Agnes Brown's new baby sobbed.

Matty lay crumpled in a twisted heap, a hand at his knee, his agonised face buried in the crook of an elbow. He wept into the grass, his dream, our dream, the county's dream, destroyed.

Old men gnawed on knuckles.

The baby took a long inhalation.

For drawn-out seconds, no-one stirred. A hush descended over the field, a panic-stricken stillness, the nearby splash of a stream in spate the only sound.

Old John Kavanaugh picked his thin frame up from the damp grass, combed back his fair hair with his fingers, and glared down at the stricken Matt Darcy. He shook his head, turned, and he limped off the pitch to the lonesome wail of a distressed newborn who cried for a county.

Chapter 16

John Kavanaugh's surveyor, James Gorman, seemed to find summer mornings a challenge. He slid his jacket down his arms. "It's like the side of a blooming mountain, Mister Cassidy. How far up do you go?" For a heavy man, he had a thin neck. An enormous Adam's apple bobbed above the knot of his tie when he spoke.

The sun scorched the stones dry in the front yard. The village glistened. Gold and green fields, cradled in the sculpted lap of the hillside, were illuminated to a shimmer by light reflected off the lake. Damp folded back from the fields in wide, rolling sheets of warm mist.

When I was able to walk in such a landscape, so perfect it caught my breath, my eyes never pointed in the same direction as my feet. A summer morning in Duncarrick.

Alma loved summer mornings.

Noleen would have loved summer mornings.

"Up onto the rise," I said. "And keep going. Past the tree. It's not the first or second bank you come to but the third. The wired one, way in the distance."

Sweat broke out on his shirt beneath his breasts as I spoke. Gorman loosened his tie.

I said, "If you see any evidence of an old castle up there, let me know, it might add value."

James Gorman had no humour. "Heritage holdings only detract from the value these days, Mister Cassidy. If the Environmental Network people get wind of it, you'll have one of their member organisations swarming over your land for the next ten years. You won't be let near it while they pick bones out the ground with spoons, and expose entire walls with toothbrushes." He unfolded a Tilley hat from a jacket pocket. "I know of a case in Ballintupper," he said. "Down below the Abbey. The poor man raised five children and died of old age before the sale of land went through. I'll get my boots."

*

James Gorman paced the meadows, pausing frequently to lift his hat and push hair back over his head, peer over stone walls, scribble notes in his jotter. He had no electro-optical scanner. At field edges, he would stretch his arms wide to the side then clap his hands together in front, before pacing in the direction his fingers pointed.

At seemingly random locations, he jagged a spade into the ground, the chink of metal against stone, and hoked around. What was he looking for? If he was checking for drainage, that wasn't a problem, the stony ground was a sieve. If it wasn't a sieve, the house would have been washed away decades ago.

I grew concerned he would unearth Alma's clocks.

He wrestled with the gate of the second field, then disappeared over the rise.

What if the land was worth nothing? What if he tells John Kavanaugh to reduce his offer, or worse, to walk away from the deal altogether?

I staggered back into the house to my chair and lit a cigarette. My knees bounced, my legs restless. I coughed phlegm into the fire, rolled my shoulders, and waited for James Gorman to return from measuring my land.

James Gorman took his time.

*

"What do you think, Mister Gorman?" I held his spade as he changed back into his shoes.

A dark line ran around his hat where the crown met the brim. "I think this weight'll be the death of me, that's what I think, Mister Cassidy." His boots were damp from dew. Spikelets of crouch grass clung to his diamond-patterned socks. He dabbed at his flushed forehead with a handkerchief. "I'll head back to the office now." He paused to take a hefty breath. "Fill out my report." He threw his hat into the boot of his car. The swept-over hair was matted to his head. "I'll have it to Mister Kavanaugh by the morning."

My heart sank. "I see."

Gorman must have noticed. "I'm sure you understand, Mister Cassidy." He took the spade from me, making it awkward for him to tie his laces. "It was Mister Kavanaugh who commissioned me, so I'm beholden to him to let him be the first to hear my considerations." He glanced at his car, eager to leave. "I wouldn't worry, though," he said.

The tension in my body eased.

James Gorman flashed a smile. "There really is nothing to worry about, Mister Cassidy." He didn't act like a pisser. Matt Darcy was wrong again.

Chapter 17

I don't know why I was invited to the wedding of young John Kavanaugh and Rhiannon Harkin. Some childish act of revenge by Rhiannon? I don't know. I went with Matt Darcy.

We knew that young John and Rhiannon had met in London, that John had his own construction company, and that this was being talked of as a 'whirlwind romance', worthy of a Hollywood movie.

Rhiannon looked sensational.

Matty thought his invite was a belated apology for the incident on the Gaelic football pitch months earlier. For this reason, he refused to buy a wedding present. He spent the day with his splinted leg resting on a bar stool, chatting to the barman, a handsome young man with freckles and a head of ruby curls that had the reflective sheen of a sucked lozenge.

Matty was lamenting his missed opportunity of a Connaught Final winner's medal and was asking the barman's view on whether he should go for the knee replacement operation he'd been offered.

Not to be outdone, old John Kavanaugh carried the hitch in his step magnanimously, limping around the hotel while boasting about how, contrary to tradition, he paid a hefty contribution to the reception costs. "They've no money, and I wanted it to be right, you know?" He shook hands and laughed with senior managers from the Electricity Supply Board and Bord na Móna while his wife slugged back gin and tonics.

I spent my time talking to the bride's sister, Alma Harkin.

Alma Harkin seemed to share my distrust of the Kavanaughs. "I hope this marriage lasts," she said.

I nearly choked on my beer. "They'll be grand, I'm sure. He'll whisk her back off to England, and she'll want for nothing."

"She's spoilt, Tom. And a spoilt child makes poor choices."

Rhiannon seemed over me, yet made a point of draping herself over young John Kavanaugh, her new husband, every time I looked her way. They were a suited couple, both ambitious, both attractive, and both young.

During his speech, young John Kavanaugh thanked his mother and father and boasted about how well he was doing in London: lots of work on, twenty-plus blokes employed, just after buying some serious construction plant. He said it was a long way off, but he was in talks with a house builder in Manchester and was hoping to buy the company out. It would make him one of the biggest house builders in the northwest of England. That got a round of applause from the guests. He made us raise a toast to his father who seed-funded his investment and who encouraged him to be, "Brave and brash and completely ruthless." Matt Darcy didn't stand for the toast.

*

The band, a girl and four lads over from London, played their third and final encore. The lads wore matching grey suits, their thin, knitted crimson ties loosened at the neck, sweat pushing through the spine of their jackets. Their beards were far too long. The girl wore a red dress that was far too short. She had long, well-muscled legs like Rhiannon.

Applause for the band segued into disco music that was far too loud. It was difficult to hold any type of conversation without your voice ending up grating and hoarse.

I leaned towards Alma and shouted above the music. "My condolences for the loss of your mother."

Alma's blank face was hard to read.

"I should have mentioned it earlier," I said. "I'm sorry."

She said, "At least you've the decency to mention it at all."

"You mean the speeches?"

"I listened to a speech from the groom's father, and another from the groom himself, and neither toasted absent friends. All we heard was how wealthy and successful the Kavanaughs are."

"Try to not let it upset you," I said. "The Kavanaughs would want everyone to believe they don't have troubles. They wouldn't want to be sharing problems in public."

The music held the conversation at a pause. As the first song ended, Alma said, "I'm not upset. My mother's death was a blessed release. But when the bride's mother has died only a few months ago, you'd think they'd pay her a tribute."

I nodded my agreement.

"Yes, ladies and gentlemen," the disc jockey announced over the speakers. "*A Groovy Kind of Love*, there by Mister Phil Collins. Number one in England and number one in Ireland. Just like the Kavanaugh family."

A cheer went up in the Kavanaugh corner of the reception room.

Matt Darcy caught my eye and mimicked shoving two fingers down his throat to vomit over the counter.

"What do you think of the groom's mother?" I said. It was mischievous, but I wanted to know Alma's view.

"God help her, she's trapped," Alma said, looking over. "The clothes. The hair. The forced smiles. The booze."

I cast around for Rhiannon. She was on the dance floor with friends, laughing, yelling at the disc jockey to pick up the pace. No-one would trap her.

"I don't want the same thing to happen to Rhiannon," Alma said, as though she could see right into my head. "But if it does, she has only herself to blame."

"Where's the main man?" the disc jockey inquired. "Where is he? Mister John Kavanaugh, you're wanted on the dance floor. The bride wants to dance with somebody. And so does Whitney Houston."

Alma reached a hand towards me, touched my arm. Long fingers. Despite the music, she said, "How are plans for the farm faring out?"

"Yeah," I said. "Grand. Thank you."

"I passed the house the other day."

"You did?" Alma lived in town. My house wasn't in the sort of location she'd pass accidentally.

"You're making a good job of the extension."

The extension was draining me, costing me much more than I anticipated. "It's slow progress," I said. "But it's coming along."

"I like it," Alma said. "You'll have a fine house when it's finished."

I wanted to lean over and kiss her.

"Have you bought more sheep?"

I was sitting with Alma Harkin, at her sister's wedding, and she was asking me about sheep.

"I have, yeah." I had doubts about the quality of the stock, but I didn't mention that to Alma. "But I'm nowhere near capacity."

"You do have a lot of land. Just keep an eye on prices. The E.E.C. are going through turbulent times. Meat markets are all over the place. I think the phrase they use is 'fluctuating'. But I think you're right, it could be the right time to invest when prices are depressed."

"You follow the meat prices?"

"I can read a newspaper, Mister Cassidy."

I laughed.

She laughed.

"You're doing the right thing," she said.

"I am?"

"Yes. Keeping on the job at the power station whilst you get the farm established."

That too was draining me, physically, but I needed the money. Hardy sheep of a reasonable quality didn't come cheap. "I thought it best not to burn my bridges too soon," I said.

"Very wise," she said.

I went to the counter, ordered us both another drink, a pint for me, a tonic water for Alma.

Alma sat straight-backed, cross-legged, hands rested in her lap, smart in her blue dress. She was watching Rhiannon.

John hadn't wanted to dance. Rhiannon had left the floor and was pressed against her new husband, feeding him wedding cake with her fingers.

I twisted my cigarette into an ashtray, told the barman to buy himself and Matty a pint and keep the change. I gathered up the drinks and virtually skipped back to my seat.

Later, when the room was hot with moving bodies, Alma and I joined the bride and groom and most of the guests on a crowded dancefloor. A disco number. I didn't recognise it, but I shuffled my feet and swung my arms in not too awful a manner.

Rhiannon worked her way behind me and bumped me with her arse. She winked when I turned around, then laughed and shimmied off through the throng to her husband.

Sometime late in the evening, Robert Palmer was crooning about a woman he fell in love with unintentionally; she was all good loving at once. It might have been the drink I had taken, but the nonsense of his lyric made perfect sense to me.

As the song faded away, I leaned my head close to Alma's and said, "Are you familiar with the Celtic saying, 'going to a wedding is the making of another'?"

Dark brown curls that bounced on her shoulder tickled my cheek. I moved away reluctantly.

Alma blushed. "We didn't come together."

"No. But anyway."

"Was that a proposal, Tom Cassidy?"

I blushed.

Alma leaned back in close and said, "I'm not like Rhiannon."

I wanted to say, "I agree with you. You're far more interesting." but Billy Ocean was shrieking through the speakers, imploring a lady to get out of his dreams and get into his car. It put me off Billy Ocean.

It was the truth, Alma was nothing like Rhiannon. There was no-one like Rhiannon.

I shrugged, drunk, unsure as a fool, and raised a thumb to Alma.

Chapter 18

"I've Gorman's valuation, Tommy. Came through yesterday." *Yeshterday*. John Kavanaugh hovered in front of the fire, his fur coat buttoned around him, his hands plunged deep into pockets. His trousers were tucked into what looked like leather-lined Wellington boots, an expensive precaution against the goose shit, maybe. He wouldn't take tea when I offered it. "Not particularly good news, I'm afraid."

I halted my cup on its journey to my mouth, placed it on the draining board. A chilling shiver of disappointment spread through me. I tried to mask it. "I'm sorry about the car seat," I said.

"Car seat? What car seat?"

"Your car seat. A few weeks back."

"Ach, that's nothin. Nothin at all. Mark cleaned it up. Not a worry. I've been sick in it myself a hundred times." He chuckled. "He's well used to it."

"All the same. Yellow seats."

"I said not to worry, Tommy."

"You sure?"

"Of course."

"I've only ever been sick once before. In a car, I mean."

"Getting back to the valuation."

"The valuation, yeah." I swallowed hard. "Not good you say?"

"Not good, no. But listen, there's no need to worry." John Kavanaugh's breath made pale-grey clouds in the cold kitchen air. "We have an agreement."

I almost reached to shake his hand. "How much did he say?"

"We'll come to that. I've a copy of the letter in the car. I'll let you have it. I meant to bring it in."

I turned to pick up my tea. Beyond the window, Mark, the handsome driver, *chauffeur* if you like, patrolled the golden car.

I was glad I didn't have to face Mark. I had made an awful mess of the back seat on the way back from Buckley's the night I had a drink with John Kavanaugh. I was no longer able for heavy nights of drink.

Mark was on the lookout. For Matt Darcy, perhaps. He was right to be wary. Matty could appear coming down the lane from around by Mulligan's bridge at any time. Though it was fair to say that Matty passed my house less frequently since we had the row over Kavanaugh buying the fields. And I was grand with that.

"But listen, Tommy," Kavanaugh said. "I want to let you in on a little secret?"

"Sorry, John. I was looking out at the car."

"No, that's fine." Kavanaugh glanced behind him at the inadequate fire, lifted the furred collar of his coat around his neck. When his hands were back in his pockets, he said, "Listen to me, Tommy. I didn't become as wealthy as I am today by squandering my gains. You get my drift?"

I didn't get his drift at all.

"I'd like to share a little trick with you," he said. "A little manoeuvre I've played several times. What do you say? It makes no difference to me whether you want to go along with it or not, but I thought I'd mention it anyway because it could save you a bit of money."

I was keen on saving money.

"You see, once you sell to me, Tommy, the Government will be after you for the C.G.T. I wouldn't do this for everyone, now, but you and I can come to an arrangement. Just between the two of us. How does that sound to you?"

This was unfamiliar territory for me. Despite the cold of the kitchen, sweat gathered beneath my shirt. The hot tea didn't help, so I put it down. I coughed to clear my throat. "I'm not sure what C.G–"

"C.G.T.? Sorry, Tommy. When you're doing big deals every day like I am, you take all the bullshit terminology for granted. C-G-T, Tommy."

Pronouncing the letters slower and louder made me none the wiser.

"Capital Gains Tax. You see, Tommy, you're under the impression that the land out there belongs to you."

It did belong to me. It belonged to my father before me, to his father before him. "It is my land."

He shook his head at my offer of a cigarette. "You'd think that, wouldn't you?" His fur coat flapped as he spoke, drawing smoke from the fire that rolled its way up the breast. "But the bloody Government has a different take on it. They allow you to think it's all yours, until you want to sell it."

I opened my mouth to speak, but I was unsure where to start with the questions.

"You see, Tommy, when you come to sell an asset like that little bit of land of yours, the Government think you owe them a big slice of the money. You get me? They want in on the action."

It wasn't the biggest plot of land in Ireland, but neither would I have described it as 'little'. John Kavanaugh was talking down its value, preparing me for the bad news in James Gorman's report. And what was all this about being 'in on the action'?

I blew smoke into the air.

"A bloody third of it," he said. "You'll have to pay the Government nearly a third of what I give you."

I didn't need Matty to work out what a third of one hundred and fifty thousand euros would be. "Why's that?"

"Because the tax man is a greedy bastard, Tommy. With an insatiable appetite for our money. Your money. You know that." He used the tone of voice you'd save for someone who was dopey but harmless.

I had very few dealings with tax. Alma managed all the finances of the farm. I couldn't say if the tax man was a greedy bastard or not, but I didn't want to give him one-third of the money I was about to receive from John Kavanaugh.

He pulled a hand from a pocket. "I'm a deal maker, Tommy. A businessman. I do very good deals." He opened a hand to me, as if he was showing me the very good deal he had sitting in its palm.

Hairs lifted on the nape of my neck. "I'm sure you do, John." I didn't trust myself to pick up the mug of tea for fear I'd spill it. I needed this deal to go through.

"Makes not a blind bit of difference to me," Kavanaugh continued, "but there's a way you can slash your tax burden." He chopped the air with an angled sweep of his hand. "What do you say, Tommy?"

Tension in my shoulders fell away. He was going ahead with the deal. "Sounds grand."

"I can't get rid of it all, but I can save you a good lump. And it's all very simple if we work together." He gave a conspiratorial smile, shrugged, and re-pocketed the hand. "Up to you, Tommy. Just tell me whether you want to go along with it or not."

"Is it legal?" I asked.

He swayed back and forth in his coat and laughed. "Isn't it between friends, Tommy?" Smoke from the fire swirled around him. "Just you and me. Not a bother."

He was allowing me into the secrets of the multi-millionaires. He had the gift, the knowledge that only wealthy people had access to, the knowledge that kept them wealthy. Matt Darcy might be able to calculate the tax I would have to pay, but John Kavanaugh could reduce it.

Matty, Alma and I had spoken about this sort of thing in the past. "If all the millionaires paid the tax due from them," Matty said one evening, "the Government could leave pensions alone and there'd be some form of a pension left when our time comes." Matty had flapped his hands in the air. He tended to be more animated in Alma's company. "Three point four billion pound, that's what I reckon the underpayment to be. And that's in a year." His hands fluttered around his head like loosed pigeons. “They wouldn’t be looking to take away the telephone allowance if the wealthy coughed up their taxes.” Alma looked on, impressed with his number work. I chipped in with, “You’d do it yourself if you had the money. They pay people to set up these tax avoidance schemes. Was on the radio.” Matty wasn’t listening to me. “The bus passes’ll be the next to go.” A wagging finger. “This country is in a mess because people don’t pay their proper tax.” “Listen to you, Tom,” Alma said. “Trying to sound like some economic analyst in the newspaper.” Her voice weighed heavily with sarcasm. “I’m sure Matty makes a valid point. It’s not as if you’ll ever be wealthy enough to be bothering with tax avoidance schemes, will you? What do you think, Matty?”

John Kavanaugh shuffled from foot to foot, a look of impatient expectation written across his orange features.

“Sorry, John,” I said. “I was just…. Sorry. What is it you want me to go along with?”

John Kavanaugh punched the air. “Good man, Tommy. We need to concentrate, now, be nimble, keep a clear head.”

His jubilance was unnerving.

“You’re a man after my own heart, I’ll say that about ya, Tommy. Only soft eejits pay tax, and you’re no soft eejit. Smart people avoid it. I avoid it and that makes me smart.” He winked, an extravagant jerk of the head.

I wanted John Kavanaugh to tell Matt Darcy that I was smart, too.

“Rules are for fools, Tommy.” Kavanaugh was rubbing his hands together for warmth, looking about him. “Have you anything left of the whiskey? Open her up. I’ll tell you what we’ll do, and we’ll drink to fools and their rules.”

Chapter 19

In the spring of 1988, Alma Harkin and I were wedded. Less than six months after Rhiannon married John Kavanaugh.

I was convinced Alma was who I needed. She wasn't afraid of hard work, had a good head for figures, wasn't obsessed with painting her nails, yet wasn't the last ewe into the pen when God was administering good looks. (Jesus, that's a stout thing for me to come out with. She was good-looking, handsome, let's leave it at that.)

Matt Darcy agreed with me. "I tell ya now, Tommy." He removed his glasses, checked the lenses for smears, replaced them, grinned. "You have the best woman in the whole of Ireland." I detected some relief in his tone. "Congtaulations, Tommy. I'm happy for you."

Alma was to be my support, my work and life partner, the one to help me realise my plans. The farm would be a success with her help.

We held the wedding reception in Buckley's Bar and Lounge. It was a modest affair, Alma didn't want it elaborate.

John and Rhiannon came over from England. I didn't speak to either of them the whole day, and I was happy enough about that.

We ate a fine buffet. Lisa-Marie Gavin made sure Buckley provided proper plates and not the paper ones he usually supplied at functions.

Alma had planned for no formal speeches, but Father Roche, who conducted the brief and simple ceremony with his usual solemnity, insisted on saying a few words of thanks to God for the food. It was good of him to bother. He spoke at length about Alma's mother, Mae Harkin, and her work at the power station. He must have rambled on for a good half-hour in all and managed to include something about it never being too late, in God's eyes, to get married and start a family.

Matty, my best man, then felt obliged to stand up and share an acceptably embarrassing anecdote involving me, an endoscope used for sheep insemination, a metal detector, and the Dublin Philharmonic Orchestra. He also said some gratifying words about how beautiful Alma looked in her wedding frock.

The drinking got underway.

There was no music. Alma didn't want music. It was the first wedding I had been to without music, but that's what Alma wanted, so I was happy with that.

There was laughter.

Neala Thomas got her husband to do the trick with the eye.

"Go on, Frank, do it." She was on her feet, laughing, garnering attention with flicking waves of her hands. "Shush, listen, watch this. Watch this, everyone, it's dynamite. Come on, Frank."

Frank Thomas had enough drink inside him to go along with it. He stood up as Neala sat down. "Right, so."

The pub fell quiet.

"I've a trick no-one else here can do," Frank announced.

Men who'd seen the trick before turned back to their conversations at the counter.

Matty came up beside me. "Not the eye trick, is it?"

"Afraid it might be, yeah," I said.

"At your fuckin weddin?"

Neala liked her and Frank to be the centre of attention, but I didn't mind. "He's all right."

"If anyone else can do this," Frank said, "I'll give them five pounds." He lifted his wife's glass from the table.

Neala screeched, "Ah no, Frank, not my drink," but she was rolling on her seat.

"Right," Frank shouted. "See this?" He pointed at the glass. "Now. Five pounds if you can do this. Okay?" He raised the drink into the air, slowly, like a clumsy illusionist at a town fair. "Everyone ready?"

Expectant faces, staring open-mouthed.

"Watch this." Frank Thomas plucked out his prosthetic right eye and dropped it into Neala's gin and tonic. "Now, can anyone here do that?"

Screams, hands covering mouths, howling laughter. Our guests rocked in their seats like there'd been a small tremor in the ground.

Alma was standing beside Father Roche, two faces of cold stone.

Matty put a hand to the side of his mouth to holler above the uproar. "I'll give you *ten* pounds, Frank, if you can do it again with the other eye."

And so the laughter went on.

*

I was surprised when Alma told me she wanted to leave early. It was the middle of the afternoon, the evening still ahead of us.

"Why? Where are we going?" I asked. "It's our wedding day." I was a little unsteady on my feet.

She wrapped her arms around one of mine and smiled up into my face. "I'm not one for all this drinking, Tom. You know that."

"But it's our wedding day, *Missus Cassidy*. We can't leave before the end. Our guests. Come on, you can't leave now."

She checked over each shoulder. No-one was watching, so she kissed me on the cheek. "I've asked Rhiannon to stay at the house with me, and John said it's okay. You're enjoying yourself. You stay here."

My heart clenched in a painful contraction. I glanced around the room. Happy people. Laughing people. Sociable people. Enjoying themselves at my wedding while my new wife punctured my pleasure with the softly spoken prick of her introverted air.

Rhiannon stood with a hand resting on the counter, her short, pearl-white dress clinging like tight wrapping around an extravagant wedding gift, and watched us from across the bar.

I shuffled around, turned my back to her. "Alma, it's our wedding day."

"Come home when you're ready," Alma said.

"But I want you here with me. With our guests."

"I'm going home, Tom."

My disappointment turned to disbelief, disbelief to embarrassment, embarrassment to anger. The drink didn't help. "This is the first time I've asked you to do anything for me. It's our wedding day and you're leaving me on my own."

"Rhiannon'll drive me out."

"Why the fuck are you leaving?"

She flinched. That hurt her. She let go of my arm, glanced over at Rhiannon. "It's arranged, Tom. I'm leaving now."

And she was gone. No fuss. No goodbyes. No hoisting her in the air to choruses of 'For she's a jolly good fellow'. No noisy serenade of tin cans tied to the bumper of the car as we drove away, the wedding party waving us off to our future together. Nothing. She slipped between our guests and out the door, without a word to anyone.

The keys to whatever BMW or Mercedes or Range Rover John Kavanaugh had driven over from England jingled from Rhiannon's fingers as she strode towards the door, her expression limp, resigned. She squeezed my arm for a second as she passed.

Matty came beside me. "It's all right," he said. "We'll have a drink."

I said nothing and allowed Matty to lead me over to the counter, him limping as he broke-in the new knee. "When one accepts the rose," he said, "one also has to accept the thorns."

I didn't know what he was talking about.

"Never understood women," he said.

"Have I fucked up here, Matty?"

"Why?" He rested a hand on my shoulder. "Because she's not an alcoholic like you, ya mean?" He put his head close to mine, whispered in my ear. "You've got the best woman in fuckin Ireland." He was drunk. He was never able to take much. "Cheer up ya miserable bastard and have a drink."

I said nothing, because I couldn't think of anything to say.

"It's yer weddin day," Matty said. An amused glint bloomed in his magnified eyes. "And don't worry. I'll go out in a while and pull all the celebratory bunting off your car."

"Fuck you, Matty."

We had a drink. I had lots of drinks. The singing started.

I smoked a cigar from a wooden box with a sloping glass lid that Buckley kept behind the bar for special occasions. I don't know why I did that. What was I celebrating?

However much I drank, I couldn't get drunk. I was the soberest person in the room. I watched them all fall away, one after another, staggering, congratulating me, shaking my hand, kissing me, wishing me all the best for the future.

I laughed with them in turn, thanked them for coming, and reddened with guilt as I made up reasons for Alma leaving early. Neala Thomas caused whoops and roars when she said, "That morning sickness can last all day, you know, Tommy."

"Fuck off, Neala," I wanted to say, but instead I laughed along.

I wanted everyone to leave, everyone to stay, the night not to end. I wanted to remain in Buckley's and have a drink.

I pictured Daddy sitting there, in the corner where Buckley had the television. That was his spot, but there was no television in his day.

I didn't want to end up like Daddy.

I threw back my shoulders, swelled my chest. There was no fucking way I was going to cry on my wedding day.

*

We must have been only a few hours away from daylight, three of us left.

Buckley poured me a fresh pint. Matt Darcy couldn't drink any more. After a few misses, Buckley managed to shove his own glass up an optic, twice, and threw back the double in one swallow. Buckley was a man of extremes. When he was working, he was a right sorehead, never took a drink, little humour out of him. When he was socialising, you couldn't hold him back. One could say he knew how to let his hair down, but he didn't have any hair. I must have been at least a little bit drunk to have thought that was funny.

"That's better," Matty said and wiped his mouth. "Why're ya smiling?" His spectacles rested on the precipice of his nose.

"No reason," I said.

"I'll leave you gentlemen to finish up," Buckley said. "Unlike ye lads, I've work..." He propped straight arms on the counter, hiccupped. "In the mornin."

"We're done here, now, too," Matty said. "Mister Buckley, sir." He saluted as if Buckley was a colonel in the Irish army. "I'll get this man home to his wife." Matty was as sloshed as Buckley, I doubted he was able to get himself home never mind me.

"Mister Cassidy." Buckley launched a wavering arm over the counter. He had to concentrate to pass it between two beer pumps. "The best of luck to you. You're a good man."

I straightened myself up on the bar stool, transferred my cigarette to the other hand. "Thank you for today, Mister Buckley."

"My pleasure. My great pleasure. Not a bother. No." A hiccup. He waved a finger in front of his face as if he had something important to say. "If either of ye two ever sees me with a glass of beer in my hand again..."

Matty and I laughed. Buckley was a publican for Christ's sake.

"If ya ever sees me in a glass..." A faltering attempt to complete his line. "Ye can shoot me."

"Ah, yeah," Matty said, drowsily.

"Shoot me in the head."

"We will," Matty said, emphatic this time. He jerked back his head, rubbed at his knee.

"Take care of this man, Mister Darcy. I'm up to my bed."

"We will, yeah."

Buckley shoved his arm between the pumps and shook my hand again. No words were exchanged this time, just a solemn nod of heads.

He staggered through a doorway and out of sight.

I watched Matty in the mirror, casting around for his jacket, and listened to the heavy creak of Buckley's lumbering ascent.

"Ya fit?" Matty said.

I reached for Matty's jacket, handed it to him. "I'll finish this. How's the knee?"

Matty twirled in a drunken limp-dance with the jacket. He found the armhole, threw back his shoulders, stared me in the face. "Right so." He reached for my arm to steady himself. "The best woman in fuckin Ireland."

"I know she is," I said. "You all right to get yourself home?"

He slapped my arm a couple of times, wobbled, adjusted his feet. "Tommy Cassidy." He gurned a drunken smile. "Married man at last."

"That's right, Matty." I wanted him to leave. "Goodnight."

"I hear she's not keen on havin the dog in the house."

"She's not, no." This wasn't a conversation I wanted to have with Matty. "I've him a new shed made. Goodnight, Matty."

"Yeah." He pushed his glasses up his nose, tried to focus on my reflection. "It's time. Time to go." He limped alongside the counter, a hand sliding its edge to maintain balance.

"You all right, Matty?"

He raised a hand without turning, lurched for the door, and he was gone, too.

*

I smoked cigarettes and pulled myself more pints, alone on my wedding night, but couldn't get drunk. I rose from my seat, felt for my keys, cursed at the thought of my car outside still covered in ribbons and lipstick and confetti. I tidied myself in the mirror.

"You look very handsome."

I turned and stared.

Rhiannon stood in the doorway. She wore a pair of woolly slippers peppered with multi-coloured pom poms. The white dress was hidden beneath a pink fleece dressing gown dotted with blue sheep. It was a dreadful sight, yet she looked beautiful. "Alma sent me in for ya."

"Thoughtful."

"She was worried."

I realised that this was the first exchange of words between me and Rhiannon since her own wedding day, half a year earlier. "How are you enjoying married life?" I said.

She pushed herself off the doorframe, shivered away the chill, let the door close out. She approached warily, peeking around the alcove wall and through the doorway that led upstairs to Buckley's living quarters. "You on your lonesome?"

"I am, yeah."

"On your weddin night?"

"Can I get you a drink?"

She was beside me, smelling of cold night air and expensive perfume. "I wouldn't say I'm enjoyin it much," she said. "Married life."

That didn't wholly surprise me. I pursed my lips, huffed. "John not living up to expectations?"

"I wouldn't say that," she said. "He's everything I expected, and less."

I laughed. It was a losing-control-of-your-face laugh. Perhaps my first real laugh of the day.

She smiled, tilted her head and swayed her body as she scanned the empty bar. Her hair was perfect, recently brushed. Her teeth were brilliant behind the fresh red of her lips. I imagined her outside in the car, stretching for the rear-view mirror before she came in. I couldn't put my eyes from her.

"You haven't changed a bit, have you?" I said.

"Same old Rhiannon," she said. "Despite attempts to change me."

It felt good to hear that. For some reason, it gave me hope. Some things should never change. "Make sure you continue to resist," I said.

"We're tryin for a kid." She propped her back against the counter, perched her elbows on it, dipped her head. Her violet eyes stared from beneath strong, charcoal eyebrows. "He wants kids."

At first, I thought it a broadside, a barbed reference to our own history, but she lifted her head and gave me the smile.

"Does John know you're here?" I asked.

"John's in a drunken stupor back in the hotel. But if we're long away, Alma might get suspicious."

I cleared my throat. "Say you stopped for one."

"Oh, yeah? Stopped for one what?"

"A drink."

She frowned, mocking. "A drink, only?"

"That's all you should say, yeah."

She parted her lips, ran her tongue over her teeth, laughed. "Bloody hell, Tommy Cassidy, listen to us. You sure we're alone?"

"We are, yeah."

"No acting group meeting in the alcove?" A smile.

"Not tonight, no."

She was Elizabeth Taylor. Elizabeth Taylor in the 1951 film, *A Place in the Sun*. My mother's favourite movie.

"What about you?" she said. "How're *you* enjoyin married life?"

I stubbed my cigarette. "A bit new to it."

"Married life with Alma." She stretched back over the counter. "Good luck with that." She looked even better than Elizabeth Taylor. "Remember what we got up to in that alcove?"

I inhaled, returned the car keys to my pocket. "I do, yeah. I remember it all right."

"I recall you were shy enough when there were people around."

"I was, yeah."

She lifted a slippered foot onto the footrail, draped her fingers over the edge of the counter. A naked knee pushed through the gape of the dressing gown. Her pearly nails matched her pearly dress.

Loyalty. That's what I thought about at that moment. It was late, or early, I had been roused from melancholy by a young woman whose beauty was real and not confined to a celluloid reel for projection onto a screen, whose beauty I remembered touching, whose beauty I craved, and I thought about loyalty.

I don't know what nameless force of magnetism caused it, but she lifted herself away from the counter and we were suddenly closer.

I stared into those violet eyes, sucked in my belly. Her scent was sweet spice.

"We're away tomorrow," she said. "We've to call to Manchester."

"I heard you were rushing off."

"And I've no reason to come back to Ireland ever again."

What of loyalty?

"And you won't be coming to England anytime soon."

"Most likely not, no." It wasn't difficult to convince myself that loyalty worked all ways. Rhiannon was risking as much as I was.

"If ever," she added with a shrug.

"No."

"We won't see each other again after tonight, Tommy."

That should have made me sad, but didn't. "I suppose."

She lifted her eyebrows, glanced left and right, dipped her chin and smiled down at the gaping dressing gown. "So what do ya think?"

She knew well what I thought.

"I don't intend leavin John anytime soon, Tommy."

"Why would you?"

"Just wanted to make that clear."

"You've made it clear."

"That's not what this is about." Rhiannon could do that, explain away a wrong to the point of it being right, that it was justified, even. “So?” she said, the question mark evident in her tone.

“So,” I said.

She smiled. Black hair, red lips, dark eyes, skin of white porcelain. The contrasts were irresistible. “Would you be up for a last pluck of the goose?”

I wasn’t shocked. It seemed inevitably right, even though we both knew that it was utterly wrong. I said, “You sound like you’re in a Hollywood movie.”

“Do I, now?”

We played the scene out, despite me not being one for amateur dramatics.

“Aren’t you supposed to be a married woman?”

“Aren’t you supposed to be a married man?”

“I heard them rumours, alright.”

“And we’re here, all alone. You and I.” She was Elizabeth Taylor of the big screen, brought to life there in Buckley’s Bar and Lounge. “On our ownsome.”

“We are, yeah.”

“And the West Coast Performers aren’t meetin in the alcove?” She grabbed the lapels of my jacket, moved her body against me, her head next to mine.

My hand found its way to the small of her back. “They’re not, no.”

She whispered into my ear. “I’ve no knickers on me.”

I wondered if Elizabeth Taylor was ever as brazen.

She leaned back her head, pressed herself against me, sighed appreciatively. “So,” she said, “Who would know.”

I would know, and she would know. Loyalty would have to turn its back or leave the room.

“I suppose no-one would,” I said.

She took my hand in hers, interlocked our fingers. “So what odds?”

Chapter 20

John Kavanaugh was true to his word and had his driver, Mark, bring me a copy of James Gorman's valuation before he left.

I took it to the light of the window and stretched my arms to focus my eyes and steady the words. Wherever I held it, the letters leaped around each other as though in a poorly choreographed céilí dance routine. Alma could have read it to me. Or, Matt Darcy. But I could ask neither.

*

For much of my time at school, Daddy thought that battering me with his fist would steady the letters.

Given my difficulties, I was relieved when he kept me away from class to help with the sheep. For me, a lambing season on the slopes of Cloonta Beg, Mammy and I working through cold nights pulling lambs from ewes and gathering cades, was preferable to the tribulation of ridicule in Mrs Joyce's schoolroom. Mammy and I would share a cigarette or dance an open-air waltz before heading down in the morning.

But time on the mountain didn't help with the reading.

Mrs Joyce complained about my lack of academic progress to her husband—her *husband* for Christ's sake—who passed the complaint onto Daddy when they met in Buckley's. It was not what Daddy wanted to listen to when out for a quiet drink. When he arrived home, Daddy complained to me.

Slapping aside Mammy's protective protestations, he hauled me from my bed and yelled his tobacco-and-alcohol-infused frustration into my face. "Do I have to listen to what an amadán you are every time I meet him out? Do I?!" He punctuated his phrases with punches. "Your. Thickness. Shames. This. Family."

Mrs Joyce kept me back a year in school. "Unsatisfactory level of achievement," she told Mammy. "Too bloody mollied by his mammy," Daddy told me.

If I hadn't got a seat beside Matt Darcy when he moved up a grade, I think I'd still be there.

*

I scanned James Gorman's report until I reached the numbers. Numbers were less of a problem. Numbers behaved themselves, unlike the fidgety letters.

I wished it was on yellow paper. It was easier on yellow paper. Alma tried to teach me to read on yellow paper, the sunny colour somehow able to exert a measure of control on the recalcitrant symbols.

Nine and eight.

Ninety-eight thousand euros.

Sweat hauled heat from my body, chilled my bones. A cold lethargy swept over me. I needed to sit. Matt Darcy had been spot on. I took deep breaths, to calm the tremor, and reminded myself that John Kavanaugh had agreed to pay his original offer. There was nothing to worry about, whatever James Gorman's valuation letter said.

If Alma was there, she would have told me what to do.

I left down James Gorman's valuation, threw two sods of turf onto the fire, grabbed a bottle of beer.

My cigarettes were waiting for me on the arm of the chair.

Chapter 21

I left sooty fingerprints on the folded sheet of blank paper that was waiting for me in my work locker at the end of my shift.

It was the simple system I had in place with the boss following several miscommunications. Two folds meant 'call up to the office'.

Brian Minnock was a slim man who hurled for County Offaly in his youth and still kept himself tidy. He'd frequently call down to the boiler house in his suit and tie and wasn't afraid to lend a hand on the barrow when the rush was on us.

He stood up behind his desk when I entered. Light from the overhead bulbs shimmered in the shallow-crater contours of his bald head. "Tommy, come in, come on in." He beckoned me with curled fingers. "How're things?"

The walls of his office were lined in layout plans for the bog fields. They looked like schematics for an unfeasibly complex airport terminal.

Old John Kavanaugh was there, seated in a dark corner, his face in the shadow of his hat. He sat back in the chair with a confident cross of his long legs and laced his fingers over the buttons of his tweed suit jacket.

"Grand, Brian," I said. "You wanted to see me?" I held up the fold of paper.

"I did Tommy. I do. I wanted to see you, all right. You got the note, that's good. I've got something to…Well. I, a…I'll come out with it straight. I've some bad news, I'm afraid."

I glanced over at Kavanaugh who said nothing, moved nothing.

"What's the problem, Brian?" I pulled at the collar of my work shirt with a sooted finger. "What's wrong?" I thought for a moment Minnock was about to tell me that Alma had had a serious accident out at the house. I dismissed that when I realised he would hardly wait until the end of my shift to let me know such a thing.

"Fields B-two to B-five are behind schedule, Tommy."

Relief. I had heard about the delays. The weather was playing havoc with the development of some new fields.

"The rain, Tommy. You know well, yourself."

"I do, yeah."

"It's just, and it pains me to say it, Tommy, it's just, with the schedule gone to hell and that, and all the shagging expense of it all, you can imagine. We were going through the books and, well…There's not the work to go round. We need to let men go."

The momentary relief turned into a sickening ache. It bloomed in my stomach, spread to my chest. I managed to disguise a stagger with a shuffle of my clogged boots. My heart burned as though I had just fed it as fuel to one of the Babcock and Wilcox boilers. "You mean redundancies, Brian?"

"You said it, Tommy, that's the word, yes. You know it. You nailed it in one."

His nodding head gleamed, so glossy I thought I could make out the dark patch of writing you find on the underside of bulbs in the reflection.

"I'll come right out with it, Tommy. It's only fair I tell you to your face. I'm afraid…"

He didn't want to tell me. It was Old John Kavanaugh who wanted him to tell me; I bloody knew it.

"Tell me what?"

"It's you and Jocky," he said.

"Me and Jocky Quealy? Jocky's here five minutes. I'm here the best part of thirteen years. How can it be Jocky and me that has to go?"

"I know, Tommy. I know all about your time here at the station. That's not in question. It's time well served. And it'll help with the package we have for you. It's just, well, how can I put it? The other men have…You know, severe responsibilities, shall we say."

Alma wasn't earning. The farm absorbed money like carrageen absorbed water. *I* had responsibilities.

"I need this job for another while, Brian. I've heavy expenses."

"Oh, I know that, Tommy. I understand. It's just–"

"Please, Brian." Heat worked its way into my face.

"Tommy, listen to me now. It's only that…Well, the others you see. They've all got children growing up." Minnock ran a hand back over his skull and blurred the reflections.

"Children?" I said.

"That's it, now." He gestured towards Kavanaugh. "John and I were drawing up criteria. We thought that was, maybe, you know, the fairest way. We're a…Look, Tommy, I'm awfully sorry."

Chapter 22

"Matty." I was short of breath from the shuffled slow-motion dash across the kitchen and out into the yard. Rain pelted down on top of me. I was gasping. I wished I had remembered my cap. "Hold up."

Matt Darcy had been visible on the lane from the turn at Mulligan's bridge, juddering down the slight descent on his bicycle. He slowed before he reached my house and dismounted. He was about to wheel past, but I hurried out to catch him. I suspect he wanted to be caught.

Wet gravel crunched beneath his Wellingtons and there was a squeak of damp brakes as he pulled to a halt.

Rain spilled from the sky. Out across the village, gusts that would strip bark from trees carried rippling dense curtains of it in off the lake and draped them over the fields. It lashed against Matty's Mackintosh and drenched his bicycle. Matty didn't seem to mind. He was how I imagined a character from one of Dexter McEvoy's stories to be, the policeman in Flann O'Brien's book: at one with his bicycle, their molecules mingled, half man, half steel frame, oblivious to natural elements.

Matty focussed his attention on the road, his neck shrunk into the shaggy up-turned collar of his coat. Water hopped into the air between the spokes of his front wheel. A naked hand shot from a handlebar to push rain-dappled spectacles back up his nose.

"I'm sorry," I said. Cold rain penetrated my jacket, but a clammy heat still rose in my neck. "Come in out of this. A drink, maybe?" I could hear myself breathing. "Please."

He looked at me for the first time. Drops streamed around hollow cheeks to be whipped by wind from the tip of his chin. I thought he was going to refuse my offer. He shouted into the wind. "Any of Kavanaugh's whiskey left?" A reluctant smile worked its way across his damp face. A blast of wind knocked him back a half-step. He raised a hand to anchor his cap to his head.

"I have, of course. Much as you want."

*

We sat in our usual armchairs, either side of the fireplace, like an old married couple on the verge of reconciliation after hostilities.

The weather blew at the house as if to devour us, like the wolf who chastised the three pigs—not a story in Dexter McEvoy's classical collection. Rain clattered against the kitchen window in squalls, the rattles like fistfuls of pebbles on a tin roof. A sonorous pipe whistle in the chimney sent a shiver along my spine.

I pulled my sodden jacket tight around me, smoothed down my wet hair.

Matt Darcy wore his forlorn look, his mouth gaping in a damp and gormless, fly-catching pose. His cap and coat hung from a screw below the mantelpiece and dripped rain onto the hearth. A tiny, almost-Ireland-shaped puddle formed on the granite surface.

We both stared into the flickering fire as though waiting for its tongues to start the conversation.

I sipped my whiskey and opened with a familiar question. "Jamieson's or Bushmills?" I knew well what his answer would be.

Matty gave a sigh of relief. The conversation was underway. "The Dew. Every time. It has to be the Dew if there's a choice to be had." He grimaced as he swallowed his first mouthful and growled at its burn. "You don't have to tell me," he said to the flames.

I did have to tell him. I wanted to tell him. I had spoken to Alma about it, but her response was indifferent. I needed to tell Matty. "I want to tell you," I said.

Matty scrunched his nose, nodded. He was ready to listen. The wrinkled skin around his magnified eyes still held damp from the rain.

I blew cigarette smoke over our heads. "You were spot on with the value of the land."

He gave no reaction.

"Ninety-eight thousand euro. On the button."

"Did muck-features honour his original offer?"

"He told me about the tax man."

Matty furrowed his brow. "What tax man?"

"Capital gains tax."

"C.G.T.?" he said. "I know it. Payable on chargeable gains over twelve hundred and seventy euro." Matt Darcy knew all about capital gains tax.

"Why didn't you tell me about the capital gains tax?"

He scoffed, held out a hand to the fire. "Why didn't I tell you? You only listen to what you– To tell the truth, I did tell you. We spoke about it. Don't you remember me tellin you about it the first time Buckley's wife got the big-C? Buckley was set to sell up, remember? And the two of them to travel the world? He was whingin like a wether about the capital gains tax he'd have to pay, remember? The pub was worth a few hundred thousand then. Vicky, God rest her, went into remission and that put an end to the round-the-world trip."

I had a vague recollection of Buckley's wife being ill. Did Alma help out? Or, was that when the cancer came back?

Matty closed and opened his hand, catching heat from the fire. "I told you all this. We talked about it. You and I. Ya must listen to only half a what I say."

I shuddered at the thought of there being as much again of the blathering verbiage out of Matty that, somehow, I manage to ignore.

"What about the tax man?" he asked. "What did Mister I've-A-Gold-Roller have to say about the tax man?"

"He calls it a–"

"Royce. I know. What did he have to say about the C.G.T.?"

“He came up with a scheme.”

Matty withdrew his warming hand, shuffled to the edge of his chair, and perched forward. He was in danger of toppling into the top of his Wellingtons. “Ya know,” he said, “that I’m not in favour of any form of tax avoidance.”

I tried to remember the details of John Kavanaugh’s plan. I wanted to put it to Matty the way Kavanaugh put it to me, to convince Matty the way I had been convinced. I wanted Matty to go along with it the way I had. But my heart thudded dismally in my breast while a lump in my throat the size of a small potato threatened to squeeze tears from my eyes. My lungs ached. I could feel the itch of inflamed tissue in my airways. A deflating fatigue threatened to silence me forever.

“What is it, Tommy? Tell me.”

“I’ve never been as reliable as you with numbers, Matty.”

“We know that.”

“You’ve been correcting me and helping me get them right for what must be the last forty years.”

“Forty-five years.”

“Yes.” I coughed to clear my throat and forced the words out. “He said we’d reduce the tax if we put a lower price on the sales contract.”

Matty was ahead of me. He groaned and collapsed backwards, his torso flat, his neck braced upright against the back of the chair. A six-year-old child would get away with sitting like that, but Matty’s age and sporting legacy would leave him with backache. The chipped cup of whiskey was balanced on his belly. He waved his bony knees from side to side. “Don’t tell me,” he said.

“He gave me a cheque for some of the money. He promised the rest in cash.”

Matt Darcy stilled his knees and asked, “How much was in the cheque?”

“Sixty thousand euro.”

“And he told you he saved you eighteen thousand in capital gains tax?”

"No. He said about thirty thousand. A third. C.G.T. is thirty percent."

"Have you cashed the cheque?"

"Yes."

"Signed anything?"

"Signed everything. Paid him back fifteen hundred euro for the legal assistance he arranged on my behalf."

"You've accepted the deal, so. Is the money in your account?"

"The deal's official."

"And the ninety thousand in cash?"

I searched for a way to tell Matty that there was no cash.

It wasn't that John Kavanaugh was yet to gather it together, I would have understood that, it was a serious amount of cash. I was faced with the challenge of explaining to Matty that John Kavanaugh wasn't going to *bother* gathering it together. Ever. John Kavanaugh told me so. To my face, as he stood in front of my fire, drinking a cup of the whiskey he gave to me. A Judas gift.

I couldn't come up with the words. I took a draw on the cigarette, shook my head.

Using a Wellington as a counterweight, Matty rocked himself upright. "Shit to death."

"What?"

"The scummy toe rag should be tied to the tails of two horses and shit to death as they drag him into town and back." He pressed a palm into the small of his back. "And to town and back again." He wound his torso left and right. "What's the hold-up with the cash?"

The damp, steaming image of Matt Darcy blurred in my teary eyes. "When it all went through, he called here..."

"Go on."

I sniffed. "I poured us both a whiskey. Seal the deal and everything. I remember feeling embarrassed. Nervous. The throat was playing up and I'd never taken that sort of money off anyone before. The time I went to England and sold all my sheep to the abattoir in Castlebar would be about the most I'd have had in my pocket in a long while. My only concern, all I was thinking about, was where I'd hide the cash to keep it safe. I told him as much, joking around." I managed a weak smile.

Matty's mouth gaped wider. I had his full attention.

"He stood himself here at the fire. In his big fur coat. Took a sip of whiskey. Placed the cup on the mantle. That's when he told me."

Matty was snarling silently, his lips drawn up, baring his teeth like a rabid dog. A look of utter disgust.

"He told me he thought…" I fought off a choke. I was scared I'd either cry in front of Matty, or die of a coughing fit. I inhaled courage. "He said he'd already paid me a fair price. There'd be no cash."

A crushed-raspberry hue ripened in Matty's face. The joints of his bony fingers grew white against the falling poppy leaves that decorated his mug of whiskey. "We'll go to law," he said. "That's what we'll do, go to law and get the gobshite locked up."

"I threatened him with that, Matty."

"And what did the stinkin pail a piss say?"

"Told me go ahead. But he said he'd expose my plan to extort Irish Tax and Customs out of thirty thousand euro. A third of the ninety in cash."

I didn't share this with Matty, but John Kavanaugh also said, "By the sound of you, Tommy, you wouldn't live long enough for a court case. You're a dying man. Look at the state of you. Take the money and be grateful. There's plenty there to see you out."

"*Your* plan now is it?"

"That's what he said."

In a movement that belied his aching lumbar, Matty shot to his feet and slung the remains of his whiskey into the fire as though it was poison. The fire flared and hissed at the same time, fine ash rising up the chimney, blue flames reflecting in the puddle of rainwater that had grown to the shape of Europe. "The numbers are all wrong, all wrong, all wrong!"

I expected the cup to shatter in his grasp.

"He's just like the father. I didn't steal any ceramic insulator from that display in the foyer." Matty spread his arms. "Why would I steal something like that? It wasn't me. It was old John Kavanaugh and his schemin." Matty swung an arm, pointed it in the general direction of Owencas Electricity Generating Station. "He made the whole thing up so that he got the foreman job. He bloody lied." Matty held up an imaginary antique ceramic electrical insulator in his free hand. "What the hell would I do with an antique electrical insulator? He nearly got me sacked! Now his dog-shit son's at the same shenanigans."

I tried to calm him. "It's all right, Matty. No-one believed you stole that electrical insulator."

He sat down. "I couldn't give two shites what people think about the electrical insulator. That's not the point. The point is the numbers are all wrong."

"Can I get you another whiskey?"

"Listen to me, Tommy. Capital gains tax is twenty percent. A fifth."

"John Kavanaugh said it was–"

"At twenty percent, he'd only have saved you eighteen thousand, not thirty thousand."

The shame was gathering. I could feel it building in my core. I wanted Matty to go no further, to stop talking and leave. When in shame, I was naked, exposed, vulnerable. I could be angry. I needed to be alone. "You need to go."

Matty didn't hear me. "But it's worse," he said and ground his dentures. A yellow flame flickered in the spidery crack of his lens.

"Don't chastise me." The lump in my throat had grown spikes. It dredged my airways. If I started coughing I would never stop.

"I'm not goin to."

"I feel a fool."

"You're not a fool."

"I feel dishonest."

"Just too trusting."

I couldn't look Matty in the eye. Even though he said he wouldn't, I waited for him to start on with the didn't-I-warn-yous. I could virtually hear him. I was afraid I'd argue back. He had been right to warn me against going ahead with the deal, and I *had* been a fool. But I couldn't listen to Matty tell me that.

"Anyone would do the same," Matty said at last. "We all think we're different, but we're not. Not really."

The restriction in my throat seemed to shrink away. This was what I wanted to hear. I took a breath without pain or discomfort.

"It's not your fault," Matty said.

Tension drained from my shoulders. I felt light-headed, a giddiness that couldn't be attributed to the whiskey. I've wondered since if Matt Darcy was put on this earth for that one single statement, that one single act of forgiveness. It was a reminder of why I loved the man. I had never hugged another man before, but at that moment, I wanted to hug Matt Darcy.

"We all like to imagine we're the straight and honest one," he said. "We all like to think we're as straight as a die, that we're incorruptible. We all think we're the straight line in a world full of curves."

He was losing me, but I didn't mind.

"But what we don't realise, is that even a straight line is a curve. A curve with a very big radius."

He had lost me.

"An infinite radius, Tommy. If you could imagine such a thing." Matty pursed his lips, creased his brow. "Can you imagine such a–"

"I don't care, Matty. Really."

"No. I'm sorry. What I mean is, we all have our price."

That's what he was trying to tell me. I got it. And my price was thirty thousand euros.

"What can I do, Matty?"

"On me solemn oath, Tommy, I don't know."

"I had plans for the money."

"I wish ya spoke to me about the tax." Matty was talking to the fire again. It felt easier, the fire sharing the blame.

"I know. I should have listened to–"

"The thunderin bastard." Matty slid his fingers up under the lenses of his spectacles and worked roughly at his eyeballs. He spoke between his hands. "No, ya don't understand." He lowered his hands, pushed the spectacles back up his nose. His eyes were bloodshot and glassy. "Legally, you didn't have to pay *any* capital gains tax on the sale of your land."

Chapter 23

I had too much drink taken, started to worry about being able to drive home, but it was pleasant to be in Buckley's with Alma there. She disliked the place, but I had managed to talk her into coming in for an hour. We'd just been to the christening service of Baby Delores Gilhooly.

The Gilhoolys were relatively new to the area at the time. Michael was a guard up in Sligo, seemed a nice-enough fella if you discounted the air of smug superiority and the accusing pin-prick eyes. Una was a doctor, or a nurse, or something in medicine.

We probably wouldn't have been invited to the christening at all if they had had time to form their clique, but it was early days. The Gilhoolys hadn't yet determined who their friends were, so cast their net wide when they drew up the guest list.

Alma had been at the reception for longer than I had expected her to stay. She sat stiffly at the far end of the counter, her arms folded.

I read the body language from the other side of the room and excused myself. I sidled over, expecting an argument.

"Why do they never say anything to you?" she said.

"About what?"

"It's always me that gets it. Weddings, christenings, even funerals. It's always me that gets it, never you."

"Alma, I don't know what you mean."

Her eyes welled.

"Hey, what's wrong?" I rested an arm on her shoulder, checked the bar to see if anyone was watching us.

She shrugged away my arm.

"What's wrong, Alma?" It was distressing to see her cry, but a relief to think I might not be the culprit.

"I knew I shouldn't have come in here. I told you that."

I knew I'd be implicated in some way.

"An hour you said. Well, it's been three. And all you've done is drink with your friends over there."

I swayed, watched her in the bar mirror. "These people are your friends, too."

"Are they? Are they really? Then why do they speak to me the way they do? They never say it when you're around. They even shut up when you bring me over a drink. It's like they're all ganging up."

"What, in the name of Christ, are you on about?"

"No need to curse." Alma wiped around an eye with a tissue.

I stuck my hands in my pockets, rocked unsteadily, and waited.

She leaned back on the bar stool to peek behind me, a quick scan of the room, then stuck out a bottom lip to blow-dry her face.

"Who upset you?"

"It was nothing."

I coughed out a laugh, held out an open palm. "Who upset you?"

"Every time we're out, and it's not that often we are out together–"

"Hey, that's not my–"

"Shut up, Tom. I'm not complaining." Her tone was sharp enough to cut through any anesthetising effect of the alcohol I had consumed. "I'd be happy if I never set foot in this place. Ever. But I'm the one always asked about children."

A sinking feeling in my stomach. "Oh, for fuck's–"

"Stop it. All you're good for is cursing. I won't tell you anything if you're going to react like that."

"Grand…Sorry." My hands were pushed down into my pockets again, my arms rigid. My fingers found cigarettes. "Go on," I said. "Tell me. Who was it this time?"

"I only paid the baby a compliment."

"Who, Alma?"

"Who do you think? The child's mother. Una Gilhooly. Her and her new sidekick, Neala Thomas."

I blew out through pursed lips.

"But don't you go saying anything, Tom."

My body tensed.

"I was telling Una how lovely her baby is when Neala started in with, 'Have you not considered having any of your own, Alma?'"

I pulled the cigarettes from my pocket.

Alma continued, "Just because she's dragging five after her. Wears it like a badge of honour. Una even asked me if we were having problems. As if I would want to be discussing something like that with her and Neala Thomas in Buckley's. She even warned me not to leave it too late. When you came over with this soda, the bitches shut up."

Bitches? I remembered coming over with Alma's drink. Una complimented me on the colour of my shirt. "Cornflour, same as Michael's. Don't tell him I think it looks better on you." I even bought them both a drink.

"I was trying to get your attention," Alma said. "Get you to stay here. Did you not see me?"

I sucked on the cigarette, pulled the smoke into my lungs.

"As soon as you headed back over to your cronies, they started again. I couldn't believe it."

I stuck out my chin, my jaw clenched.

A corner of an old red crepe-paper wedding decoration was still sellotaped to the yellow-tarred ceiling. A forgotten remnant from our own wedding party, seven years earlier. I blew smoke at it, hoping it would burst into flames. It didn't. "Listen," I said. "Take no notice."

"No notice? Easy for you. It's always me they say it to. It's just…" She dipped her head, dabbed at a corner of an eye with the tissue. "What is wrong with us, Tom?"

"Thought you didn't want to talk about this now?"

She lowered her hand, stared me in the face, her mouth set in a scowl. I shouldn't have answered her like that. She said, "You never want to talk about it, do you Tom? John and Rhiannon don't seem to be having any problems."

Heat, from adrenaline and alcohol, flushed through me.

"Twins, Tom. Rhiannon wasn't a year and a half married before she had her first. Then a second. Now she's so good at it, she's producing them two at a time. And here we are, married seven years and–"

"Alma, stop it. Please." I looked around to see where Michael Gilhooly was. I wanted to have a word with him.

He was standing square-shouldered by the entrance to the alcove. His feet were set straight. His head was shaved close up the neck, his chin lifted so that he peered down his nose. He looked, for all the world, like he was lecturing half a dozen delinquents he'd caught driving a stolen car. His audience listened intently, arrested in his stare.

Someone offered him a fresh pint that he seemed reluctant to accept. Gilhooly looked the class of a guard who found it difficult to leave his job at work.

Alma rooted in her bag for a clean tissue. "It was Una drew down about it."

"About what?"

"She asked if I envied Rhiannon and her newborn twins."

I scanned the counter for an ashtray. None. I dropped the cigarette to the floor, ground it to death with my shoe. "What the fuck did she say that for?"

"Tom, calm down."

"No. Something needs to be said."

"You'll say nothing, Tom. That's what you always do."

I turned too fast, staggered against the bar, roared. "Here, Michael!"

Conversations halted. People turned.

Now, I don't have the peripheral vision of sheep, but I remember, as I strode towards Michael Gilhooly, I was aware of everyone in Buckley's watching me.

Gilhooly turned, lifted his chin. "Yes, Thomas. What can I do for you?"

"Michael, you need to arrest that bloody wife of yours before she upsets every woman in the bloody room."

Gilhooly glanced over my shoulder at his other guests, gave an easy smile. "Thomas, I don't think there's any need to be shouting. What's the problem?"

My arms quivered. "Have a fucking word with Una, will you?"

Gasps in the bar. Hands to mouths. Shared looks of shock. I could see everything. Peripheral vision.

Michael Gilhooly lowered his chin, adjusted his stance.

His tiny eyes were buried deep beneath thick, menacing eyebrows. He looked like he was ready to bust my face with his forehead. "Thomas–"

"Tell her to mind her own fucking business." I was useless at confrontation. "Before someone else minds it for her."

The bastard flashed a smile, then tilted his head to the side a fraction. "Thomas." Michael Gilhooly was calmness personified. "There's no need for the swearing. Please lower your voice."

I didn't. "While you're at it, have a fucking word with her bloody…Her bloody sidekick, Neala Thomas."

Alma was swinging her coat around herself.

Neala Thomas's husband, Frank, put down his drink, straightened himself at the counter. He might have had only one eye, but I could see everything.

"You've drink taken, Thomas," Michael Gilhooly said. "You should calm down."

"Or else, what?" That's what I said. I stuck out my chin and said 'Or else, what?' We were at the christening reception of this man's baby daughter, and I stuck my chin in his face and said, 'Or else, what?'

Gilhooly broadened his smile, not in a mocking, challenging way, but in a sincere and genuine way. In a relaxed, loud whisper he said, "Or else I might have to take you into custody at the counter and buy you another drink."

Relieved sighs around the room, some forced smiles. An awkward laugh behind me.

The red burn of shame rose from my neck. I had two options. I chose the wrong one and decided that Michael

Gilhooly wasn't taking this seriously enough. I lifted the pint he held in his hand and tipped it over his cornflour shirt.

"Fuck," from Gilhooly.

Gasps from around the room.

A strong hand grabbed my arm from behind. "Easy, Tommy," the voice familiar.

"All right!" I shook my arm loose, raised my hands in the air. The universal sign of surrender.

Michael Gilhooly didn't hit or arrest me, so I staggered my way back to Alma.

Alma had taken a small, silver-paper-wrapped parcel from her handbag and placed it on the counter, She was pulling on gloves, her eyes fixed on her wriggling fingers.

When I turned, Una and another woman were drying Michael Gilhooly off with a tartan shawl and a bar towel. Matt Darcy stood beside him, shaking his head at me, a hand on Michael Gilhooly's beer-stained shoulder.

Alma strode past the pool table and out of the pub, the door clattering behind her.

"I'm sorry, Michael," I said. "Una." Everyone was staring at me. "I'm sorry." The mirror behind the counter doubled the stares. "There's a small present here for the baby." I tapped my pocket for car keys. "We both think she's gorgeous, by the way." I dropped my chin to my chest and followed Alma out.

Chapter 24

Vibrations woke me. The house rattled. I raised myself up in the bed and waited for the shock of light in my eyes to subside.

A chugging cacophony of engines assaulted my house in heavy waves. Big engines, like on a building site.

Men yelled.

What time was it?

Juan de Juanes' statue sat in shadow, useless.

Banging on the back door made me jump.

"All right," I called. But it was not all right. I'd slept fully dressed. I swung my legs off the bed and landed a booted foot in a wok of my own vomit. "Christ." A vague, pained memory of last night's solitary drinking came to me like a chilly mist from the lake.

I had let John Kavanaugh make a fool of me with the capital gains tax. Matt Darcy knew that, and I was sure the whole village knew it, too. I was ashamed, full of regret. Repentant drinking, especially alone, is always the worst kind.

I let my boot drip.

More banging. "Tommy. You in there?"

I thought I recognised the voice, but I couldn't put a name to it.

"Hello?" Bang-bang. "Tommy?"

I summoned a ragged breath. "Wait." I pushed off the bed. My head reeled. The cough got to me as soon as I was upright. It ran its course, folding me, unfolding me, doubling me over in spasms, hacking air through decrepit airways, my lungs collapsing and inflating like leaky bellows. I spat into the wok. A coppery taste of blood. I let it dribble.

I steadied myself with the bedpost and ran a rough hand over my face. "I'll be there."

I could barely tell which way was up and which way was down. I blinked to rid my eyes of twisted black lines that floated in my vision, and I headed for the back door. I yawed on and off course, a meandering path like sheep on a slope, and reached the table. I shook a few bottles for dregs and swallowed back a mouthful of stale something, cider, maybe, or stout. I reached the door, lifted the latch.

The enormous hulk of Ryan Matthews was walking away from the house. He turned, came back. "Jesus, are you all right, Tommy?" The look on his face would have been no worse if I'd shown him the contents of the wok.

His belly was slung in a thick, faded-tartan work shirt unbuttoned down to the bulge. The shirt sleeves were rolled to thick wads just below the swell of his shoulders. His curly red hair was mad, his face ruddy, his frown huge.

He had his dog with him, a dog that might be good with sheep, astute looking. But Ryan didn't need a dog that was good with sheep. He didn't need a dog, at all. My father would have dismissed it a 'pointless, shaggin ornament'.

I wondered at the absurdity of me standing there, thinking about such things.

"You don't look the feckin best," Ryan Matthews said.

"Yes," I wheezed. "I'm middling, Ryan."

"Right." He drew back his immense head, appraised me.

I managed a smile.

"We're here to start work," he said. "For John Kavanaugh. Me and the lads. Out the back there. I know it should've been yesterday, but we had a problem. That old JCB he left us wouldn't start. On its last legs, I reckon." Ryan threw back his shoulders and laughed.

My mind raced. What work for John Kavanaugh?

"It's on wheels, Tommy, not legs." He looked disappointed I wasn't laughing. "The machine. It's on wheels." His shoulders settled. "Ya do know about this?"

I shook my head. A ball of pain bounced between my temples.

"Ah, ya do."

"What work?"

"Feck." Ryan dipped his chin. "Tear me up and throw me away." An I'd-rather-be-somewhere-else smile, unmistakable amid his blush. "Declan," he shouted and beckoned with a thick arm. "Step and fetch the big envelope out a Bogsey's cab?" He slipped his two hands in under his armpits. "Are you sure you're all right?"

I said nothing.

"Thought you'd know about this, Tommy." He waited, smiled, kicked at stones.

The front yard was alive with the throaty knocking of big-engine tappets. I could feel the hammering in the door jamb coming up from the ground. The air smelled of burnt diesel.

Declan O'Dea rushed up the yard, a black mobile phone in one hand, a large envelope in the other.

"Come here with it." Ryan Matthews snatched the envelope. "And put that bloody phone away."

"I've a signal." Declan looked only a little older than when Alma used to mind him for his mother, his face still a fall of freckles, his hair cut tight to his skull. He'd stuff jam sandwiches into his mouth, sat on the chair at the table, his feet swinging clear of the ground. "How ya keepin, Mister Cassidy?" he said. "Ya did well out the land, I hear."

Ryan Matthews elbowed Declan O'Dea in the shoulder. "Here, Tommy." Ryan handed me the envelope. "John Kavanaugh said give you this if there was any confusion. It explains it all."

Declan O'Dea pushed buttons on his phone.

"Explains what, Ryan?"

"The quarry," Ryan said. "He said it's the legal papers authorisin the quarry. We're startin on it today." He nodded his great head towards the field. "Preparatory work, just."

"It's me," Declan O'Dea said into his phone. "I'm out by Tommy Cassidy's now, and I've a signal."

I felt nauseous. "A quarry?" The floaters were back in my eyes. A shiver ran through me. The hairs on my arm prickled.

"Three bars coming up the path, I swear to God."

"Feck off with that phone, Declan," Ryan said. "We won't be drawing from it yet, Tommy, don't worry. There's enablin works to be done, but give us a couple a months or so and there'll be wagons flyin in and out past your door. I can see it being a great success, all right, what with all the new road works going out to the gas depot. Area's cryin out for it. Make a few bob for John Kavanaugh, I know. Shrewd businessman, that buck, you've to give him that."

"I…I don't understand. There must be…" The din of the engines inflamed the pain in my head, made me squint. "Someone's made a mistake."

Ryan shook his head. "No. No, there's no mistake, Tommy."

"It's as we thought," Declan O'Dea said into the phone. "Not his place no more, and not a clue what's going on. But listen, I'll save the minutes. So long." Declan O'Dea folded the phone in half, shoved it in a pocket, and walked off smothering a giggle.

I wanted to clip his ear, or kick his arse, but I was incapable of doing either. "John Kavanaugh mentioned putting in a few sheep." My voice was weak, unconvincing. "Said nothing about a quarry."

"Might have *mentioned* sheep, Tommy, but he always intended a quarry." Ryan kept his eyes steady on me for fear I'd collapse. "We wouldn't be here, else. Did you not hear him say it the night we met in Buckley's? Look, I've a number for him in England. Call him if you like, but it's all laid out in that envelope."

I turned the envelope over in my trembling hands. Brown, the colour of officialdom, the colour of authority, unquestionable authority.

"Notification." I coughed the word out. "John Kavanaugh should have sent me notification." I gripped the door jamb. I needed to sit.

"Told me he did, Tommy. Ages ago. Ya not get it?"

I glanced behind me at the jumble of letters and leaflets, circulars, and free newspapers built up on the kitchen table, unread and unopened and surrounded by a forest of empty bottles. I pulled the door close to my side. "No, I didn't…I didn't receive anything like that."

"Tear me up and throw me away. I'm sure it's all in that there envelope." Ryan Matthews took a step and stooped over me. His nose wrinkled, and he straightened a little. "If you want me go through it, I'll come back once I get the lads started." He stepped away and rubbed a thick index finger back and forth beneath his nostrils.

"Thank you, Ryan. That won't be necessary. But, thank you."

We were joined by a middle-aged man I didn't recognise, stocky build, height up to Ryan's shoulder, olive skin.

"Meet Bogsey, Tommy. From the E.U. Lithuania or someplace. Great worker, but don't let him know I said that." Ryan Matthews laughed his giant laugh. "Isn't he here beside us, he'll know well I said it."

The stranger reached forward, offered me a hand to shake. The hand was calloused but gentle. "I was born Latvia. My name is Zhoro Boguslav." He bowed his head when we shook.

"Drove machines on some mighty construction projects over there," Ryan said. "Yet to make his mark in this country, but listen, when he does, Tommy, it'll be the mark of–"

"Pleased to meet, Mister Tommy." Zhoro Boguslav's English sounded broken, though not as broken as I felt.

"Best we make a start," Ryan said. "These men are stealin money off me. Can't afford to have them standin round all day pissin up against the wheel of a digger."

I smiled at Ryan Matthews to let him know that I knew his men were not really pissing up against the digger wheel.

He smiled back. "It might get loud, Tommy." And he was gone.

Zhoro Boguslav dipped his chin, then followed Ryan Matthews, nudging the dog before him with his leg.

I wanted to step out into the yard and block the machines. I wanted to challenge Ryan Matthews. I wanted to demand some sort of right to deny these machines access onto my land. But I was sick. Drunk and sick. I stood wheezing in the doorway, my head bobbing as I breathed.

And it was no longer my land.

My hand trembled against the door frame, the purpled skin all veins and tight tendons, the knuckles grimy and gnarled. Dry blood sat against the quick of several cracked nails. I barely recognised my own hand from a divot in the sod.

The strength I needed to step into the yard evaded me.

Revving engines shook the ground. The jamb vibrated in my grip. The front bucket of a digger hovered into view, on its way to my field. Zhoro Boguslav was closeted in the cab, hands swinging left and right with the unresponsive steering, concentrating.

Declan O'Dea followed, sitting atop a dumper truck, phone in hand. There was writing emblazoned on the side of the bucket skip. I thought I could make out the letters 'KAV' against the yellow paintwork. Declan grinned and waved as he bounced on the sprung seat.

Ryan Matthews strode behind, taking giant steps, the dog at his heel.

The dog paused to lick at a strip of goose shit.

Ryan stopped at my door and said, "You're sure you didn't know nothin about this, Tommy?" He scratched under an arm and leaned down an ear.

My voice was hollow. "As sure as I can be."

He grunted and tossed back his huge head, his rust-coloured hair flouncing like a horse's mane. "We'll only start widening the entrance today." He pointed. "Take it back a few meters. There's a gate to go in. Is that the children's rest, Tommy?"

It was as much as I could do to nod.

"We'd better avoid goin too near that. We don't want to be disturbin the graves of the babies."

I didn't want that either. I wanted to explain who was buried there that was close to me, that it was a cillín, that it was un-consecrated ground that meant something to people, that it mustn't be touched. But I couldn't round up the words.

"We've to clear a space for a big metal bowser at the back of the house, Tommy. To hold the fuel. Have ya any need of that old shed?"

The shed had been empty a while, barring a few dog blankets, maybe. Ryan might have had use for it, but I was in no mood for generosity.

Ryan gesticulated with a bare arm. "We'll be diggin away a bit of the bank and we'll need to dig out for the footings. We'll be workin close to the house, but Bogsey will be safe enough. I'll try to keep him from puttin the rear bucket through the wall." He laughed, threw back his big red head. "I was jokin, he won't put the bucket through the wall." He gave a brief smile. "We'll get on, so, Tommy. By the way, ya know yer door knocker is broke, ya do?"

As Ryan Matthews walked out of my view, a grey goose waddled into it, the gander we'd had for over twelve years, that Alma insisted we got to warn of burglars that didn't exist. Alma had given it a name I couldn't recall. It crossed the yard, its steps wary and hesitant, eyeing Ryan Matthews's dog. It turned its sienna-orange bill towards me, adjusted its head. I knew what it was thinking. 'What the fuck have you done?' is what it was thinking.

"If Alma heard that language out of you–" I coughed against the envelope. "She'd pull your neck and feed you to the fox."

Chapter 25

"Easy, Tom. Go easy."

The night snow was prickly cold on the back of my neck. A north wind blew in off the lake, threatened to lift the cap off my head.

I helped Alma around to the passenger door of the Austin 1100.

She collapsed into the seat, blowing hard. "Wait!" She held her breath, curled her head forward. Her thin hands were freezing, the knuckles blanched from the grip around my fingers. She blew out air and groaned, a deep guttural groan, a groan born of tolerated agony.

"Alma?"

She forced herself straight, juddered in pain, her breath clouding in the icy air, and squeezed words out. "It's too early, Tom. Something's wrong."

Wind tore at my ears. "We'll be there in no time. They'll take care of us." I didn't think she could hear me. I ducked into the car to shelter from the gusts. "Why is she early?"

"Hurry, Tom. Just hurry."

I eased her hand free of mine and placed it on her swollen belly. "Hold on to that little one."

Despite the sub-zero temperature, sweat ran from her temples.

I picked my steps to the driver's side of the car, slipping on snow, buffeted by the wind. I was short of breath—an affliction I had noticed worsening—but when the cold bit at my face I couldn't breathe at all.

Snow settled in my lap as I shrugged the door closed. I coughed.

"The car stinks of sheep," Alma said.

"Sorry."

"You all right?" she asked. "That cough."

"Grand." I fumbled the keys with frozen fingers.

"Be like you to die on me when I need you most. No more smoking if you're to be a father to this child."

Minutes later we were clear of the lane and on the lake road.

The blower struggled to demist the front windscreen, its fan a wheezing rattle behind the dash. The headlights picked out mounds of snow that flanked our route and narrowed the road. In the rearview mirror, lit by taillights, two lonesome wheel tracks marked where we had been before being filled by billowy drifts and disappearing into darkness.

The diagonal fall of snow came in fat, swollen flakes, a mesmerising dump of white cotton from a sinister black sky. The wipers cleared the debris, but I drove blind, the road a white desert in the blackness of night.

*

I think Alma entered the new millennium having given up any hope of becoming a parent. I know I did.

Her younger sister, Rhiannon, had no such problems. Two children within two years of getting married, now both teenage lads, and twin girls a few years later. That's the way of it, be times. Some women are born fortunate.

The twins had been a complicated mix of emotions for Alma, not helped by the row at the christening that was still raw after half a dozen years. I repeatedly tried to reassure Alma that it was Rhiannon's age, eight years Alma's junior, that made all the difference. It wasn't Alma's fault she was the age that she was.

Nor was it mine.

Unlike Alma, I hadn't suffered the indignity of being questioned about the lack of children. I was never asked, in hushed tones, "Did you not want kids?" Or, with a mildly accusing frown, "Do you not like children?" Or even, "Is there something wrong? Can ye not have a family?"

No, I was never asked such questions. Only Alma. Yet, for me, there was still a shame to it, an ache of ignominy. As if not having a child, evading the responsibility of parenthood, was dishonourable, selfish even. It sometimes seemed as though offspring would have provided public testimony of a functioning marriage.

I had developed a grudging appreciation of the opinions of Rhiannon's former professor. The improved social status I noticed in others. It was subtle, no-one went around tugging at forelocks and calling them Your Majesty, but it was there. It was as if parenthood brought you a certain entitlement to measured respect. It could keep you in a job, for one thing.

Having an heir to inherit your worldly goods began to make sense to me.

Continuation of my genetic imprint? Things weren't going particularly well with the farm or with Alma, I was hardly a success, yet I was conceited enough to think, 'Why the hell not?'

But more than anything, I wanted a child for Alma. She needed a child. I needed her to have a child.

Alma announced it over breakfast.

I missed my mouth with the teaspoon of egg yolk. "You're what?"

"Here." She handed me a tea towel. "Clean yourself up. Dadda."

"How long have you known?"

"A few months, only. Are you happy now?"

"Months? Why…? Yes, I'm happy." I rose from my seat, threw fists into the air, and raised my face to the heavens. "You know it's all I ever wanted. For us to be a family."

We clasped and shook each other's hands, and giggled through tears, joyous at the unexpected gift. When we settled, we raised a toast to the baby and to God with sips from mugs of hot tea.

*

It was gone six o'clock—I recall the Angelus—when Alma came out of the bedroom and mentioned the pains.

"It can't be, Alma. There's a foot of snow on the ground." That's what I said, as though a foot of snow on the ground precluded the possibility of childbirth on the basis that you can't get to a hospital when there's a foot of snow on the ground. "Will we give it a while to see if it eases?"

Alma had a defiant look that said she'd take herself to the hospital, if only she knew how to drive.

I was sitting counting weeks on my fingers when Alma shouted from the bedroom.

"We have to try, Tom."

I shoved snow from the car with a brush, put tools in the boot, and locked the dog away in his shed. It took longer than I expected, the cold catching my breath, forcing me to stop and rest.

It was treacherous underfoot as Alma and I made our way across the yard to the car. I slipped twice in the darkness and came close to toppling, but Alma managed to shake her arm free in time to avoid me bringing her down on top of me. She yelled in frustration.

*

Narrow wedges of yellow, liquidy light tried to pierce the blackness but were soaked up by the cotton snow. We snaked along the whited-out lake road like blind mice in a maze. I wiped a hole in the screen's condensation with my cap. A murky, faint glow of orange from a roadside dwelling inched by like a watching spectre. The Thomas's house, Neala and Frank sheltering inside with their big family. I knew where we were.

"You comfortable, Alma?"

She took shallow breaths. "I need you to talk to me."

Talking wasn't something we did a lot of anymore. "About what?"

"About anything. Anything to distract me." The strain was in her voice.

“Never seen snow like this.” The weather. That’s all I could think of, the bloody weather.

The weather wasn’t distracting enough for Alma. “Why do you think the baby’s a she?” she asked.

“What?”

“You said ‘she’. Why’s *she* early? How do you know?”

I hadn’t realised. “You’re carrying high. Girls sit high.” My voice lacked any authority.

“You seem to know a lot.”

The Bakelite steering wheel stroked my chin as I steered us between the walled banks. My hunched shoulders ached, my eyes strained to find a route. “Is it not true?”

“You’ll be telling me next it’s a girl because I was sick in the mornings.”

She surprised me when she said that. “That was to be my next piece of evidence.”

Alma groaned in pain, folded forward. “Heavenly Father.” She forced herself back, blowing hard breaths. “And who fed you all this?”

“What?”

“The obstetrics.”

“I don’t–”

“The childbirth stuff. Who told you all about–”

“Lisa-Marie Gavin.”

“I see,” Alma said. “Discussing the lift of my belly and my morning sickness you are when you go for messages? I’m surprised you didn’t suspend a wedding ring from a thread. I hear that works.”

“Thought about it.” A constriction in my throat made me cough.

I thought I heard her cackle a derisive laugh despite the agony.

“Wait!” She twisted in the seat, pushed at the dashboard with a straight arm. “Holy God.” She eased herself back. “Might be calling on more of your midwifery knowledge before the night is out.” She rubbed sweat from her brow with the back of her wrist. “I only hope I don’t have to rely on you.”

Thick clumps of snow slanted down in the pale glow of the headlights to swoop at the windscreen in some concerted ruinous ritual of last-second self-destruction. Their bulk taxed the wipers. Everything beyond the confines of the Austin 1100 became uncertain, veiled in a white deadly shroud.

"I didn't know," I said. "Left or right, boy or girl." When she didn't reply, I said, "The ring. The way it turns."

Alma shuffled in her seat. "I need the toilet."

I tightened my grip on the wheel.

A swirl-away of snow gave the illusion of an abatement. I pressed on the pedal, accelerated into the clearance. The car slithered like a rat's tail and veered sideways.

"Tom, go easy! You'll ruin us and I'll never forgive you."

I used gears to slow us as we neared where I thought the bridge on the bend was. The dark parapet came into view. Adrenaline made my legs quiver. I leaned my body with the steering wheel as we negotiated the turn.

"Careful, Tom."

The turn was mushy but the wheels held the road. We crested the bridge and the car pitched and rolled as if on water. I coughed out a relieved laugh.

Alma moaned.

Midwifery knowledge exhausted, I said, "Did you notice the hydrolastic suspension, Alma?"

Alma blew shallow breaths, grimaced. "Machines? At a time like this?"

The car bobbed forward.

"Up and down, Alma. Like a boat."

"Explains the sea-sickness."

I laughed, too loud and too long, and coughed, and wiped another hole in the misted window with my hand.

I had travelled that road a thousand times, but we moved in a weak huddle of light beyond which there was only a swallowing blackness. I felt lost.

I kicked the floor-mounted dip switch to adjust the headlight beam. Main. Dipped. No difference. Try again. I pressed with my foot. The headlights went out.

"What are you doing?"

"I'm trying–" I kicked the switch. Nothing. Kicked again.

"Tom, slow down!"

I kicked several times. "It won't bloody come on!"

Kick.

The lights returned.

"What did you do?"

We must have travelled almost fifty yards in pitch darkness.

"The cold," I said. "The electrics are playing up in the cold."

Alma screamed, "Stop messing with the electrics!"

"A faulty connection…I'm sorry to scare–"

"For God's sake, Tom, just drive!"

The wheels of the car crunched through the thickening blanket of snow.

"We'll be there now in no time."

"Tom, you're not going to make it." She pushed both arms against the dash, bowed her head. "Holy Mary," she breathed. "Mother of God. Pray for us sinners."

"Hold on, Alma."

"Now and at the hour of our death." She lifted her head and shouted, "If we left in time, we'd be there by now!"

"I'm doing–!" I searched the road for a route, smarting from the accusation. I regretted raising my voice. "I'm doing my best, Alma." I was desperate. "It'll be grand. It's all right."

But it wasn't all right. The engine strained then raced then strained again as the tyres gripped then slipped in the deepening snow. I backed off the accelerator, kept the gearing high, and steered us between the snow banks.

"Tom, the baby!"

"Hold on, we're close." I had no idea where we were.

The car struggled on, the crunch of snow like as if the road was gnawing at the wheels.

Alma gasped. "Sweet Jesus." An agonised mantra. "Sweet Holy Jesus."

The tyres lost grip and we slid sideways.

"Tom!"

I changed gear, murmured encouragement to the car. The car regained traction.

In a flash of light, the car was tugged backwards like a bolting dog ran out of leash. We jolted forward. I shot an arm out in front of Alma to prevent her hitting her head.

The engine stalled.

"What have you done?!"

The car rocked to a standstill. Headlights flickered then extinguished altogether. Red warning lights on the dashboard threw Alma's face into a haunting relief. Her skin was moist with sweat.

"Are you all right?"

Alma gulped air. "I knew you couldn't do this."

I wiped the window, could see nothing. Blackness. The storm was still there. We could hear its hollow roar.

"I knew I couldn't trust you."

"Please, Alma."

"No, I knew it." Her look of antipathy told me all I needed to know about how much Alma trusted me.

I cranked the engine. The car shuddered. The engine died.

"It's easing," she said. "Thanks be to God, the pain's easing."

"We've hit something," I said.

Alma glared at my hand, willing the key to save us. "Try again. Try the key again. Why did we not leave on time?"

I twisted. The engine took. I kicked the floor switch. The headlamps ignited and a wall of drifted snow bounced the light back into our eyes. I took a second to recover from the glare.

Flakes settled on the windows, the build-up even and rapid. We were being buried.

"I'm going out there," I said. "Call if you need me."

Alma grabbed a sleeve of my jacket. "Don't fail me, Tom."

I tapped her hand, eased her trembling fingers free. Sweat ran down the side of her nose, but her fingers were icicles in my gentle squeeze.

Sucking cold air swirled thick globules of snow around the inside of the car.

“I need you to get this right,” Alma called.

I slammed the door, lost balance, stuttered for grip.

Snow swallowed my feet, calf-deep. Snow topped my shoes, nipped at my ankles. Snow smothered the car’s roof, burned at my hand. Snow was everywhere. I was blinded by a billion swollen flakes of whirling snow.

Wind wrapped itself around my throat and squeezed. I drew shallow breaths and shielded my eyes to search the landscape.

The blizzard gusted and parted.

I glimpsed the dark shadow of a steep incline off to the side of the road. A crack of a flag in wind. I recognised the mound: the giant’s grave. Legend decreed a giant lay buried beneath its humanoid-shaped mass. I have no explanation for why people stuck an Irish tricolour in its belly, but I was grateful for its signal. We were nowhere near the hospital.

Exhaust fumes thawed my legs as I retrieved the shovel from the boot.

With an arm across my mouth, I ducked into the gusts and trudged to the front of the car. I dug from the base of the tyres. The engine chugged weakly with a warm-oil smell. I clanked the shovel against bumper and bodywork.

The snow grew deeper as I worked away from the car. When I turned to empty the shovel, the wind blew it back into the gaps. I had no idea how deep the blockage was, nor how far it stretched. My shovel wasn’t up to the job. I wasn’t up to the job. Alma was right.

I kept digging, the snow light and soft yet obstinate and uncompromising, the storm a hectic squall. My fingers burned. It was like shovelling white soot. I made little progress.

Flakes cooled the nape of my neck. Clouds of warm, panted breath were whipped from around my face and off into the night. The wind stung my ears. All I could hear was the gusting wind. All I could think of was Alma and our baby.

“Let me do it.” Alma stood beside the car, one hand on the bonnet to brace against the gusts, the other holding the bulge of her belly. “You’re incapable of even this.”

I stood erect, flexed the spasm from my back, stuck the shovel upright in the snow. "What are you doing?" I yelled. I pointed. "Get back in the car."

"I'll do it. You're too useless." She turned her head, blinked away snow.

I stumbled over to her. "Alma, please. You're in no fit state."

Her face changed. I read fear in it. "The baby, Tom. I'm losing the baby!"

She didn't lose the baby. She lost what sounded like a splash of fluid. It sank into the snow between her feet. A momentary waft of steam before the wind blew it from beneath her skirts. She wrapped both hands around herself and screamed, "It's too soon, Tom!"

"Ahoy!" The shout came from behind me.

Alma stepped backwards. "Jesus Christ."

A hulking silhouette looked down on us from the top of the snowdrift. Backlit snow swirled around it. Its head was on fire.

It was the giant, risen from the dead. He had a shovel over his shoulder, and he had a dog with him. A ghostly orange glow of death, milky in the snowstorm, emanated from around the two shapes. Is that how the dead looked after being buried under soil and granite rock for a thousand years? I was curious about the dog, having never heard mention of it before.

The giant yelled, "Isn't it great to be alive on a night like this?"

"We're hitting for the hospital," I called back. "My wife's about to have a baby."

"Holy Sweet Mother of God and all the feckin angels in heaven." The huge silhouette rotated, its orange glow momentarily lost to the storm. "Connor, two choices," it hollered. "Dig like hell or go back to the house for hot towels. Diggin'll be less messy."

In three strides the giant descended the slope of snow and was beside us, panting clouds of whiskey breath into the storm. The man stood head and shoulders over me and was as wide as the car. Hair roiled around his huge head like flames in a furnace, long strands of red lashing his ruddy features. God went wild with the hair when He built the giant's head.

Apart from the lack of a hat, the man was dressed for bad weather. He shouted into the wind. "If ya sit in, missus, we'll have ya on yer way in seconds." He yanked the car door open and hoisted Alma into the seat.

The roar of a heavy engine went up the other side of the drift and the dog darted. The drift inched towards me and then lifted off the ground. A hand wrapped itself around my shoulders and dragged me backwards over the bonnet of the Austin 1100.

The man yelled into my ear. "He'll cut ya in two if ya don't move."

The drift retreated. An opening appeared. The snow thinned. The wind gusted through the gap. I clamped my cap onto my head with a numb hand.

The tall stranger bellowed alcohol fumes into my face, "Tear me up and throw me away, but I never seen a year with snow this feckin big."

The digger revved and shifted the drift sideways. A floodlight beamed from the top of the cab.

Words on the loader arm. The changing light, the mayhem of the storm, and the adrenalin that panicked my body must have all combined to hold the letters steady. 'Ryan Matthews Plant Hire.'

"Is that you?" I shouted. "Your name Ryan Matthews?"

"You have me." The giant crushed my hand in his warm fist.

The digger tipped its loaded bucket, its revolving beacon casting loops of milky amber light into the maelstrom of the night, and returned for another scoop.

Our way was clear.

"I've got to go."

"I'll leave you to it," Ryan Matthews said. "Take yer time, just go as fast as ya feckin can."

I knew what he meant.

Chapter 26

She was a fighter. Our tiny fighter.

Tubes protruded from her mouth and abdomen, yet she fought for life with a conviction that confounded the nurses.

We watched her pull air into undeveloped lungs, her ribbed chest fragile as a weave of Belleek china, the swell of her belly rising and falling in shallow lifts.

A crocheted hat, small enough to just about keep a goose egg warm, covered her head. Tiny wisps of black hair leaked out from under the hat and down over the red, wrinkled forehead. Her podginess surprised me, folds of flesh encased in yellow-hued skin.

We peered through the Perspex canopy, Alma in a wheelchair, her arm through the iris of an access port, her fingers, huge by comparison, stroking tiny toes.

Our baby girl lay on her back and ignored us, her shuffles drowned by the soft hum of the incubator fan drawing in air to heat.

If she were a little lamb I'd have known what to do. Keeping her warm seemed the right thing. Premature lambs are vulnerable to hypothermia.

Her limbs jerked occasionally in fitful frustration, swatting and kicking at the air. She was annoyed. Then she'd settle for long periods, and we'd sit and observe, and wait for her to stir again.

I saw Alma in the curve of her chin and the shape of her eyes.

Alma named her Noleen. Noleen Mae Cassidy, after the child's grandmother.

*

Alma jerked a wheel and spun the chair around. She set off, reached the wall, then was back at the side of the incubator.

Back and forth, back and forth, mumbling an incoherent prayer. Her strained face glowed with a grey sheen. Several times she started sentences that she couldn't finish, ran out of words, distraught.

*

In the early hours of the second day, she called me away from our daughter to the side of the room where the light was brighter. "Tom, listen to me," she whispered. "This is my fault. Don't you see? All my fault." She didn't want the baby to hear her confession.

"Alma, stop."

"Shush, now. It is. Can't you see its all my–"

"Don't say that."

She raised her hands, waved them in front of my face. "No, no, no." She spoke rapidly in an urgent whisper. "Stop. Stop it. Listen to me for once, Tom. For the love of God, listen." Her eyes were wide and damp and bloodshot. "I know what happened. I know. And it's all my fault. I know it is. I've let her down."

"She'll be all right, Alma. She's safe now. Look at her. She's beautiful."

Alma shook her head. "No. Don't do that. Stop. It's too early. I couldn't carry her, Tom. It's my fault. She's not strong enough. Not yet. She's not strong enough to survive. Not on her own. Not without me."

"The nurses are taking care of her." As I spoke the words, the conviction in my voice faded away. "She'll be grand."

The appalling glare of the tubular strip lighting was reflected in the traces of Alma's tears. "How long, Tom?" she whispered. "How long have we got with her?"

The fluorescent tubes hummed.

I had no answer for Alma.

*

"Ask, and it shall be given you; seek, and ye shall find; knock, and it shall be opened unto you. For everyone that asketh receiveth; and he that seeketh findeth; and to him that knocketh it shall be opened." That's what it said in the hospital's copy of the *King James Bible*. Matthew, chapter seven. Alma read it to me, several times.

She told me to ask God for help, so I did. No, I begged God for help. With everything I had. I drove through snow to the church and lit candles. My knees ached from the marble step of the altar while the wicks burnt out. I coughed in the cold of the church while I explained to God that our baby girl was innocent, pleaded original sin was not her doing, asked that He not take retribution on her for any of her parents' misdemeanours. She was pure, I told Him, pure as the snow driven into the church around my feet as I dipped two fingers into the stoup.

But God knew all of this already.

Chapter 27

"It's time. Your tablets."

"They make me…"

"Make you what?"

"Not sure."

"They'll help."

"Yeah."

"Here, then."

"Seems a lot."

"We'll take it steady."

Chapter 28

“Please God, let her live.” My candle-lit prayer, over and over. “Let our baby Noleen live.”

Father Roche cited the heavy snow as the reason for not being able to make the journey to the hospital to christen Noleen. When I offered to drive him in, he told me he was two days into a bronchial infection and on a course of very strong antibiotics. He didn’t want to pass it on to the patients who had been unfortunate enough already, spending Christmas and New Year in hospital.

He changed the subject, asked me how I was getting on with the new euro banknotes and coins. “The price of everything has gone up with the exchange rate. Have you noticed that, Thomas?”

The longer our baby lived, the more the doctors learned of her condition. A heart murmur and a suspected brain bleed added to the confusion of her complications.

*

The shrill of the single-tone warning bleep pierced my heart.

We were ushered hurriedly away from Noleen’s incubator by two nurses.

I stood behind Alma’s wheelchair in the corridor and watched Alma scrub at her face with her fists.

“Alma, go easy.”

She rose from her wheelchair. “I’m going back in.”

“Alma.” I grabbed at her as she fell. Her complexion went from red-raw from rubbing to powder-white. I gripped her clammy hands. “Alma?” I thought she had died.

A porter helped her back into her chair. We wheeled her into the visitors’ room. The porter pressed lighted buttons on a vending machine, gave her water to sip. “There you go, missus. I’ll get a nurse.”

Alma didn't want a nurse. She rose from the wheelchair, her dressing gown gaping, and threw the beaker of water at the wall. "Let me in there!"

"Missus!" The porter punched a fat red button by the door.

Three buzzers went off simultaneously somewhere along the corridor, the frail sound like faulty fire alarms.

I didn't know what to do, I'd never seen Alma like this, so I did nothing.

Alma charged at the porter, kicked him in the leg, beat him with clumsy slaps.

The porter cowered. He had no idea how to fight back.

Two nurses entered, both wide-eyed and red-faced from their sprint, both wearing pale blue tunics. They halted next to the porter.

Alma backed away, hands clenched in tight fists, feet apart in a fighter's stance.

The older nurse took the lead, trying to calm Alma. "Missus Cassidy, it's all right." The nurse tried to push the tension down onto the tiled floor with flat hands. "There's no harm." The nurse edged closer. She was twig thin, greying hair, no physical match for Alma. "Missus Cassidy, I can only imagine how you're feeling right now, but please be reassured." Her voice was placating. "Your baby is being seen to." She inched towards Alma. "The doctors are with your little girl right now."

"Don't come any closer, ya fucking bitch ya."

I couldn't believe what was happening.

Two more nurses arrived, different coloured tunics, navy blue and white. A range of ranks had responded to the alarms.

Alma swung with a fist, caught lead-nurse on the ear.

The nurse crouched away, a hand to the side of her face. Her colleagues closed in around Alma.

White-tunic dashed from the room.

Navy-blue took the initiative. "Alma. Calm yourself down, please." She sounded less tolerant. "Everything is being done to help your baby. You're only making it worse. Sit back down and we'll–"

They rushed Alma, grabbed her arms, wrestled her backwards into her wheelchair.

Alma fought them, wriggling and writhing and jerking like a sheep caught for slaughter. Her gown slipped down an arm. "Leave me be!"

"Watch her," the porter said. "Watch her, or she'll kick the shins off ya."

The situation felt surreal. I was living through one of my own nightmares.

White-tunic was back with a syringe.

Alma calmed down after they stuck the needle in her thigh.

A bed was wheeled in, but the room wasn't set up to accommodate a hospital bed. Chairs, tables, a wire stand of torn-cover magazines screeched and scraped as they were dragged out of the way. This room was for visitors, not for insanely sick people that needed sedating.

"Get the bed out," Navy-blue yelled. "The chair'll do."

Confusion as the bed was reversed out into the corridor.

"Maureen, take her back to the ward. Go along with her, Fiona."

Alma was wheeled out, her head lolling.

The older nurse, a palm pressed against her reddened ear, tried to explain what just happened and where they were taking Alma.

Stupefied with emotion, I couldn't make sense of anything she said, my head filled with doubt and fear and the incessant buzz from somewhere out in the corridor.

I righted a chair, sat down.

They gave me tea in a brown plastic cup that crackled when I held it, and a sealed three-pack of biscuits that I didn't touch.

I didn't realise it then, but I think that when they wheeled Alma away, her will to live spilled off the chair and fell to the floor. Her desire to carry on with life, to keep going, was left behind in the visitors' waiting room to lie, hidden forever, in the curls of gathered dust beneath a tall, grey machine vending drinks and sugary snacks.

Noleen Mae fought for another four hours. Her tiny, tiny body was eventually overwhelmed, unable to cope.

*

I buried Noleen at night, while Alma was still in hospital, beside the children's rest, the nearest cillín to home, un-consecrated ground for the un-christened, within sight of the lake. I decorated a cake tin with ribbon to use as a coffin.

Noleen was gone.

I had asked, I was denied, my incantations pronounced in vain, rejected.

I was angry with God, I was angry with the hospital, and I was angry with Alma.

The shame returned.

*

When I next drove in to check up on Alma, a junior doctor stopped me and asked that I step into a side room. We sat on low, worn-padded chairs typical of hospitals.

Elf-like features gave the doctor the look of a child dressed up and playing at being a doctor, the stethoscope around her neck an expensive Christmas playtoy. She drew narrow eyebrows together, a warning that this was not going to be a good-news conversation, and fidgeted with the scope's tubing. She asked how I was coping.

I wanted to tell her that she was too young to appreciate any of this, that I couldn't understand how God had let Noleen die, that I couldn't comprehend how they, the medical staff back there with their millions of pounds of modern technology, had let Noleen die. I thought about asking her why it was that, unlike her sister, Rhiannon, Alma couldn't carry a child, the one thing I asked of her, the only thing she had to get right. I nearly asked the young doctor why I married the wrong sister.

Instead, I told her I wasn't sleeping much, but otherwise, I was grand.

She said, "To be expected in the circumstances, Mister Cassidy." Bluntness made her sound more mature than she looked. She told me, "Alma is still under sedation and is comfortable. I'm pleased to have caught you. I'd like to update you on our findings."

The doctor's words washed over me. Some I heard, others I didn't. She called it a "geriatric pregnancy". *Geriatric?* I'm sure we both were geriatric to the doctor, but Alma was only forty-five. I learned that "An extremely preterm baby is more common for mothers of Missus Cassidy's age". I had been "unfortunate".

I sat forward and asked the doctor-who-looked-like-a-child about Alma and I having another baby.

"Your wife can't have another baby, Mister Cassidy. She's been left medically incompetent. I'm sorry, I thought you knew."

Medically incompetent? "You mean she's barren?"

"She's not a sheep, Mister Cassidy."

"Infertile?"

"Your wife had a hysterectomy. She can no longer have a child."

I sat back. There would be no more children.

"I'm sorry for your misfortune, Mister Cassidy."

None of it seemed to be my fault.

The doctor wanted Alma to remain in the hospital. "We'd like to monitor her progress."

I left without calling in on Alma.

*

Four days later, I returned to the hospital.

Traffic tyres had cleared tracks in the roads, but snow frozen into obstinateness lay banked at the sides and over the fields, whiting out features. The journey was like driving through a chilling, bad dream in which your whole life had been erased.

I must have driven over the bridge on the bend and past the giant's grave, but I had no recollection. When I parked, I sat in the car, the engine running, the windows misting, trying to remember where I was and how I got there.

Before I could collect Alma, I had to wait for another meeting with the same doctor. We sat on the same tired chairs.

"We were concerned your wife might be suffering from postpartum psychosis, Mister Cassidy."

I nodded, but my face must have betrayed me.

"It's sometimes called puerperal psychosis, or postnatal psychosis."

I wondered if the doctor might prescribe something for my cough. "I see."

The doctor knew that I didn't see. "It's like baby blues, but not at all like baby blues at the same time. It's much more serious."

My head was gone, fogged. Thoughts froze then raced. I had sheep outside in the top field. I needed to get home to the sheep.

"Mister Cassidy, are you all right?"

"I'm grand, yeah."

"We can't be one hundred percent with these things, but our opinion is she hasn't got it."

"That's good," I murmured. "Got what?"

"Postpartum psychosis, Mister Cassidy. You sure you're okay?"

I nodded. Words required too much thought.

"Then I'd ask that you watch out for signs of manic or low moods. Or hallucinations. Be wary of any loss of inhibitions, compulsiveness, unusual behaviour, that kind of thing."

I was too numb to react, though I wanted to stand up, move my legs, and walk away.

"Anything like that," the doctor said, "we need to treat as a medical emergency. We do think your wife is suffering from depression, and there are symptoms of post-traumatic shock."

The doctor prescribed antidepressants for Alma. I told the doctor that I, too, would benefit from a prescription of antidepressants. The doctor said, “You must speak to your G.P., Mister Cassidy.”

*

Time is a great healer. More than one person said that to us. Matt Darcy said it. Father Roche said it on more than one occasion, others too, including one of the doctors.

Alma took the sentiment to heart, clinging to it to subdue the injustice. Her literal interpretation worried me, but I thought it perhaps typical of someone with an anxiety-related disorder. She bought a clock.

We had a clock. Two clocks. One on the granite mantelpiece in the kitchen, the other in the bedroom on my side of the bed on top of the small cabinet. Without mentioning it at all, Alma transferred the bedroom clock to her side of the bed.

I went to sleep watching her peer at its hand movements, the juddering click of the second hand dragging the minute hand reluctantly around the face until morning dragged Alma from her bed.

She watched the hours, and she waited to be healed.

Other clocks appeared in the house, then more clocks. There were clocks in every room.

No two clocks were the same, a variety of faces and displays. Some had Roman numerals, others had no numbers at all. Most had the westernised Arabic numbers I was most familiar with, but the size of the numbers varied. Some displayed only four numbers, like points of a compass. One didn’t use numbers at all but had twelve pictures in a circle. Twelve pictures, twelve babies, cherubic faces, waiting for hands to stroke them.

Alma bought art deco clocks that looked like they belonged to an earlier era. She bought Italian clocks that looked like they belonged to the future, clocks with metal numbers on the end of golden sticks that burst from behind the face like crepuscular rays, a clock with its numbers fallen in a heap beneath the dial like a face shook naked of features. There was a plastic salmon clock with white hands, a ceramic sheep clock with black hands. Before long, every wall in the house bore two or three or four clocks.

I put up shelves and nailed hooks into walls to carry them. I thought about notifying the doctor about Alma's behaviour, but didn't.

I will admit that as the volume of the second-by-second ticking of the clocks grew, so did my irritation.

Chapter 29

I could list you the emotions I went through when we lost Noleen. Anger, guilt, betrayal, disbelief, rage, shame—I'll stop there.

The loss was in my stomach, my centre, my core. A heavy, swinging gnaw that I carried with me everywhere like I'd swallowed a shovel of shingle.

Alma and I didn't talk about it. I couldn't tolerate seeing her cry, and I was too afraid I'd break down in front of her to challenge her about what had happened.

I let my emotions simmer.

Alma got some relief from the antidepressants, blue elliptical-shaped tablets with '20' written on their sides, and some other pills that helped her sleep.

I spent many hours reflecting on what had happened—was there anything I should have done differently? Could I have prevented any of this?—and waited for my emotions to ease in their own good time.

Time, the great healer.

Occasionally, Alma lifted a clock from its shelf or unhooked one from the wall, and took it apart. Its innards were inspected as a mystic might examine runes. I'd sit and watch her, unsure of what she was looking for. There was no explanation, and I didn't ask. If its reassembly frustrated her, she brushed the parts onto the floor with the sweep of an arm.

I lacked the imagination to come up with my own distraction.

Talk ceased in the house. All but the most rudimentary exchanges were replaced by sideway glances as we tried to read the other's moods and moves.

Alma spent a lot of time in bed.

We drank our tea alone or in silence.

The world tilted, the winter snow melted, spring was but a few spins of the earth away, but the icy tension lingered.

*

Alma was crying in the bathroom.

I overcame my hesitation and tapped on the door. "Alma?"

No reply.

"Alma. What's wrong?" Pointless, I knew what was wrong.

"You've been trying to keep it from me, but I know." The locked door deadened her slurred words.

I pressed an ear closer. "What, Alma? Keep what from you?"

"You know, you know, you KNOW!"

I heard Alma collapse against the door, the rub of her back against the panels as she slid to the floor and wept.

"Alma?"

"Noleen should have been born today."

*

I took Alma to the G.P.

The G.P. was reluctant to increase the dosage, so I gave Alma my tablets.

Alma stopped eating, lost weight. Her eyes sunk into her skull, her face all angles and bony edges. Her hair grew long, she tied it back with a band that pulled it severely off her face, and almost completely white. She wore black. Only black. She stopped being handsome. She stopped caring. The burden of guilt aged in the space of six months. She had become what men in the pub call *once a fine-looking woman.*

*

I gave away the last of my sheep, sold the dog and the car, erected another shelf in the bedroom, and left for England. I took all the money from the car to help me get established in London.

I can't remember who suggested I go. The idea just fell out of the conversations Alma and I were not having.

*

The steel vessel *Jonathan Swift* was an hour and a half out of Dún Laoghaire when the panic set in. My first time on a ship. My first time away from Ireland.

A new place, new people, no work. A boiling heat emanated from my gut, lodged itself in my throat. I loosened the top button of my shirt. I looked about me, wondered what the hell I was doing, and let the fear build.

The horizon bounced in the landscape windows of the ship's lounge, the white tips of inky waves giving way to the washed-out grey of the gull-strewn sky.

Grown men staggered angleways back from the counter with pints that slopped their shoes.

I had an unsettling awareness of my own heartbeat. Dizziness forced me to lie down. I closed my eyes and hoped I wouldn't die.

My nerves were in an awful state by the time I arrived in Holyhead. I walked past the railway station and spent the night lying on a bench in a graveyard.

Leaving Duncarrick was as terrible as I always feared it would be.

Dawn laid tombstone shadows across grassy graves. As the shadows shrank, I gathered my wits and steadied my resolve.

The train was packed and ran out of sandwiches before Crewe, but I was on my way to London.

*

London was a shock and hectic. The buildings, the noise, the traffic, the lights, people racing. Confusion. Too many people.

Red double-decker busses charged around the streets, thousands of them. Black cabs prowled for fares, millions of them. Cyclists hopped onto pavements and wound their way between startled pedestrians, hundreds of them. A man, old enough to have grown out of rollerblades, glided along Euston Road as though rocket-propelled.

I moved in my own myopic tunnel of intent and tried to shut out the chaos.

Rhiannon was the only person I knew in London. I found out how to get to Camden and went to find her.

She wouldn't see me. I had called at a bad time. She had to collect the children from school and wouldn't be back until late. She had someone coming around later to fix a leaking tap.

Bogus excuses.

She questioned what I was doing in London, then didn't wait for an answer. She adjusted the clasp in her hair, now tinged grey at the temples, and avoided eye contact. She twisted the heavy gold rings on her wedding finger, told me to go home, told me to go back to Alma.

*

The room I found was expensive. I needed to find a job before the money ran out.

I walked, and I smoked.

Marylebone, Mayfair, Soho. Covent Garden and its colonnaded opera house where an Asian busker gave a rendition of *Dirty Old Town* on an out-of-tune guitar. Waterloo Bridge and the River Thames causeway, wide enough to swallow Duncarrick in its odorous mid-afternoon tidal swell.

Rhiannon had changed. The children had changed her. John Kavanaugh had changed her. Despite her resolve.

After several more lame-excuse rejections from Rhiannon, I knew my trip to be a waste of time, an embarrassing disaster. I scolded myself for my naivety, my stupidity. I blamed Alma for putting me in that position.

I walked some more, smoked some more.

London at night lacked the blackness of Duncarrick at night, its urban streets lined with stark white and amber bulbs, highlighting my shame, relaying me on to the next lamppost to shame me more. In London, there was nowhere to hide and there was everywhere to hide.

I took refuge in the pubs. Crowded, rowdy, laughter-filled pubs, full of people sharing time together, full of people talking about children and bemoaning the fact that they had to get back to childminders. I drank unfamiliar beer and smoked unfamiliar cigarettes, on my own, unapproached and approaching no-one.

I was in London, a million times the population of Duncarrick, and I never felt more lonely.

The excessive drinking worked against me. Respectable people steered clear of the drunk-who's-in-here-every-day. People that did come near asked for spare cigarettes, or matey change for a coffee, or ten pence for bus fare. They hovered, hand out, swaying, sallow-faced, struggling to maintain control of their glazed eyes.

I spent my days thinking about Noleen, about Alma, about Rhiannon, and about God.

I concluded that Rhiannon's reaction was not a rejection. There were signs of something else in her face. Surprise, certainly. Embarrassment, maybe. Hope?

In the middle of one of those long intervals of drunken rumination, during a self-obsessed period of inebriated introspection, I convinced myself that God did not exist.

How *could* God exist? How could He allow Noleen to die? How could He allow *my* Noleen, my little girl, to die? I ran through the arguments in my head. It brought relief from the rage. I didn't have to be angry with Him anymore; He didn't exist.

I explained all this one afternoon—I think it was a Tuesday. There was mid-week horse racing on the television—to a lay sister who was playing bridge in The Old Bell, a pub on the edge of the Queen's Park area of London.

She listened, quietly and politely, as I explained my reasoning. She shuffled uncomfortably in her seat, her wide eyes shifting from one card-playing friend to the next, her gaze imploring them to sit still and not to react.

When I went on to criticise the size of the cross on the chain around her neck, her bridge partner decided enough was enough and stood up. He told me, "Kindly go home and sober up."

I tried to meet with Rhiannon again. She was too busy, wouldn't buzz the vestibule door open, or even come down to talk to me.

After two more weeks of drinking and getting lost in the lanes and thoroughfares of London—and having a packet of cigarettes and forty pounds 'borrowed' from me by a girl with a Stanley knife and a grey, drug-addict's face—I decided it was time to return to Duncarrick and face up to Alma.

I had my suitcase standing beside me, packed and ready for home, when I spotted Ryan Matthews in a pub in Soho.

His big, red head of hair floated above the fog of cigarette smoke. He didn't recognise me. Why would he? I wasn't with a pregnant woman who was about to lose a baby, or driving an Austin 1100, or carrying a shovel in a snowstorm.

He roared when he made the connection, "Tear me up and throw me away!", and belted my back so hard I thought he dislodged vertebrae. It was Ryan that reminded me about the shovel, a gentle tease. "Remember the feckin shovel? You were a brave man takin on a drift of snow twice yer height with a shovel." He bought me a drink and two for himself and asked after the baby.

I told him she died.

He bought me another drink, and two more for himself, while I regathered my composure.

"You have kids, Ryan?"

"Five of the little bastards." He threw back his big head and laughed, probably relieved we were on a happier subject of conversation. "When I say 'bastards'," he said, "we did get married first." He roared again and slapped my arm.

"What ages?"

"Oh, Lord, that's a good one…Connor, I think, is twelve. He's the oldest. The others're under that."

"Twelve's a good age." I just said that, unsure why.

"You met him. You met Connor. He was drivin the J.C.B. the time we cleared the snow. Remember?"

"At twelve years old?"

"Probably only eleven at that time. He's a devil for machines. It'll all be his one day, the business. Connor will inherit the lot." He shoved back his leg-of-lamb shoulders and thrust out the barrel of his chest. "That's the only reason I'm here, another machine to hand down to him."

Ryan Matthews was in London to buy plant for his hire business. "Half the feckin price, Tommy. And there's a fella up in Inverness that'll sort out the paperwork for fifty notes."

"There much work, Ryan? For the likes of me, I mean."

"Up in Scotland?"

"No, here in London."

"I was jokin. Much as ya want. Eriksson's buildin a new football stadium at Wembley. They need to knock down the old one."

"Are Erikssons taking on men?"

"Who?"

"Erikssons," I said. "The people building the stadium."

"Eriksson's not a builder."

Talking to Ryan Matthews could be like clearing snow in a drift. "What are they"

"Football. Soccer. England manager. Surely, you've heard of Sven-Göran Eriksson?"

"He doesn't sound English."

"He's Danish, like the bacon. Or Swedish, maybe."

"And he's over here building a new football stadium?"

Ryan boomed out another laugh. "Bless me little heart, you've it all wrong!" He giggled like a twelve-year-old boy. "He won't be building it. He's only the manager. Of the team."

"The England football manager? I understand now."

"Imagine that, the manager building the new stadium, eh?"

"Who is building it?"

"What can ya do?" he said. "They'll be lookin for labourers, and I know ya fancy yourself with the shovel." He grinned, a giant, childish grin. "What's in the suitcase?"

I dragged my suitcase in under the table. My plans had changed. "I need a cheaper place to live."

"Where are ya now?"

"Kilburn."

"You need to go feckin south, young man." Ryan nudged my shoulder. "Go south, young man? Ya get it? Most people say go west."

I rebalanced myself on the stool. "I have it, Ryan."

"Don't do nothin until I put you in touch with James Taylor first. He's a rotten old cockney but he's decent with it. Great time for the Irish."

"Is James Taylor the man building the new stadium?"

"Not on his own." Ryan's laugh was loud enough to fill a hay shed. "He'll have *you* on the shovel to lend a hand."

Ryan Matthews seemed to be the person who would appear when I needed help the most. My giant guardian angel. I spent most of the money I had left buying his beer for the rest of the night, in gratitude for his gallant rescues.

Sometime later that night, a sober Ryan Matthews eased my face from a urinal, picked me up off the toilet floor and carried me and my suitcase to a taxi.

Chapter 30

I had been dreading his call since Matt Darcy mentioned the inspector was about the town asking questions. The Duncarrick rain beat down so hard on the roof tiles, I nearly missed his knock.

Inspector Michael Gilhooly was examining the broken metal goose when I got to the door. He lowered his gloved hand and drew back his head when he saw the state of me. His tiny eyes narrowed.

I could only imagine how I looked.

"Mister Cassidy," he said.

I wasn't sure if it was a greeting or a question.

The air smelled damply of plant oil, lifted from the fields by the pounding rain to permeate the valley.

Gilhooly hadn't changed much since his daughter's christening, maybe a tinge of grey at the extremes of the cropped sideburns, and he still held himself well.

He peered out from under the rain-dappled peak of his inspector's cap, his bank-vole eyes set close together, predatorial, honed to chasing down prey. Matt Darcy was right, there was something of the *creature* about Michael Gilhooly.

Raindrops darkened the shoulders of his uniform.

"Been a long fucking time," he said.

I tried to hide my tremor.

"What way are you, Thomas?" He could see how I was. I was dying. "Heard you were having work done about the house." The cold eyes never left me. "I'm almost ashamed to admit it, but I don't think I've ever been out to Duncarrick before. It has a beauty. Even in this." He held out a hand, as though to catch a sample of the weather and present it to me.

The weather was such that Ryan Matthews and his men had been rained-off work for the last two days. Water from springs that Ryan had unearthed in his excavations ran freely off the field banks. Beneath Inspector Gilhooly's boots, the flow was strong enough to cut a shallow channel.

"Not going to invite me in?"

I stood my ground. My mind had the incident with the pint of beer and his cornflour shirt on rapid repeat. "How can I help, Michael?" I said.

While Gilhooly assessed the croak of my voice, I allowed myself, for that second, to entertain the possibility that all this might only be about the shirt. I remembered hearing that the christening reception disbanded shortly after our little altercation. He would have blamed me for spoiling the event. That's all this was, maybe, revenge for me ruining his cornflour terylene shirt and his daughter's christening.

"Work, Thomas. An official call. It's concerning the death of your wife."

My stomach rolled. I had anticipated his visit, had imagined how it would run, yet I thought I was going to vomit on the doorstep with the shock of its reality.

"Missus Alma Cassidy." He used her full name as if Alma was someone neither of us had ever met, a stranger from the other side of the country.

Raindrops tapped the plastic peak of his cap. The wind fell light. His eyes maintained their scrutiny, gauging my reaction.

"You never were interviewed about the circumstances of Alma's death, were you, Thomas?" *Alma*, that time. It was as if Gilhooly played me like a tug-o-war, slackening to give ground and then drawing me back when I was unbalanced. Was it some tactic he learned at Inspector College?

I didn't answer.

"Staffing," he said. "Cutbacks. They've the force fucking ruined."

I wanted to close out the door and for Inspector Michael Gilhooly to go away. Gilhooly, on the other hand, settled his stance, like we'd met on the lane on a summer's afternoon with nothing to do but lean on a gate and watch sheep eat grass whilst we chatted like old friends in the sunshine.

"Not everyone realises," he said, "that government austerity measures come at a price." His mouth, but not his eyes, smiled at his own humour. He had probably used the same line arguing with his superiors against cuts to his budgets. "Especially out here in the boglands," he said. "So I took it upon myself to do some investigating."

Water from the springs backed up against the side of one of his boots. It would have been fortunate for me if at that moment a flood came roaring off the bank and washed Inspector Gilhooly away.

"If you don't mind," I said. "I've a shiver coming on me."

"I bet you do," he said, but he wasn't referring to the cold and the damp. "I won't keep you long. I'm sure everything's in order. I doubt there'll be anything to worry about."

I tilted back my head. "Grand."

"It's just good to tie up a few loose administrative laces, if you know what I mean." Gilhooly seemed oblivious to the rain and the wash around his boots. "It'll all be sound. Providing, that is, the toxicology report doesn't reveal anything untoward."

What toxicology report?

"You look shocked." He adopted his down-the-nose look. "Standard practice in these circumstances. Doctors report their concerns to coroners. Coroners refer on to pathologists. Pathologists do what they have to do, and a while later, a toxicology report makes its way back to the coroner. Simple. Drawn out and fucking time-consuming, but simple."

I had no idea if what he was telling me was the truth or not.

"Bloody cutbacks don't speed it up any."

"Who authorised it?"

"Pardon me?"

"The report."

"Oh, you don't worry about that, Thomas. I don't need your consent. Check your post. You would have been notified. Did you not get a letter from the coroner's office?"

I didn't reply.

"I'd say you did. Probably came with the Interim Certificate of the Fact of Death. It was all explained in the letter."

The undertaker for Alma's funeral, Dessie Manghan, had mentioned such a certificate. I took it to be Manghan's over-elaborate name for a death certificate. Manghan liked to make things sound more complicated than they needed to be.

"I understand Alma was taking medication following what happened with the baby?"

I swallowed hard.

He observed me.

I wondered if he had waited these eight long years for an opportunity to take his revenge for Delores's ruined christening. It entered my head to ask how many more children he had running around at home, but I didn't.

He resumed. "There's an over-sensitivity to the misuse of drugs, these days, Thomas. All the suicides." He spoke in the captured-audience lecturer tone I remembered from the christening. "Poisoning through overdose is a very serious issue. But as I explained to my men back at the barracks, where would you, or Alma for that matter, have access to sufficient quantities of tablets to effect an overdose? Certainly not from her doctor, I've checked that. Alma's prescription ended over three months before she died. So, my money's on there being some kind of misunderstanding."

The animal eyes bore into me. Is a rodent bank vole carnivorous? Probably not. Cats are. Inspector Michael Gilhooly was a cat, toying with his prey to exhaust it before pouncing. I was no more than a mouse to him.

"I understand how awful it must be," he said. "It must have hurt you both."

He had no understanding.

"And I was going to let the matter pass," he said.

In a movement that spilled rainwater from the peak of his cap, he leaned towards me. I swear to Christ, it seemed like he was about to bear his teeth and deliver a fatal feline neck bite to sever my spinal cord.

"But then I called London," His breath smelled of stale coffee. "And spoke with Missus Rhiannon Kavanaugh."

A shiver worked its way into my legs that threatened to topple me in a heap at the door. I was afraid I'd drown in the small ravine of rushing brown water at Gilhooly's feet.

"Your deceased wife's sister. But you know that of course. She told me she had concerns."

I couldn't think what concerns Rhiannon would share with Gilhooly, though I was in no fit state to be thinking anything.

"So I'm chasing the tox report. I wanted to let you know I'll be in touch when I receive it."

"Grand," I said, but I wasn't grand. I hoped he couldn't see the pound of my heart through my jacket.

"I've my eye on you, Thomas Cassidy," he said, with no attempt to disguise the menace in his voice.

He straightened. "I'll let you on with your day." He saluted, two gloved fingers. "Don't fucking think I forgot what happened at the christening." And then he was gone.

I fell against the door frame, held onto it, my cold fingers burning at the clutch. A sickening sourness formed in my mouth. It's ache worked its way to the back of my throat, up into my skull. The rain, the fields, the running water, spun and tumbled together in my head. My legs gave way like ruptured shuttering on an excavated field bank. I collapsed onto the kitchen floor.

Chapter 31

I was sick in the back of the taxi.

"Let it all up, Tommy," Ryan Matthews said pawing my back.

The driver pulled to the side of the road and insisted I leave his cab.

I stumbled onto the pavement, raised a hand in apology. "I'm sorry, Ryan."

The driver swore in a foreign accent as he circled behind me with a dustpan and brush from the boot.

"Do ya know where the feck you are, Tommy?"

"I do, yeah, Ryan. I do. I'm just down here a bit." I forgot I had left my old digs.

The driver sprayed the seat and the floor with disinfectant and rubbed with a rag, still cursing.

"Now listen, Tommy," Ryan Matthews said. He shuffled his huge frame to the edge of the seat. "Be sure and call James Taylor tomorrow afternoon, ya will? There'll be a job for you at Wembley Stadium. I'll call him in the morning and let him know the craic." He hiccupped, the first sign he'd taken any drink. "He'll be expectin yer call. Ya won't let me down, sure you won't?" It was a big step to recommend anyone for a job in London. Ryan Matthews's reputation was at stake.

I leaned myself against a lamppost and felt for the scrap of paper in my pocket. "I've his number."

"Listen, Tommy. Could ya do with a few pound for your wallet?"

"Ah, Ryan." The heart in me swelled despite the shame. "I'm grand."

"Just, ya mentioned money is all. Would ya take a few pound until James Taylor coughs up?"

My giant guardian angel. "No. I'm grand."

"Take this. A hundred. I wish it was a grand." Ryan chuckled to himself. "Grand? Ya spot that one, Tommy?"

I crushed the notes in my fist. "You should never lend money to a man when he's drunk."

"Give James Taylor a call tomorrow afternoon and you'll be sorted."

I rubbed roughly at my chin, determined not to tear up. "You're a gent, Ryan."

"Sure yer all right to get home?"

I waved him away.

His big face grinned. He tapped the driver's screen and sat back in the seat.

The driver waited until I closed the door, then drove off, leaving me lost and alone in London, my suitcase still in the taxi.

I wrapped an arm around the lamppost, breathed in the cold. The night air still smelled of antiseptic, reminiscent of a neonatal care unit in a small-town Irish hospital. I lit a cigarette, clumsily, challenged to coordinate movements and tools and materials.

A youngster stepped rapidly along the opposite pavement, his head down. He wore a knee-length black coat with the hood up, his hands in the pockets. He was on his way to a nightclub, or from a nightclub, or the home of his girlfriend. I didn't know.

I sucked on the cigarette, inhaled.

A couple ambled past, linked and laughing, on their way back from a pub, or a picture house, or the ice bar where everything you touch is solid ice and you can only stay in there for about twenty minutes because it's just too bloody cold.

London was full of the unusual. There was always something to do, somewhere to go, and for most, someone to be with.

I willed Rhiannon to appear, walking down the street towards me.

Where would she be going this time of night?

To find me.

Unlikely. Rhiannon no longer wanted me.

A coincidence then? Of all the streets, in all the towns, you had to walk along this one. Another favourite film of my mother's.

I laughed out loud, clutched at the lamppost to stop myself from falling.

"Hello, Rhiannon." I checked to make sure no-one was close enough to hear me.

"Hello there, Tommy." She whispered it, but I still heard her in my head. She had dressed herself up and looked a bit more like her old self, a young Elizabeth Taylor.

"Good to see you," I said. "The children well?"

"They're grand. I want to apologise for shouting at you when you came around the other day." And then, "The kids miss you."

No, she wouldn't say that. The children didn't know me, never met me. They could get to know me if their mother would only allow it.

Rhiannon needed to know how I felt about her. And how Alma felt about me. Why wouldn't Rhiannon see me?

"Alma's given up." That's what I told Rhiannon.

"I can understand that. It was a tragic loss. Mammy was the same. Never right after losing the baby. I feel sorry for Alma. I feel sorry for you both."

"I've given her time to sort herself out."

"Mammy had all the time in the world. Never really got better. Got worse, if anything."

I considered this. Would Alma ever get better?

"You'd make a lovely father, Tommy. I've always thought that."

Rhiannon wouldn't say that, either. When we were together, children were the last thing she wanted. It took John Kavanaugh to change all that.

"I know you've always wanted children, Tommy."

That sounded better, more like what Rhiannon would say.

"It's all I wanted."

This would not be the time to mention the time I paid for Rhiannon to come to England. No. That was best left forgotten.

A young couple in matching heavy, black army surplus boots passed behind me, giggling. "First sign of madness," the lad said.

I reversed around the lamppost to watch them walk away.

The lad stopped and turned. "A problem, grandad?"

The girl tugged at his arm. "Leave it, Wayne."

I shook my head. "It's grand, son. Walk on."

"I'm not your–"

"Wayne, come on." The girl pulled him away.

He gave a final look back and threw an arm over the girl's shoulders.

I dropped the cigarette to the ground, twisted my foot on it.

Should I go to see Rhiannon?

She had refused to see me several times already.

If only I had a chance to explain.

I should have gone to London with Rhiannon. The arse fell out of farming as soon as I got into it. Something else that conspired against me. It was always a struggle after I lost the job at the power station. I only wanted a viable farm and a family. My own family.

I had taken too much drink to see Rhiannon now. I stuck out an arm.

A taxi drew up in front of me, as if by magic. The omens were good. I was meant to do this. I wiped my mouth clean.

The diesel engine's rattle filled the street. A standard Nissan 2.7 litre engine, according to the previous taxi driver.

The driver stretched over, pulled down the window. "Where to, mate?"

"Rhiannon's flat."

The driver shrugged. "Gunna have to be a bit more general, mate." He reached to close up the window.

"No, sorry. Sorry. Camden. Camden Town."

The driver narrowed his eyes. "You got enough money?"

I could only imagine my drunken, dishevelled look. I lay a hand on the bulge of notes in my pocket, threw back my shoulders. “Of course.”

“Better climb in then, mate. Don’t wanna keep the lady waiting.”

Chapter 32

From the confinement of my fireside chair, I could see the sun-strewn view of the southern flank of Cloonta Beg through the grimy kitchen window. Mulligan's land, the ground not as stony as mine. I wished it was my land. Then, perhaps, John Kavanaugh wouldn't have cheated me out of it.

Ryan Matthews called my name from outside.

I gathered my strength, pushed myself off the chair.

I had taken to using Daddy's old walking stick to get around the house. Its handle was a rubbed-smooth bulge of wood that, when I was young, used to resemble the head of a goose. Many a time I felt the stubborn flex of its knotted ash-bark shaft across my back.

Movement was exhausting. My feet pained most of the time, especially when I stood, and squelched when I walked. The skin of my swollen legs was stretched paper thin, and my left leg wept a clear fluid that trickled from its ulcerous spring down my shin to be gathered in a tea towel tied above my ankle. The leaky ulcer stung like a bastard.

My body was closing down.

I unlatched the door, and the heat of the day rushed past me.

When Ryan Matthews lifted his head, his smile slipped. "Tear me up and throw me away." His face was a concerned frown. "If you were a dog, Tommy, I'd be inclined to sink a bullet in yer skull. Compassion, only."

I forced my body to straighten, pushed back my shoulders. Tendons pulled tight in my legs and groin. I wanted to ask Ryan how he expected me to look after he and his machines had confined me to the house for the best part of two months.

"Yer feet, Tommy. Are you able to walk at all?"

I had on me the pair of sandals Alma bought when we visited the beach at Enniscrone, shortly after we got married. We ate ice cream, drank tea in a café sitting by a window overlooking the beach. I wanted to remove my socks, worried they would take on sand, the same way the youngsters did when they wore sandals. Alma told me to keep the socks on. She said I'd look like Jesus with corns. She laughed.

I was without socks now, unable to bend to get them on. My feet bulged around the straps, my toes a rainbow of indigos, blues and greens.

Ryan's dog extended its neck to sniff the doorway.

"With the stick, Ryan," I said. "I walk a bit with the stick."

"Yer chest sounds like it could do with a squirt of easy-start." He smiled again. "You know, the stuff we used to spray into engines when they wouldn't–"

"I know it, Ryan." I gazed down at Ryan's dog. It was licking my damp toes.

"Come out of that, ya bastard," Ryan yelled. "Sorry, Tommy." He hesitated before moving closer. "Come here. Hold onto me. You should see this. I never thought I'd see the feckin day in this village."

I reached up to clutch his tartan-clad arm, felt the bulge of bicep.

"Steady does it," he said.

I was born in that house, grew up running around it, brought my wife here to live, and raised sheep on its acreage, but I no longer recognised my surroundings.

The yard was no more, it's uneven, weedy surface dug out and relayed as a wide, flat sandstone apron the colour of biscuit. The goose shit was gone. Sunlight bounced off its rolled surface, made me squint. There was a car and Ryan's dirty white van parked where the dog's shed used to be.

"Easy," Ryan said.

The hedge of briars had been ripped away, the trench that ran beside it filled in. The field Daddy called The Rise had become a boggy expanse strewn with ruts and hollows and spotted with puddles of bronze bog water. The vegetation had been peeled back and piled up on a bank, the mound a sandwich of soil and white stone and black peat. I could no longer see the hazel tree.

It was carnage, the field a cratered swath of ruin hacked into my mountainside. A livid scar on the flank of Cloonta Beg.

Ryan led me between two stout metal posts daubed in red-oxide against rust, to the track.

I glanced over to the children's rest. It was gone, covered in rolled stone, eradicated out of existence. Ryan had forgotten his vow to keep his men away from it. The shock of it took my breath and I staggered.

"Easy, now. You all right?"

There was no point saying anything to Ryan about Noleen and the children's rest.

"See." Ryan straightened to his full height, pointed down the track, pushed out his chest. "Look at that, Tommy. Would ya ever think it?"

I raised my head and squinted. Reflected light from the jade-hued lake pained my eyes, made the image shimmer.

They had widened the track. Matt Darcy would be able to meander his way along it without catching a wheel in a ditch.

"What ya think, Tommy?"

My eyes focussed, my vision cleared. I could make out the front end of an articulated lorry emerging from the haze, moving slowly towards us. It filled the track from edge to edge, its bulk rocking gently from side to side as it rode the shallow dips and rises.

"A low-loader, Tommy. In the village. Wait'll ya see what's on her back."

Vertical exhaust pipes coughed black fumes into the air. Between the pipes, the thick yellow boom arm of a giant excavator, an iron fabrication of destructive power. Whatever carnage Ryan Matthews's men had done to my field and my mountain, their work had only just begun.

Declan O'Dea and Zhoro Boguslav were there to watch the excavator arrive. Young O'Dea had his arm aloft, holding up his mobile phone to photograph the occasion for posterity.

"Kavanaugh got it brand new for this job," Ryan said. "Reckons the money he'll make from the quarry will cover it.

He says it cost a million quid, but you'd have to allow for the bullflation. Brought it all the way from England with him."

Brought? I clenched Ryan Matthews's forearm to prevent me from collapsing onto the stone. Was John Kavanaugh back in Ireland? I wasn't sure I could face John Kavanaugh, hadn't the strength to meet him. I eased my grip, steadied my breathing.

Ryan worked his arm free. "All right on yer own a minute?"

The excavator's boom loomed high above us as it neared.

Ryan took a step towards it. "It's fitted with a super-long reach," he said. "Sixteen meters, Tommy. Bet that's over fifty feckin foot."

Matt Darcy could have confirmed that for him.

Ryan hadn't finished with the accolades. "The cab's like a four-star hotel. I've stayed in rougher bed and breakfasts in Mularanny." Ryan jigged around like an overgrown child eager to get the wrapping off an early birthday present. "Didn't you drive one a these in London, Tommy?"

I had. Wembley Stadium. This machine was built for demolition.

Ryan beckoned the low-loader off the lane. It drew to a halt with a hiss of air-brakes that lifted dust from the rolled-stone apron.

The ground beneath my swollen feet became still.

An awestruck Ryan Matthews read the large black lettering, heavily shadowed in gold, emblazoned along the length of the boom arm. "Kavanaugh Developments, Construction That Cares." He grinned back at me. "The man couldn't care a shite about anything."

It was the glint of sun off the sloping top edge that drew my eye. Handmade by craftsmen, according to Mark. Its shape derived from Greek temple architecture. The vertical lines appearing perfectly parallel thanks to the entasis bulge of the metal strips. Straight ahead in the distance, the stainless-steel grille of a gold Rolls-Royce Phantom turned in off the lake road and glided towards us.

My heart cramped in my chest from its sudden hammer. It beat at a terrific rate.

The gold phantom drew noiselessly level with the apron and halted, blocking the lane.

Mark, the driver, capless in the heat, climbed out and hefted a rear door open.

My hand juddered on the walking stick. I felt my body flood with adrenaline.

John Kavanaugh, the multi-millionaire from Manchester, swung his thin legs out of the car and pushed himself erect. He pointed two fingers at me like a pistol, closed an eye to aim, and jerked his arm. He nodded to Mark and limped towards me, the grin engulfing his face full of deprecating contempt.

Chapter 33

I overpaid the London taxi driver.

He held up the notes. "You sure, mate?"

I waved him away, and the Camden street fell silent.

A night freeze thickened the air, but a fire burned in my belly. I staggered across the road.

The red-brick, multi-storey wall of windows and balconies towered over me, immense in the dark.

A string of washing was slung below a balcony near the top. Two shirts, some underpants and a towel hung stiffly, like a small family of frigid phantoms.

I draped myself over a metal railing, rested my arms on the hedge. My legs buckled, but I managed to stay up. "Rhiannon."

No response.

I shouted louder. "Rhiannon!" I peered through a cloud of my own breath in search of a pebble to throw.

On the balcony below Rhiannon's, a door of rectangular glass panes flashed a reflection of street lights onto the street. A man bulging out of a string vest gripped the metal rail of the parapet and in a whispered yell said, "I got kids, buddy. Can you cut the shoutin?"

The man clearly believed that having kids gave him the necessary status in society to ask me to shut up. (Whenever I later reflected on this incident, I accepted that deep down I agreed with him.)

"Nothin to do with you," I said back to him.

"You wake my kids and it will have." He flexed an impressively sized arm, sleeved in dark tattoos.

Rhiannon appeared on her balcony. She tied a dressing gown around herself as she eased the door to the flat closed and tiptoed to the edge. Her hair was loose about her face, an adorable slumber-mess of curls.

"Rhiannon."

"Still too loud, buddy."

Rhiannon leaned over her parapet and spoke down to the man. "Mister Hughes, I'm sorry about this."

Mr Hughes scowled down at me, unperturbed in his string vest by Camden's night-chill, and said, "We're fed up of men callin here, but he looks about the worst. If you're runnin some kinda business from your rooms, you need to improve your clientele."

"Watch yer mouth!" I shouted and pointed a wavering finger at Mr Hughes.

"I'm warnin you." Hughes dipped back his head to check his flat.

"Go away, Tommy," Rhiannon said. "You're embarrassing me."

That hurt. "I came to London to see you. I told you. That's why I'm here. We need to talk."

"It's half-two in the mornin," Rhiannon said. "And you're stupid drunk. What're you doin shoutin up from the street at half-two in the mornin?"

"You didn't answer the buzzer thing. Here. The other day. I called here. You didn't answer."

Hughes stuck his chest out over the balcony. "She's closed for business, buddy. So I want you to piss the fuck off." He pointed an arm back up to the junction.

I ignored the muscle-bound bastard.

A light went on in the flat above Rhiannon's.

"I don't want to see you, Tommy," Rhiannon said. "How many times do I have to tell you?"

"Alma and I, Rhiannon. She's had time. It needs ending. It's time. It's all too late."

"I don't understand what you're on about," Rhiannon said.

"Best shut this Irish twat up." Hughes was making more of a racket than I was. "Before I go down there and do it for–"

"I love you!" I declared it loud, for all of Camden Town to hear.

A glow of light from an opened door temporarily lit up the balcony on the fourth floor. An old man, naked above the waist, shuffled to the rail and leaned over. "What's going on, Al? Nigerians again?"

"The Irish this time, Joe," Hughes said. "Paddy Boy, here. I'm on it. Just need him to shut the fuck up."

The curtain stirred in the lighted window of Hughes's flat. A silhouette appeared between the metal mullions, shook its head, disappeared.

"I'm sorry I didn't come to London with you," I said.

"Bloody here now," Hughes said. "And I'm about to make you sorry you are."

"Yer gunna have to go down to this one, Al. Here to see our little colleen of a workin-girl is he?"

"I'm sorry, Mister Manning," Rhiannon said, her neck stretched out over the parapet rail, looking up. "You should go in, you'll catch yer death."

I looked around for bricks to throw at Mr Hughes and at the old bastard on the fourth floor.

Rhiannon said, "You need to leave, Tommy. Don't call again. Please."

I spotted an empty bottle impaled on a railing to my left.

Hughes shook his head and tutted. "No way to treat a customer."

"I made wrong choices, Rhiannon. The farm. Alma."

"Tommy, you're married to my sister."

"What the fuck?!" Hughes was making a lot more noise than me.

"Hear that, Al? If you don't go down, I think I bleedin well will."

"I wanted children. We couldn't. Alma couldn't. We lost Noleen." My fingers gripped the hedge. Thorns and twigs stuck my skin. Tears ran cold on my face. "She lost Noleen, Rhiannon."

The howl of a baby escaped Hughes's flat and spilled down into the street.

"Get him gone, missy, or I'm goin down and I'll bury him in the bushes." Hughes was fortunate babies cannot choose who their parents are.

"Rhiannon, let me in. Please. We'd be better off without Alma. I'll think of something. A plan. Something. I will."

"Go, Tommy." She was pleading. "For fuck's sake."

The baby screamed, louder this time.

"You woke my baby, you prick!"

I reached for the bottle and launched it at Hughes. It struck the metal bar of his balcony and shattered into a thousand pieces. The noise in the dense night air was like a bomb exploding.

Hughes retreated into his flat, picking steps to avoid glass splinters.

The old man on the fourth floor wrapped scrawny arms around his saggy chest. "For it now, Paddy Boy."

Flats lit up at random locations on the multi-storey wall of windows. Curtains shifted.

"Leave, Tommy," Rhiannon said. "Go before he comes down to ya."

I backed into the middle of the road, looked around for a magic taxi. There was none. I swiped a forearm at my tears.

More lights in more flats, flickering on, blinking like the whole building had been disturbed from hibernation.

"If I go now, Rhiannon, I'll never come back."

"Good." She didn't mean it.

"I won't leave until you see me."

"Jesus, Tommy." She peeked over the balcony, saw Hughes had gone. "Tommy. I won't meet you. Please go."

"Why?"

"Just go!"

A lad joined Rhiannon on her balcony, mid-teens, thin arms, a black t-shirt that read 'AC/DC' and depicted a schoolboy impaled on a guitar. There was a familiarity to the lad's features, but I was sure we'd never met.

"Ronan, go back in."

"Who's that man, Mum?"

"Never mind. Go back to your bed."

The lad positioned himself in front of his mother, shielding her from the street danger. His young eyes bore down on me.

A light, downstairs in the entrance vestibule.

I gazed up at Rhiannon and shouted. I can't remember what. I was drunk, and frightened, and confused. I wanted to tell her to say goodbye to the children for me, but the children didn't even know who I was. "I'll call when it's done," I said.

She shouted back, but I had turned and was heading towards the junction, staggering, almost tripping in my urgency, hoping for the safety of a taxi.

Hughes was out on the street, striding and string vested, arms spread threateningly wide. He held what looked like a tourist-shillelagh gripped in his fist.

I picked up my pace.

The shillelagh bounced hollowly in the street and slid to a halt next to me, a wooden mallet of varnished trunk, the handle snapped off on the road.

I kept up my drunken run.

Chapter 34

"Mister, bloody, Cassidy." John Kavanaugh said. "Wasn't sure if you were still alive. I'm only here to see if Ryan can knock the house, yet." The Mayo-accent affectation was gone. There were no hissing s's.

He wore a dark-grey suit, navy shirt with a white collar, and a red tie with a small-linked chain looped beneath the knot. There were beads of sweat on his narrow forehead from the sudden heat. "Are you pleased with the developments taking place?" He spoke in a whisper, inches from my face.

I shivered in the sudden chill of his shadow.

"Hope you're keeping an eye on Ryan and his men. I expect you to be onto them if there's any sign of slacking." He arched back his spine to look me in the eye.

The sun warmed my face.

"Nothing to say for yourself? No?" He gazed over my head to survey the village, took an extravagant nasal breath. "Love this place," he said. "You know, I reckon there's enough stone in that mountain to cover the whole of Ireland in roads. Just wait until we start with the explosives."

I kept my eyes low, stared at his chest, tried to breathe. There was a diamond-shaped Freemason logo on his tie, a square and set of compasses embroidered in gold thread.

"Spent all the money yet?" he said. "Of course not. Told you I gave you enough to last. Probably more than you need. You know, if I were you." He adjusted his feet and whispered, "I'd spend it a bit faster.

I stared at the ground.

"To be honest, Tommy, I've never seen anyone deteriorate as much as you have. I remember you as a fine, good-looking man. And look at you now. You smell like a drunken corpse, and you're breathing like an ass with bloody asthma. To be honest, it don't look to me like you've long left."

I suppressed a rage-induced cough.

"What's wrong with you anyway, Tommy? Is it the cancer?"

I recalled a simple story Dexter McEvoy read to me of a girl who was raped by a gentry man in nineteenth-century Ireland, the time of the Land Wars. The girl beat the man around the head with a stick. I clenched the handle of my father's walking stick.

"Rhiannon phoned me," Kavanaugh said.

I felt my throat tighten, my legs wobble. It was all I could do to stay upright.

Ryan Matthews was talking with Zhoro Boguslav, both taking turns to point at the excavator.

John Kavanaugh adjusted the knot of his tie. It didn't need adjusting. "Couldn't fucking believe what she told me." His lip curled in an amused grin. "You. In London. A couple of years ago, was it? Round at the flat. Roaring up like some drunken banshee from the bog." He shook his head, pursed his lips. "It's people like you that give us the bad name. And all that happening well before Alma died."

I hefted the stick, gripped it in sweaty hands. My fingers rooted for purchase on the knobbly shaft.

"If Alma could only see you now," he said.

I wanted to ask Kavanaugh about the woman in Manchester. I wanted to challenge him about the child. I wanted to beat him about the head with Daddy's stick.

"Fuck," he said. "If *Rhiannon* could see you now."

Ryan Matthews walked towards us.

"You're a mess, Tommy. An embarrassing mess of a loser." Kavanaugh was smirking, goading me to lash at him. "Rhiannon's been thinking about what happened to Alma, Tommy. And she's angry. I mean pissed-off, roaring-mad angry. She's on about going to the police to–"

Ryan shouted before he reached us. "Mister Kavanaugh. Good to see you." His voice was still full of glee. "She's a beaut."

I eased my grip on the stick.

Kavanaugh turned to face him. “Pleased you like her, Ryan.” *Pleashed.* The cloying ingratiating was back. “Thought I’d call to see she arrived safely. And check over my land, of course. You’ve tidied it up a bit, I see. Moved things around.”

“It’s goin well, right enough,” Ryan said. “I wanted Tommy to see the machine arrive in the village.” Ryan gripped my arm. “Come over. Take a closer look.”

I shuffled my way around John Kavanaugh.

“I’m heading back today, Tommy,” Kavanaugh called after me. “I hope I have another chance to call in, discuss the house.” He strode past us towards the gold Rolls-Royce. “Look after the machine, Ryan, sure ya will?”

“No bother.”

“Good man. It wasn’t cheap.”

“Don’t I know that well, Mister Kavanaugh?” Ryan gave me a sarcastic nudge with his elbow that nearly toppled me. “Sorry, Tommy.”

Zhoro Boguslav was up on top of a track and had the cabin door open. Declan O’Dea pointed his mobile phone at him and walked in slow motion.

I stretched my neck to watch John Kavanaugh sit into his car.

“You’d recognise her, Tommy, ya would?” Ryan wanted me to like the excavator. “It’s the CAT three-twenty-D. What did you operate? The three hundred, was it? I bet ya never thought you’d see one turnin up outside yer own house?”

Kavanaugh’s car turned, three-pointed and noiseless, on the apron.

“It’ll pull that mountain to pieces,” Ryan said.

That hurt. I had a grá for the mountain, an affection passed down through my family. But it was no longer my mountain. I reminded myself of that.

“The cab’s got adjustable everything.” Ryan was bobbing again. He extended an arm to point. “There’s an automatic throttle in her, Tommy. A fifty-foot reach. Did I mention the fifty-foot reach before? Sixteen meters.”

The old gander waddled up behind us and barked. Guilt prevented me turning to face it. I knew what it would be thinking.

"Come on," Ryan said, calm now. "I'll walk you back in. Wanted ya to see it arrivin is all. Would ya ever think it, no?"

I stood my ground and watched the gold Rolls-Royce Phantom dissolve into the lake's gleam. I closed my eyes against the image.

Emotions melded in my mind. My body felt empty, numb, my limbs too heavy to move. I was exhausted, breathless. The taste of dust and diesel fumes was sour in my mouth, the stink of it seeping through to my alcohol-destroyed gizzard.

I allowed my eyes to open. At that moment, that very moment, staring up at the monster of a machine, I grasped the enormity of the horror I faced. I foresaw the inevitable devastation of everything that had once belonged to me, everything that we, generations of my family, ever had. The major, significant decisions I made many years ago to remain here, the sacrifices that I made when I took those decisions, all counted for nothing.

"Mister Cassidy!"

I had lost everything. I wouldn't be able to stay in the house much longer. Kavanaugh would get my house as well as my land. Where would I go? I had nowhere to go.

"Mister Cassidy. Smile for the camera." Declan O'Dea approached in a quarter-crouch. "A few words for the viewers, Mister Cassidy?" He was focussed on his mobile phone, his mouth curved in a grin of devilry. "How do ya feel about Johnny Kavanaugh takin yer land and sellin it off as hardcore, Mister Cassidy?"

To think I used to feed him jam sandwiches.

"Any words for the viewers, Mister Cassidy."

"Declan!" Ryan waved a fist at Declan O'Dea. "Feck off with that! Every thrupence I give him, Tommy, goes on mobile phones."

Declan O'Dea swung his arm towards Ryan. "Mister Matthews is feeling left out. What about you, Mister Matthews? A few words–"

"I swear to God, Declan. If ya don't put that thing away, I'll crush it in me fist and shove it up yer hole."

"Thank you, Mister Matthews," Declan said. "The viewers'll be delighted to hear that."

"The phone, not me fist," Ryan said. "I'll shove the phone up yer hole."

"Too late now, Mister Matthews," Declan said. "The viewers can all see the sort of man you really are."

"Away!"

Declan O'Dea laughed and dropped his arm. "That'll be thrown up on YouTube by tonight."

Out of the churn of drink-addled emotions, the germ of a plan swirled into my head. An incredible, outrageous, improbable plan that would withstand no scrutiny, but a plan nonetheless. When you have nothing, such a plan will do, because with the plan, came hope. Of revenge.

And revenge can be fatal.

"Ryan," I said as we made our way back to the house. "Would you pick up a mobile phone for me?"

"For feck sake, Tommy," he said. "Now you as well?"

The gander was following us. It wanted to know my plan. I turned my head, winked a rheumy eye.

Chapter 35

Matt Darcy pushed open the door to my house. The engine-roars of John Kavanaugh's heavy machinery throbbed their way in behind him.

He closed out the intrusion, waddled in, paused at the table. "Drink all this yerself?" he said. "Or are they usin it to fuel that excavator?" He surveyed the debris, leaned back in his Wellington boots to glance at the battalion of bottles beneath the table, their corkless eyes staring skyward.

I hadn't the strength to fall out with him again so let his interference wash over me.

"It's a pity they don't still give a shillin back on the empties. There'd be enough here to buy back the land. What's this?"

A conical black bottle stood among the ranks of brown and green glass. It looked like it didn't belong, like it had snuck in to get away from the racket outside.

Matty picked it up, read the label. "Rigas Black Balsam. What on earth is this?"

I didn't answer.

"You didn't get this from Buckley's, I know." He held the bottle close to his face and squinted at the small print. "Sacred Heart a Jesus, ninety percent proof. And from Latvia?" Matty studied the label. "I reckon it's one a them herbal pick-me-ups. Catherine the Great was cured of some malady during a visit to Latvia by drinkin somethin like this."

I was in no mood for Matty's banal chatter.

"I've heard these foreign herbals are like liquid Viagra."

I'd heard enough. I wanted him to shut up.

He didn't. "Rub this on yer oul fella before bed, and I reckon you'd be up all night."

I had no use for it.

As if he read my thought, Matty said, "I'll have this if ya don't need it." He slipped my bottle of Rigas Black Balsam into the pocket of his jacket and took his seat by the fire. "By the sounds of it, you could do with rubbin some on yer chest."

If I was strong enough, I'd have wrestled the bottle from him. Not that time. I pointed at a crate of beer on the floor. "Have one."

Matt Darcy surveyed me from the chair, his look an uneasy mix of care and contempt. "Does gettin drunk make ya deaf?"

I glared at him and noticed for the first time the sticking plaster wrapped around the shattered lens of his spectacles.

"Is that yer reasonin?" he said. "Holy be to God, look at you."

I rasped in air and said, "Subdues the injustice."

Matty smacked his lips. "I hear ya made yer film debut on the world wide web. YouTube. I understand yer all over YouTube. All the town's on about it. You've a fine head on ya for social media. Have ya had anythin to eat?"

I said nothing.

"I've sausages." Of course he had. He reached across himself to wriggle the packet free of a pocket. One of his wrists was in bandage. The man was falling apart.

"Food's a waste," I said.

"Since the light broke in my toilet," Matty said, "sittin on the throne's a waste a time with no newspaper to read. But I still need to shite." He stood, walked to the hob. "Slow down with the breathin, Tommy. I can hardly hear the roar of the engines outside. Fryin pan. Where is it?"

"Thrown out." My throat ached. My skin itched, and a pain in the back of my head spilled down and across my shoulders. Talking took an effort I resented.

"Why?"

"You burnt it."

"When?"

I couldn't be bothered with this. "Last time."

"When last time? The sausages? I didn't. It was all right when I finished with it. Burnt it yourself, more like."

I couldn't remember, didn't care.

"I'll use this."

I closed my eyes but couldn't shut out the rumble of revving engines. The floor vibrated beneath my chair. The constant drone was deep in my skull, behind my eyes, in my temples, aggravating, the reverberations like an angry ram bleating against the wall of my inner ear. My head ached with a dry, throbbing pain.

I had learned to interpret the tones. Their variety told me the story of the devastation outside my house. The CAT 320D ripping into the hillside with the clank and squeak of metal-pin joints. A beeped warning as Declan O'Dea found reverse gear and forced his fully laden dumper truck into motion. Zhoro Boguslav easing the throttle of the excavator. A wait for Declan to return empty before getting ready to rip again.

Matt Darcy yelled, "Have ya seen the mess they're makin?"

The sausages sizzled in fury as they landed in the burning fat.

"I think they're tryin to move the bloody mountain closer to the lake." Matty laughed.

I could smell the smoke from the wok as it crawled across the ceiling. Matty was going to burn my sick bowl.

My world was being destroyed. And my vague plan for retribution no longer seemed feasible. I grew increasingly aware that it was only ever a grim plot for revenge, an ill-conceived act of morbid vengeance, thwarted before it ever commenced, too improbable to ever succeed. Another failure, in a long list of failures.

"Are you listenin?" Matty was beside me, shouting. "I'm askin how are you gettin on with the phone?"

Ryan Matthews had programmed three numbers into my new mobile phone: Buckley's, a solicitor who worked out of Gortcastle, and Buckley's son, Raymond. Raymond had his own taxi service, and I knew he could be discreet.

"It's here," I said.

The telephone was plugged into the electrical socket, the wire the thinnest I'd ever seen.

"Ya must be givin it some abuse if it's needin chargin."

"I keep it plugged in."

The chug of the dumper truck engine, straining as it pulled away, loaded.

"You can unplug it, ya know? Carry it around with you. Use it outside the house if you want."

I couldn't go outside.

"Ya have the least-mobile mobile phone in the country."

Matty produced a mobile phone from his pocket, frowned at it.

"You've one too?" I said.

"Yeah."

"Because I got one?"

"Yeah."

"Any text messages?"

"No-one has me number."

I smiled. "Put it in my phone."

"Why do you want my number?" He was eager for me to have his number.

"I'll send you a text message." I didn't know how to send a text message.

"I sent you a text message," Matty said. "Did you not get it? You can get my number from that."

I didn't know how to access a text message, never mind get Matty's number from one.

He returned his new phone to his pocket. "Anyhow, textin is only for the Devil. It won't catch on."

I reached my hand down and groped for the top of a cider bottle. As I pursed my lips to receive it, Matty pulled the bottle from my hand. I glared. Who the hell did he think he was?

Matt Darcy didn't want an argument, so returned to the sausages that squealed in rage at their scorching. "I've tea for you. And sausages."

"The lens of your glasses." I wasn't sure if he could hear me through the commotion. "What happened your glasses?"

"I need them fixed. Been lookin through cracks for the last month but they're ruined altogether now. The glass is fallin–"

"What happened?" I managed to turn my head to face him.

His magnified eye watched me from the other side of the kitchen. "Ya don't need to know."

That meant that I did need to know and that Matt Darcy was going to tell me.

"Go on, so," I wheezed.

"That skunk, John Kavanaugh."

My breath crackled in my throat. I curled into a fit of coughing, my neck strangled, the airways clogged.

Matty thumped my back. It didn't help.

The coughing subsided. I wiped water from my eyes, rasped in a breath. "He broke your glasses?"

"You know he's back?"

I hawked phlegm into the fire. "He was here."

"I called up to the house," Matty said. "Kavanaugh's house."

Zhoro Boguslav's muffled shout made it through the wall. "Keep the fecking back. No good parking under me." He must have been shouting at Declan O'Dea.

A bitter memory, painful, regretful, crowded my mind for a second or two. London. The dumper driver was too close. People yelling my name, shouting into phones for an ambulance. Angry people. Time to leave London. Did that young man die?

Matty mumbled something incoherent in the background.

This memory was not for now. I pushed it away. "What?"

"Latvian guy," Matty said. "I said his English is comin…You all right, Tommy?"

I gaped at Matty. Cool air draughted in and out of my open mouth, drying my tongue. A cold sweat pushed out on my forehead. I moved my lips. "Yeah. Grand."

"Ya look like ya just died."

"No, it's…" I remembered where I was. Alma didn't like cursing around the house. I'd have to speak to Ryan Matthews about Zhoro. "Why?" I said.

"Why what?"

"John Kavanaugh's. Why did you call up to John Kavanaugh's house?"

"I went to the house. We argued. He chased me down the drive in the Rolls. I came off the bike. Simple as that."

I shook my head. "Argue about what?"

The sizzling stopped, a rattle of drawers dragged open and pushed closed, the chink of forks on plates. Matty appeared beside me bearing food.

I took the plate, sat it on my lap. I couldn't eat.

"About you," Matty said. "We rowed about what he did on you. After what you told me happened, I needed to have a word with him."

My head fell against the back of the chair. I closed my eyes. "Matty."

"Several scores needed settling. Wasn't all about you. What he did to you was a disgrace but there's Rhiannon. Left her and the children, not a penny to scratch themselves with. The father was a thug and a bully and he's turned into one himself. He had to be told. Don't know how he has the nerve to set foot back in this country."

I was speechless. I wanted to scold Matty for going to challenge John Kavanaugh at his house. I wanted to shake Matty's hand. I wanted to get up from the chair and challenge John Kavanaugh, myself.

An intense warmth overwhelmed me that, for a moment, brushed aside my sense of despair. I held my head in a hand.

"Tommy, what's wrong?" Matty put down two mugs of hot tea and knelt on the floor beside my chair. "What is it? Shall I tell them stop?"

"No." I snorted back a sob.

"What then?"

"No, Matty, no. It's not them, it's you."

His bandaged hand rested on my shoulder. "Have I annoyed ya again?"

"No. No, you've not annoyed me." I lifted my head, gazed into his face.

The white hair was a mess from his cap. The thin face was drawn, and his frown added deep lines. A red-veined eye, magnified by the unbroken lens to comic proportions, searched my face. An edge of sticking plaster curled away from the other lens. A recent red shaving scar ran horizontally over the ridges of the cleft above his top lip. He looked like a perturbed pirate.

I reached and eased the spectacles off his face. The shattered lens flexed when I pressed down the sticking plaster. "Too old to be picking fights," I said. "You could've been killed. No telling what that man is capable of."

"Tosspot needed to be told. I showed him the scar on my knee." Matty's face looked naked without his spectacles. "Told him his own father was responsible for it. Told him he should be ashamed of himself for abandonin Rhiannon and taking up with another woman in Manchester. And I said I'd go to the Guards over what he did to you unless he paid you the rest a what he owes ya."

A blush rose in me. "You didn't have to do that."

"He came at me with a blackthorn shillelagh."

"Jesus, Matty."

"Ya know the glossy, touristy ones they sell at the seaside? Look like mallets. All the wankers have one on their wall. Anyhow, didn't I dodge the first swing. It was like I was back on the football pitch. Dodged a few blows in my day as I danced around half-backs. Bastard caught me on the wrist with the second. I think it's broke." Matty held up the bandaged hand.

"That need looking at?"

"I ran for the bike. On it in a second, Tommy, and away. Couldn't feel the wrist at all. I was completely oblivious to the pain."

"And it broken?"

"The adrenaline."

"Adrenaline?"

"Adrenaline, yeah. I think so. Pedalled like hell down the drive. Nearly pulled a hamstring."

I flexed the lens of his spectacles again, heard it crunch. I should pay to get these fixed.

"His car caught me halfway down the drive. Thought he was goin to run me over, I swear to God. Instead, didn't he draw up beside me and nudge my front wheel with the bumper. Ended up with my arse in the air up against the oak tree we used to knock conkers from. Ya remember it? Must be the biggest tree in Mayo. Twisted the handlebars. And I had to replace a mudguard. Have ya noticed how in Ireland, only the rich bastards have big trees? Been like that for centuries." Matty's knees cracked loud enough to scatter crows as he stood up. He took the spectacles from me. "Smashed my glasses, too, he did."

"Lucky it's just a lens and a wrist that's shattered."

"And my pride," Matty said. "And come here, you'll never guess what he did then. Before he reversed the car back, the window glided down and he shouted out at me. 'The old man always said you were a gay!'"

I smiled.

"Bastard's stupid enough to think that's an insult." Matty settled in his chair with his plate of sausages. A frown flashed across his face. "What are we goin to do?" The magnified eye glared. "If this carries on, ya won't be able to stay here in the house. Ya used to plan. Where's yer plan? It's not like you to give in so easy."

I watched Matty chomp on his sausages. He loved sausages. And I loved him. "It was a horse chestnut," I said.

"What was?"

"The conker tree."

"What about," he said, ignoring me but still trying to right the wrong in it all. "What about I run a key down the side a the Rolls-Royce?"

"No, Matty, you won't do that."

"Or set fire to the big house. Do something. I know, get the bastard kneecapped. Your old I.R.A. friend from the pharmaceutical company could arrange it."

"I'm doing it already."

Matty stopped chewing, sat up in his chair. "You're gettin him kneecapped by the I.R.A.?"

“No. I have another plan.” I scratched at the bristle on my chin. “At least I *had* a plan.”

“To get the rest a the money?”

“I won’t get the rest of the money, Matty.”

“Tell me, then.”

“I have to wait.” Matty would have ridiculed my preposterous plan.

“You’re goin away, is that it? Where will ya go? Yer not thinkin a goin far are ya? Will ya buy a place local? House prices are booming, but you’ll get nothin for yours now. Not with a quarry to look out on in its back yard. You might get a good deal if ya buy local. Ya could negotiate, you’re a cash buyer.” He paused to load his mouth with sausage, then spluttered, “Ya have some cash left, I hope?” He glanced at the empty bottles.

I had divided up the money. A little for me, to see me through to the end, and the rest in the hands of the solicitor to pass on. My attempt at righting a wrong. I still had some of my share left, but beer, cider and whiskey didn’t come cheap.

Outside, the engine noises ceased. Lunchtime.

“I’ve some.” I managed a wry smile.

“You don’t have to tell me your plan,” he said wiping his plate with a lump of white bread.

That, of course, meant I did have to tell him. But I couldn’t.

“Good,” I said, and I watched the bread soak sausage fat from his saucer.

Chapter 36

Wembley Stadium, the venue famous for staging the England soccer team's victory in the 1966 World Cup Final, the stadium Pele called 'the cathedral of football', the iconic home of English soccer, was to be levelled. A new stadium was to be built on the same site, but for that to happen, the old one, with its famous ferro-concrete twin towers, had to be demolished.

James Taylor forced me to listen to him telling me all that before he agreed to take me on.

"You're dressed like a man just off the Holyhead train," he said. "You any work clothes with you?"

He kitted me out in yellow trousers, a jacket with fluorescent patches, a hard hat, and a sturdy pair of toe cap boots.

I started on the shovel.

After only a few days James Taylor took pity on me, worried about my shortness of breath and constant coughing. "Can you drive a machine, Tom?" He brought the considerable bushes of his eyebrows together in question to form a small black hedge below the peak of his white hardhat.

I was confident with machines. "A dumper truck, maybe, James."

"A pity. I've need of a man to drive an excavator," he said.

The excavators were enormous. I needed the work. "I could pick it up," I said.

James Taylor's eyebrows did a little dance before he huffed a breath and put a thumb and finger to his mouth. He shrilled a whistle across the site and waved a man over. "Dave, give Tom here a go at the CAT. You can then use him on Section D and get it back on programme."

"Dave Morrisey," the young man said as he shook my hand. "You worked one before?"

"A long time ago," I lied.

Dave Morrisey glanced at Taylor, doubtfully. "Come with me, then." He walked me to the excavator, pointed out all the controls, gave me an hour to drive it up and down a corner of the site.

He waved me to a halt. "You seem fine at that. I'm impressed."

"Thank you, Dave. It's grand."

"Follow me over," Dave said. "And stay away from the Health and Safety Officers until I find you a ticket, or they'll string us both up by the balls."

I had no idea who the Health and Safety Officers were.

*

My new lodgings were south of the River Thames, close to where Brixton becomes Clapham. In a fortuitous turn of fate, I befriended the man who lived in the flat above mine.

Dexter McEvoy was a little over five foot tall, had a plump, childlike face framed in tight black curls, and worked in a bank on Bond Street. He kept his flat as hot as a boiler house and invariably wore an untucked calico shirt in maroon and white over white trousers, the legs rolled to his calves, and no shoes. He was the first black man I ever had a real conversation with.

Dexter kept me out of the pubs. We spent evenings talking. I wanted to talk about Rhiannon. Dexter McEvoy had other ideas.

He told me he was a bibliophile, and he waved an arm at the walls of his flat. They were clad in shelf after shelf of what he called, "The best stories in the world."

"You've read all these books, have you?"

"Of course, Thomas. That's what they're for."

I explained my difficulty with books.

"Then I will read them to you."

"You don't have to do that."

Dexter smiled up at me. "I'm thinking I do. Lay your hand on one for me, Thomas. We'll make a start."

The Great Gatsby came first. I was drawn to its slimness by my hesitancy.

His voice came from a mind that was travelled, the breathy timbre wrapping me in a warm world where everything seemed to make sense. I enjoyed listening to Dexter read.

Night after night, in tropical temperatures, he read. We talked about the stories, filled the room with cigarette smoke, drank tea and coffee, and talked some more. *Don Quixote*, *The Bonfire of the Vanities*.

He knew the stories inside out. "My mother read to me. Every day she do it. Taught me to love books."

When Dexter grew tired, I took to the streets and walked. I had no need for sleep.

London at night. Fewer people. Mild summer weather. Less rain than Duncarrick. It gave me time on my own. Time to think.

I replayed the meetings with Rhiannon in my head.

I pieced together the sequence of events of my last visit, what was promised, what was offered, what was accepted. I'd cringe, pick up pace, pull hard on chained cigarettes, smile, cry.

My memory was missing a whole exchange of words, somewhere between me throwing a bottle at Rhiannon's neighbour and running away from his murderous intent.

*

Dexter McEvoy was easy company. I fed off his contentment, his ease with the world. He read me a story by his favourite Jamaican author. "The end," he said, and he folded the covers closed. "What you think of that, Thomas?"

"'The end' indeed," I said. I loved the way Dexter said 'The end'.

Dexter expected more. "But what do you think of it?"

"A bit gruesome."

"Gruesome?" Dexter collapsed over the arm of his chair and exploded a laugh loud enough to wake a house. "What could he do? He wanted a son to inherit his great wealth. In my country, it is important for a man to have an heir. It is the woman's duty to provide him with an heir."

"Even if that were true," I said, "killing off three wives is excessive."

Dexter smiled. "You think so?" He slapped a hand down on the book. "Would it have been more acceptable to you if he had just killed off one wife?"

I didn't answer.

"What do you think of the twist, Thomas?"

"There you go," I said. "It was his fault all along. It must be easy to make things up when you write fiction."

"Let me tell you something, Thomas. Kenise Brodber was a contemporary of my mother. Yes, true. They both grew up in the same town in Jamaica. They played together as young children, went to the same school. Alexandria is a small town, where everyone knows everyone's business, and you know, Thomas–" He sat forward, held me in his stare. "When Kenise grew into a beautiful woman and she got married, everyone waited for the babies to come along. Everyone in Alexandria would look at her, expecting to see her great with child."

"Which book shall we do next?"

"But the babies didn't arrive."

I didn't want to cry in front of Dexter. Crying was for when I was alone, on the night streets.

"And the people waited some more. And still there were no babies. 'What is wrong?' people asked. And you know what? It turns out that the man Kenise married could not give her a child. So she killed him."

My jaw dropped.

"You see, Thomas, in my culture, there is no appreciation for a man unless he has children. The more children he produces, the more the appreciation. And a woman without children can be thought of as…unbalanced. We have a saying." Dexter paused as though weighing up options. "I'll spare you the patois. It translates to, 'a marriage without children is like a garden without orchids'. We have a lot of orchids in Jamaica." His face smiled, his teeth a radiant pale-yellow in the middle of his cherubic face.

"What happened to Kenise?" I said. "After she killed her husband."

Dexter shrugged. "Nothing. She went on to be a famous writer. Maybe it was because the authorities could not prove anything, or maybe it was because the authorities thought her husband deserved it." Dexter McEvoy raised a hand and the book got another slap.

"You're making this up."

"Maybe I am, Thomas. And maybe I'm not."

I shook a cigarette loose, took it between my lips, passed the packet to Dexter.

"Don't mind if I do," Dexter said through his grin. He swung his legs back and forth. I noticed, for the first time, that his bare feet didn't reach the floor.

*

The Shakespeare books were hard work. I had no time for the dense prose of The Bard of Avon. I complained to Dexter.

Dexter said, "One day, Shakespeare will touch your heart."

Only a few weeks later, he was dragging me through the treacle of another play when he read, "And though she be but little, she is fierce."

Dexter was right. I wanted to share Shakespeare's words with Alma. I wanted Alma to write those words on the upright stone that marked Noleen's grave.

*

I sent a letter to Alma. I wanted it to be right and spent many evenings not writing it.

Dexter McEvoy wrote it for me. It pleased him that I included the quote from *A Midsummer Night's Dream*.

Three weeks later, the yellow-papered reply arrived.

The cursive loops of the handwriting were recognisably Alma's. So too the fat, lowercase '*a*' she favoured in her signature, and the resolute underscore, a residue of the confidence she once had. I laboured over the first reading. I thought about asking Dexter to read it for me but instead tried again, then again, a fourth and fifth time, before putting it down. I gave in, brought it to Dexter.

He was hesitant. "A letter from your wife? Are you sure?"

"Please, Dexter," I said. "Read it as if it's a story."

I found good and bad in every line of the short letter.

Alma was more even-handed in apportioning the blame. Unlike the doctors and the nurses, she thought we both had a responsibility to bear for what happened. She accused me of not allowing her to talk about our loss, of being unwilling to listen, of choking off her grief with silences and tablets. That was hard to listen to.

After having time on her own, she said, she felt a little stronger. She was still taking the tablets, too scared to give them up.

Matt Darcy was erecting shelves for her and nailing hooks into the wall. She wrote, 'I'm managing well without you.' She hoped my cough had got better. She didn't think she would be able to get all of Shakespeare's words to fit on Noleen's stone, so she didn't attempt it.

Alma was coping without me, getting better, while I was still in turmoil. Something else troubled me about her words. It took Dexter to point it out.

Dexter folded the letter back into its envelope as though it was written in liquid gold on the finest parchment. He touched my shoulder lightly. "Thank you, Thomas," he said,

"For what?"

"For trusting me," he said. "Your wife's letters. They are very personal." He offered me the envelope.

I should have been thanking him.

In his steady reading voice, he said, "But I am very worried."

"You are?"

He looked at me with the same burdened sadness in his eyes as had the doctor who informed me that my child had just died in an incubator. "There is much anger in her words," he said.

It must have been my reaction that prompted it, something in my face or in the slump of my shoulders, but Dexter said, "I am so sorry, Thomas, I'm intruding. I will not make a remark again. Forgive me, please."

"No, no," I said. I took the envelope, used it to wave away his apology. "You're grand." My best smile. "I'm grateful for your help, honest to God. Where would I be without you?"

"If you want me to help you again, I will." Dexter said. "But I will write without reading, and I will read without listening."

I paused while I made sense of his offer. "One more," I said. "Please, Dexter. Will you do one more letter?"

Dexter penned a reply. He brought me fifty-euro notes from the bank. I folded four into the envelope. Guilt money, but I told Alma it was for her medication and to buy all the clocks she needed to satisfy her horological obsession—Dexter came up with the word 'horological'.

I ended the letter by informing Alma that I would not be returning to Ireland.

Dexter looked up from the papers. He couldn't help the reading. "Are you sure, Thomas?"

I smiled. "There's nothing there for me now."

Alma sent the money back with her next letter. The letter was longer, several pages, and, according to Dexter, free of the elementary grammatical errors and spelling mistakes of the first one.

Over the following weeks, more letters arrived, with increasing frequency. I opened them, but I didn't ask Dexter McEvoy to read them.

I kept Alma's letters together in a drawer. Every single one. Paling yellow letters from the 'medically incompetent' Alma, banded in a fat, friable stretch of elastic.

I asked Dexter to read me an information leaflet on the tablets Alma was taking. I wanted to know if they could be dangerous.

Chapter 37

In my late-night fog of rambling wretchedness, a few streets of London became familiar to me. It gave me the false impression that I knew the city well. I grew confident, or complacent, and ventured further afield. I'd pace Acre Lane, on up alongside the terraced family homes on Abbeville with their white-painted stonework, past the all-night Asian supermarket on the corner where I'd buy cigarettes, turn onto Elms Road, then arrow-straight onto the common.

One day at work, Dave Morrisey asked if it was me he saw entering Clapham Common at night.

"Could have been me, yeah," I said, scrabbling my pockets for the key to the excavator. "Not sleeping too well."

"It was half-one in the morning. You should be careful."

"Why? Is it not safe?"

"The common's safe enough if you've a big dog with you," he said. "And maybe a gun. Have you lost the bloody key again?"

"No," I said, holding up the key. "I have it."

*

Dexter McEvoy introduced Irish authors. Wilde and his Dorian Gray story, Flann O'Brien and his, what Dexter called "humorous but maddening", *The Third Policeman*.

I told Dexter about my friend Matt Darcy and his love of cycling.

Dexter said, "It's good to hear you laugh, Thomas."

Time with Dexter became my distraction from despair, from utter abjection, from sadness, but I found it increasingly difficult to concentrate on his stories, my mind drawn away. Noleen, Rhiannon, Alma, in that order.

If it wasn't for Dexter, I think I would have gone insane with the grief of it all.

*

"Tommy!" James Taylor ran across the building site towards me, arms waving, fluorescent jacket flapping. "No!"

Noleen was in my arms, gurgling, trying to talk through the noise of the machines and the yelling. At least I thought she was.

Taylor shouted, "Turn it off. Kill the engine."

Noleen dissolved away.

I resented Taylor's interruption.

He leapt up onto the track, yanked open the cab door, screamed into my face. "Kill it!" He reached across me, cut the engine. "Fuck's sake, Tom!"

He was gone, running around to the front of the excavator.

The rear end of a dumper truck was visible around the boom arm. It was up close, too close, in under the bucket.

Men from all corners of the site rushed towards the dumper.

I climbed down from the cab.

Dave Morrisey was wedged between the excavator bucket and the seat of the dumper, his face fixed in a rictus of utter horror, the only man not shouting.

Men pushed buttons on mobile phones, clamped them to their ears.

James Taylor stared me in the face. "What the hell were you thinking? Why didn't you see him?" He grabbed the collar of my jacket, dragged me away. "If I were you, Tom…Fuck, this is bad." He drew off his hat, rubbed an arm across his forehead. "If I were you, I'd get out of here, fast. You hear me?" He glanced back at the crowd around Dave Morrisey.

"I don't know what happened, James."

"Half asleep and not bloody watching what you were about. That's what happened." Taylor was shouting again, his spittle splattering my face. "Might've bloody killed poor Dave."

Noleen, Rhiannon, Alma. I hadn't slept properly for weeks, couldn't think straight, couldn't understand. Now Dave. It was all too much. I couldn't explain. I was lost, empty.

"I'm sorry." A cold shiver worked its chill through me.

James Taylor was snorting like a distressed ram. He stamped his boots, adjusted his stance to scan the frantic site. "Listen, Tom." He screwed his face, rubbed a thumb and forefinger through eyebrows that had grown as wild as old yard brushes. "Right now would be a good time for you to fuck off back to Ireland."

Chapter 38

"I think I'm hungry."

"I'll get you something."

"Thank you."

"I'll bring it when it's ready."

"Yes."

"Now, take your tablets."

"The place…The farm…Are you looking after the farm?"

"The farm's gone. It failed, remember? Drink this."

"Is it alcohol?"

"It'll help you with the tablets."

"You're trying to kill me."

Chapter 39

I returned to Ireland after almost a year's exile.

The first thing Alma said to me was, "You look tired, Tom."

I was shocked by how well she looked. She had gained weight, there was colour in her cheeks, she had dyed her hair auburn.

It was as if Alma's grieving had been played out to resolution on yellow parchment while my grieving had grown inside me. Alma had recovered from our loss. It had been her fault, yet she was the first to recover.

After a couple of weeks, she asked about Rhiannon.

I told her Rhiannon and the children were grand.

We argued. Nothing important enough to remember.

Alma still took her tablets, though the doctor was trying to wean her off them. We agreed the tablets brought her some relief, and she shouted when we talked about whether she should increase her dosage.

Alma made it clear that she considered Noleen's death to be my fault. Everything was my fault, according to Alma.

Dexter was right: Alma was angry.

As the weeks passed, she seemed to regress, to fold in on herself. She became preoccupied, secretive. Her hair fell out when she brushed it, she slept throughout the day, lost weight. She was dissolving, in front of my eyes, to the tick of a thousand clocks. Time was no longer the healer. Time was the destroyer. But it wasn't time, of course. It was the tablets.

Hostilities continued between Alma and me.

Many of her waking hours were spent with her clocks, watching time pass, still waiting for part of her to heal.

I said nothing.

And she said nothing.

I took a note from Alma to the doctor, asking for her prescription to be increased. The doctor couldn't, or wouldn't.

Alma took tablets. I took tablets. What was our house becoming?

*

"I've been having the dreams and visions again," Alma said one evening. She sounded more lucid than I had heard her for months. "She's two years old. Standing over there." She pointed to the door of the spare bedroom. "Her tiny hand is reaching out to me."

*

Alma filled in the application form on my behalf. It took a while. Her handwriting had deteriorated, reminded me of the first letters in London. She ruined the first copy. It was a frustrating process.

The job was driving for a chemical factory based in County Cavan.

"I'll come home at weekends," I said.

I drove a lorry delivering 'agricultural intermediates'. When I asked, I was told, "Worry not, old timer. It's only produce. Grains and flours and oils and shite. For chemical companies and farms and the likes. You know?"

"So, it's safe?" I asked.

"Don't worry. There are chemicals under your sink at home that can be more dangerous than what's in the back of that lorry."

*

After five weeks of furtive inquiries, I found what I was looking for.

Collins was a security guard with a gambling addiction and a willingness to please. He wouldn't tell me his first name. "Call me Collins," he said. "A good I.R.A. name."

"Just Collins?"

"No, not Just Collins. Collins, just."

He laughed, and I laughed. "Grand," I said, still laughing. "Very good."

Collins worked the night shift at PharmaCraft, a pharmaceutical company based just over the border in County Fermanagh that specialised in turning 'agricultural intermediates' into pills.

Collins appreciated the late-night company. We sat in his draughty, single-window cabin, me perched on two six-packs of industrial-grade blue tissue rolls that seemed to be a forgotten delivery, Collins on a cracked-leather captain's chair. Both of us shuffled for dominance of the single-bar electric heater.

Collins took a drink, so I joined him. Nothing excessive, I kept it moderate. He liked to talk of racehorses. I waited for the right opportunity to talk about what I needed.

"Twenty-six racecourses in Ireland," Collins said, one evening. "And I've won money, big fecking money, in every single one of them." He placed his beer can next to the key chest. "Best wager I ever had was Punchestown. A year or two ago now, before the bloody euro fecked-up everything."

The grey key chest on the wall was unlocked, its metal door ajar. Collins was careless. I let him talk. I needed to be patient.

"Seeing as you haven't asked," he said, "I'll tell you. It was a six-race accumulator. Lady of Lir. The most beautiful fecking horse ever to grace a racecourse." The captain's chair creaked as Collins settled into his recital.

"She was in the fifth race, and hadn't I gone through the card. Four winners. I had picked four fecking winners." His eyes were glassy and glowed orange from the fire. "By the time the Lady was under starter's orders, I had eleven hundred and twenty-three pound riding on her. Guess the odds."

I shook my head.

"A bloody guess'll cost you nothing. Have a fecking guess."

I pursed my lips, shook my head.

"Thirty-three to one," he said. "Imagine that. Thirty-three to one. I had eleven hundred and twenty-three pound riding on Lady of Lir at thirty-fecking-three to one."

"Sounds good odds." I blew cigarette smoke at the scratched Perspex window.

"Don't you want to know?" he said.

"Know what?"

"What happened."

"How did you get on?"

"Thought you'd never ask." Collins's chair squeaked as he sat up and swigged from his beer can. "The Lady led from the off. Never looked to be under any pressure, no-one near her. It looked like she'd built up…What's that fecking word they use? An unassailable lead."

I wondered if I'd have to get Collins drunk enough to pass out before I gained access to the key chest.

"The Lady was romping home." He took another swig. "But at the last hurdle, didn't she fecking stutter. And didn't this little whore of a brown filly make up ground on the inside." The metal can clinked from the squeeze of his fingers. "But fair play, didn't the Lady push back. And pushed and pushed to the final furlong. The little brown filly up with her neck-by-neck. Me screaming like a fecking banshee on acid in the stand." He sat back in the chair, rested the can on his belly, gazed down at the single-bar electric heater.

I waited.

Collins turned his solemn face towards me. "Didn't my Lady of Lir take it by a fecking nose. Eleven hundred and twenty-three pounds at thirty-three to one."

Collins threw back his head, took a long swallow of beer, pulled the ring on another can. "She was a beautiful horse. The most beautiful horse I have ever seen."

I didn't have the heart to ask what happened in the sixth and final race of his accumulator. Instead, I asked if he had access to any of the pills produced inside.

"For your cough, is it?"

"No, not the cough. Yeah, maybe."

"I have access to everything," he said. "I'm the fecking security guard." He reached over the small table, the rough material of his uniform scratching against the broken leather of his chair, and tapped the top of the key chest.

We came to an arrangement.

The pills he supplied had not yet reached their blister packs. They came to me in a paper bag, their sharp edges ground away in the crush of concealment.

I helped finance his gambling addiction.

"Don't know why you're buying these off me," Collins said. "You can get them on prescription."

"Not in the quantity my wife needs."

*

I heard through my dispatcher at work that Collins lost control of the drinking one evening, drowning his sorrows after a big loss on a horse at Listowel. Collins was caught by PharmaCraft's Head of Biostatistics urinating into a vat of chelating agent and lost his security job.

I was not motivated to carry on. I had enough of what Alma needed. I quit working at the chemical factory.

They bought me a clock.

Chapter 40

"It's Alma. She's dead." I couldn't think of any other way to say it. I focussed my fogged mind on the soft click that bounced back and forth on the telephone line connecting Buckley's Bar and Lounge with Rhiannon's Camden flat.

After nine clicks Rhiannon said, "How? What happened, Tommy?" Her London-accented voice sounded choked.

"An accident." My head was still a ball of wool, but I was certain that was what happened. "In the house." It was an accident. I was sure of it. "Sorry to be calling with–"

"I can't make it over," Rhiannon said. "She was my big sister, but I can't make it over."

"If it's money, I can send money." What money could I send her?

"That's not your place," she shouted. "Not your place to be sendin me money to attend my sister's funeral." She rushed her words. "I don't want your money." I let her anger run its course. "Technically, I'm still married to a multi-millionaire. *He* should be sending me money. If for no other reason than to help bring up his bloody kids!"

A brief period of clicks, no speech, then muffled sobs. I imagined the phone tucked into her neck.

I sucked on a cigarette, blew smoke at the ground, waved a hand to disperse the smoke. It was good to be back on the cigarettes. "Rhiannon?" I thought I'd lost her.

"I'm here," she said. "Sorry. It's a shock is all. I only got a letter from Alma two weeks ago."

I could hear her breath so clearly. She could have been there beside me.

"It's all right."

"It's not all right," she snapped. "What did you do, Tommy?" She was suspicious.

"I don't know what you mean."

"Alma. What happened to Alma?"

"There was an accident. Hit her head." A vague memory of an argument. Decided not to mention it. "We were taking strong tablets. For the sorrow, I think. Something, anyway. Because of what happened. Noleen, and everything."

"Are you drunk, Tommy?"

A reel in my head set me woozy. I rolled my back against the wall. "No…No, I'm not."

"You don't sound right."

"They sometimes made it difficult," I said. "The tablets. She tripped and fell."

Rhiannon's breathing became synchronised with the clicks, as if she was inhaling and exhaling the electronic signals. "I'm sorry, Tommy. I didn't mean what I said about the children. God forgive me, my children are my life. I'm sorry." She believed my version of events.

"I'll get money over to you," I said.

"Tommy, I can't come."

"I'd like to see you."

"The last time you came to *see* me, you were too drunk to see past the end of your nose." Her shouting drowned out the clicks. "You had no right to say what you said, Tommy. No right. I nearly had to move out after that. You're lucky that thug downstairs didn't kill you."

Her words made little sense.

"He's made my life hell, since. All that shite about giving Alma time to heal. Jesus Christ. All that bullshit about having regrets. Well, too bloody late. I'd moved on. You could see that. It was too bloody late because you chose Saint Alma."

Who made her life hell? I lost count of the clicks as I tried to remember what happened.

Rhiannon hadn't finished. "I've thought about what you said that night. Was that really why you gave me up? For a farm and a load of sheep? Sheep? For fuck's sake. You coming round to where I live was stupid. And what would Alma have said? And listen, did you even tell Alma you came to *see* me? Did you?"

The fog cleared a little. I remembered throwing a bottle. What in hell possessed me to go throwing bottles? "Rhiannon, I'm sorry."

"Why was Alma still taking tablets, Tommy? I thought those things were only supposed to be a temporary measure. It's been bloody years."

I didn't want Rhiannon to be angry with me. "I'm not sure."

"Mammy wasn't on antidepressants that long after she lost her baby."

"No."

"So why was Alma?"

I didn't know. My head was spinning, thoughts whirling. I squeezed my eyes shut, drooped my head. "I can't be certain."

"You're making no sense, Tommy. You sure you've not been drinkin?"

The signal on the line bounced, clicking time like one of Alma's wall clocks.

"I won't be coming over," she said.

"I have money." I'd find the money, borrow it from Buckley if I had to. "I'd like us to be together." I glanced up and down the hallway in case Buckley overheard.

"You know it's not just the money."

"Come. Please. Stay at the house." I'd need to tidy the place. "You should come. For Alma."

There was a pause. A long pause. I thought I could prevent myself from collapsing if I counted the clicks. I got up to thirteen. "How did she sound?" I said.

"Who?"

"The letter. How did Alma sound in the letter?"

For some telephonic reason, the clicking stopped.

Rhiannon's breath. I could only hear Rhiannon breathing down this wire that stretched from her flat to Buckley's. I prompted her again. "You said she sent you–"

"I didn't open it." She sounded defensive.

I sighed, relieved. I lifted a trembling hand to my face, drew heavily on the cigarette.

"I recognised her handwritin as soon as I saw it," Rhiannon said. "She hadn't bothered with me for twenty years. All the shit I've been through, and she did nothin to help. I got on without her long enough. I didn't need a letter from her. I feel bad now, but I wanted nothin to do with her. When it arrived, my first thought was she could shove her letters up her hole."

If Rhiannon had thrown Alma's letter away, it was for the best. Who knows what it might have revealed? I exhaled the smoke.

"I shouldn't be talkin about her like this," Rhiannon said. "I'm sorry."

I had a faint recollection that I had a bundle of Alma's letters hidden somewhere in the house. Was that true, or was I just imagining it? The London letters.

"Alma was the only family I had left." Rhiannon was conflicted. She wanted to come, whatever her dislike of Alma. "My big sister."

I could feel a pulse in my throat. I wanted to reach down that wire and touch Rhiannon, hold her. "I'll pay your fare," I said. "Bring the children."

"Work won't let me." Her voice had softened and she was trying to be reasonable, but she was making up excuses. She always made up excuses.

I jerked my jaw, tried to make rings with the cigarette smoke, failed.

"You still there?" she said.

"I am, yeah."

"I can't come because of work. That bitch of a boss won't give me time off. Not at this short notice. She likes at least a month. There's no-one to cover me. You'd think the bloody Post Office would grind to a halt if I messed with her duty roster. She won't allow it."

I didn't believe a word. "Come, anyway."

"I got rent problems, Tommy." Another lame excuse. "I'm behind."

A knot of disappointment tightened in my chest. The pain in my head flared.

“I’m sorry,” she said. “I can’t risk the job. I need this flat. I’ve the children to think of.”

“I can help.” I called her bluff. “You don’t need Kavanaugh. Let him keep the money he’s making up in Manchester. We don’t need him.”

“Big John Kavanaugh,” she said, snorting. “The multi-millionaire from Manchester.”

“That what you call him?” An image of an old friend formed in the smog of my confusion. We were discussing books. What was his name? “There’s a word for that,” I said

“A word for what?”

“Multi-millionaire from Manchester.” I mined my memory for the word.

“He’s got four children down here in London,” Rhiannon said. “And, technically, *a wife*. I’ve barely heard from him since he moved to Manchester.”

I recalled that I’d heard her husband, John, had taken up with another woman in Manchester. There was rumour of a child. But I’d just informed her that her sister had died. Enough bad news for one phone call.

I said, “I can’t remember the word.”

“What word? What’s wrong with you, Tommy? You’re makin no sense.”

“Sorry.” She was right. I wasn’t making sense.

“Listen,” she said. “You know John’s dad died a while back?”

Did I know about that? “I heard, yeah.”

“It’s just, you didn’t…No, don’t worry.”

“No,” I said. “You’re right. We should have got in touch. I’m sorry.” I sounded lame. “For your loss and everything.”

“We didn’t get on.”

“You and John or you and the dad?”

“The dad. Both.” She laughed. “Both of the bastards. Oh, God!”

The ticks resumed, as if counting me down, the lifeline between us about to snap and sever all contact with Rhiannon forevermore.

Her breathing fell back in time. "You don't sound well, Tommy."

"I'm grand."

"You're all slurred. I think you're drunk."

"I'm not drunk."

"What's wrong with you, then?"

"I'm just…" What was wrong with me? "I'm tired is all. Alma and everything, I suppose."

"You sound a packet of fags shy of your own coffin." She laughed again, a soft chuckle. It was good to hear her laugh. "Listen," she said. "I won't come over." She'd made up her mind.

Buckley's bald head ascended from the cellar. He had a crate of red lemonade with him to stack a shelf in time for opening.

I turned my back on him, crushed the cigarette in the curl of my hand. "It's on Wednesday."

"I can't make Alma's funeral, Tommy."

I lowered my voice. "There's a reception into Manghan's the evening before, but the mass is on Wednesday. Eleven o'clock, I think." The wheeze of my breath echoed through the handset. My mouth felt dry. "Please. I want you–"

"I'm not coming over." Her tone told me she was losing patience. "How many times do I need to say it?"

"Then I'll come to London after the funeral." I sounded desperate.

"Don't ever come to London again. That was the deal."

I said, "I hear John has another woman in Manchester."

A pause. The bounce of an electronic signal, back and forth, daring each of us to be the next to say something, counting down the time left to say it.

"That's only talk, Tommy."

"She has a child by him. Is that talk, too?"

The line went dead.

Chapter 41

Matt Darcy strode to the head of the queue. "Excuse me," he said. "Sorry."

A man whose name I should have known, but didn't, held back and waited.

Matty cupped a hand to his mouth and whispered into my ear, "How ya feelin?" The grey velvet collar of his Chesterfield overcoat glistened with silver raindrops. His funeral-black tie and handkerchief matched the black sheen of his spectacle frames. He looked like a benevolent gangster. "Are you all right?"

A line of people stretched out before us to the door, their clothes drenched from the rain, their damp, sorrowful faces glistening under the stark lights of Dessie Mangan's Funeral Parlour.

"I am," I said.

"You look better than ya did the other day."

"Must be some dose of flu or something I had."

"Want me to stay with you?"

"I think I'm grand."

"I'll stay with you, but ya need speed up. They're queuin up past the garage and back as far as the chipper. They're all out tonight and the weather a holy show."

Though I knew most of the people, my head was still not straight, and it became an embarrassing test to remember everyone's name, so I stopped trying. They all took a turn passing on their condolences and shaking my hand.

"I'm sorry for your trouble."

"I know that."

"Tommy, sorry for your trouble. Take care of yourself."

"Thank you."

"Alma was such a dear woman. So shockingly sudden."

"It was. Thank you for coming out."

"Sorry for your trouble."

There came a pause.

A face from another era limped forward, a friend of my mother's. Margaret O'Brien leaned unsteadily on her daughter's arm, her shuffling gait afflicted and arthritic.

I waited for her to reach me.

"Hello, Thomas." She looked smart in a bottle-green coat, a black mourner scarf wrapped around her neck and tucked beneath the lapels. She threaded rosary beads between gnarled fingers and clasped both my hands in hers. "I'm so, so sorry for your trouble. Alma, God rest her soul, was such a lovely, lovely woman."

It was the same sentiment I'd heard all evening.

Margaret O'Brien shook my hands. "This is my daughter, Pauline. Would you remember her, no? You wouldn't, she's too young I think."

"The resemblance is there, Margaret. Thank you for coming all this way. Both of you."

"We're in Galway now," Margaret O'Brien said. "Pauline drove me up. Wouldn't have missed it. Alma was such a lovely, lovely woman. We're staying at my sister's tonight so we can make funeral mass in the morning."

Pauline tucked a dripping umbrella under an arm. It left a small puddle on the wooden floor of the funeral parlour. She leaned in. "Sorry for your trouble."

"Thank you."

"I'll pray for you and Alma, Thomas," Margaret O'Brien said. "God will understand her grief." She closed her eyes and moved her lips soundlessly.

My hands prickled at the sudden heat. It was as if the rosary beads were embers, hot in our hands.

Margaret O'Brien opened her eyes and held me in a stare that penetrated the carapace of my coping. Her look delved deep, as if to my soul.

I tried to pull free, but her hands squeezed over mine, unexpected strength for such an old woman. The heat of her grasp intensified.

It was Margaret O'Brien who broke the connection.

"Mammy, what's wrong?" Pauline said.

"We must go." Colour drained from the old woman's face. There was a tremor on her thin lips.

"Do you need to sit?" her daughter said.

"We won't delay," Margaret O'Brien said. "The roads…The roads are atrocious this weather." She was trying to convince her daughter, not make up excuses for me.

She shuffled away, ignored Matty, and only paused for a moment to lay a hand on Alma's coffin, the rosary beads rattling against the brass-coloured, plastic handles.

My hands blanched as though they had been plunged into a basin of hot water.

*

It was late when we left the funeral parlour.

The undertaker, Dessie Manghan, commented on the size of the crowd. "Some woman, Tommy. To see so many out on a night like this."

Matt Darcy patted my shoulder.

I needed to thank Dessie Manghan. "It's of great comfort, Dessie. I'm grateful for all the arranging you've done."

"Not a bother. A bit awkward at the hospital, right enough. Unusual circumstances and everything. Took a bit of time to sort things out, but that's the way it is. Once we got over the delay, it wasn't a bother at all. It'll take an hour or two to get this floor mopped, now, but it's really not a bother. See you in the morning, Tommy. I'll have everything sorted out and ready. All taken care of for you."

*

I folded a pillow in half, curled onto the bed, rested my eyes. Clarity of mind was returning, the haze lifting. I felt stronger, but I was glad to lie down. Stronger but exhausted, that was how I felt. Does that even make sense? Nothing made sense.

I flexed my fingers to ease the ache in the joints and counted mourners in my head. I must have shaken hands almost three hundred times.

I wondered if Rhiannon would make the funeral.

Before I turned out the light, I looked again. Tiny red bruises where the burn of the rosary beads broke blood vessels dotted the backs of both hands.

Chapter 42

On the morning of Alma's funeral mass, Matt Darcy and I called into Buckley's so I could pay for the buffet. An enduring lethargy slowed my reactions, but I thought I was improving.

The pub wasn't yet open for business. Lisa-Marie Gavin was behind the counter, bent over and twisted, a hand up under her skirt. When she noticed us, she brushed down her skirt and said, "What's the face for, Matty? You'd think I had a tit out or something."

"Can ya not get dressed before ya come to work?" Matty propped me against the counter.

"Shaggin new drawers are stuck in me. How you bearin up, Tommy?"

I coughed into a handkerchief.

"He's a bit unsteady is all," Matty said.

"Small wonder," Lisa-Marie said. "The day that's in it. Ya frightened Buckley when you were in phonin Rhiannon. Said you were as white as a ghost. I told him he should understand, him not long after losing his own wife." Lisa-Marie placed her hands on the edge of the counter. "Come here now, gentlemen. We're not yet open, but as yer man once said, will ye have one while you're waiting?"

Matty glanced at his wrist where a watch would sit if he had a watch. "Might do him good," he said, talking about me as though I was incapable of answering for myself.

"Is he in, Lisa-Marie?" I asked.

"Out on an errand." She reached beneath the counter for an empty glass, spun it expertly in her hand like a London cocktail maker. "He left ya this." She plucked an envelope from between two gin bottles and lay it on the counter. My bill.

"How are the children?" I asked.

"Doin great, thank God. The eldest is winnin prizes in the ice skating every week. It'll be the Olympics next for her."

"She's kept it up?"

"I have a million miles put on the car, up and down to Galway." She pulled at a beer pump. "But listen, Tommy. How're you really doing? You've lost weight."

Everyone seemed concerned about me. "I'm middling," I said. "Thank you."

"Good, good." She seemed unconvinced. "A mighty crowd for a parlour reception," she said. "Last night I mean."

"I found it humbling."

"In that weather, too. That where you caught the chill?"

"Cough's with me a while," I said.

"The smokin ban will help you, so."

"Are people stickin to it?" Matty asked.

"Bloody right they are, with a three thousand euro fine." Lisa-Marie flicked a thumb at the sign pinned to a shelf of glasses, presumably a warning to potential violators of the heavy financial consequences. "Will Rhiannon make it over?"

I shook my head at Lisa-Marie. "Has her hands full."

"Shame. Be nice to see her again. Where is she now, Manchester or still somewhere in London?"

"London, yeah."

Lisa-Marie scowled at Matty. "Are you goin to a funeral dressed like that?"

Matty glared. "It was pissin rain all day yesterday." He grabbed his soiled jacket at the chest. "I'm just back from digging the grave."

"With *your* knee?"

"Not on my own. I was there in a supervisory capacity."

Lisa-Marie sat two pints on the counter in front of us. "Ah, yeah? Who was with ya?" She was drawing news.

"Neighbours from the village." Matty denied her.

I tried to pay Lisa-Marie for the beers.

"I'll get these," she said. "Not every day ya bury yer wife."

I made my face smile at Lisa-Marie.

Matty raised his glass into the air. "To Alma," he said.

Matty and I touched pints and we both sipped. As soon as I swallowed, a pain that could split rocks pulsed behind my eyeballs. I put down my drink, gripped the counter with both hands, swallowed back the vomit that built at the back of my throat, and waited for the ache to subside.

Into the silence, Lisa-Marie said, "Weather's better today."

Matty lifted a Wellington boot onto the foot rail.

Lisa-Marie arched an eyebrow at the scrape of grit on metal. "Ya fuckin bitch, ya," she said. "I've just mopped that bloody floor and you're bringin shite in on top of it."

"I've often thought," Matty said, staring into his pint, "what it would be like to be at your own wake."

Lisa-Marie parked an elbow on the counter, ran fingers through her tawny hair. She looked tired, as though she'd done a day's work already. The counter was the right height to support her heavy bosom. "Sure, you will be at yer own wake, ya fool ya. Only question is do ya want the coffin lid left off or nailed down."

"I mean alive," Matty said. "What would it be like to have yer wake when you were still alive? Before ya die."

Lisa-Marie creased her brow. "It wouldn't be your wake if you were still alive, would it?"

While I half-listened to their verbal jousting, I imagined Rhiannon walking in the door of Buckley's and leaning against the doorframe. Hard to believe that I was about to bury Alma, and I was fantasising about Rhiannon like that.

Matty said, "You could have a *living* wake, couldn't ya? See what I mean?"

"What the fuck?" Lisa-Marie said. "Why would ya want to do that? Tommy, have a quiet word with Matty here. I think he's lost it, big time."

"Think about it," Matty said. "There'll be fifty or sixty people in here later on this afternoon, all tellin stories about Alma. They'll be some tellin Tommy here what a wonderful woman she was. They'll be people who went to school with her weepin into their gin and tonics about the great laughs they had together as kids. There'll be others who worked with her at the lace factory, full a stories about the time she negotiated an extra shilling a week for the girls in the laundry. Amn't I right, Tommy?"

I didn't know the lace factory story.

Matty's mourner numbers made me uneasy. I hoped Buckley had ordered enough food.

Matty continued, "And someone will say, because someone always says it, someone will say, 'She would really enjoy today if she was here herself'."

The beer made my head worse. I would drink no more of it. I needed my wits.

"A livin wake?" Lisa-Marie was incredulous. "If Tommy won't say it, I will. You, Matty, need to sit down and have a quiet word with yerself. No-one would turn up. And if they did, they'd treat it just like any other piss up."

"How do you know?" Matty said. "Have you ever been invited to one?"

"There's the first fuckin problem straight away," Lisa-Marie said. "You don't invite people to a wake. They just fuckin turn up. Isn't that right, Tommy?"

I glanced at the door. Rhiannon wasn't there.

Lisa-Marie took my silence as an endorsement. "See? And, who's goin to be comin out with stories of how brilliant ya are when yer still alive and standin at the bar next to them? Or, or." She raised a finger into the air. "Are ya now suggestin that ya don't attend yer own livin wake at all?"

"What would be the point of not attendin?" Matty said. "That defeats the whole object of the exercise."

"Would you send out invites?" Lisa-Marie asked.

"What's wrong with that?"

"And would ya expect presents?"

"No. Why would I expect presents? I'm about to die."

"Holy be to God. You're about to die, and ya want to hold a party in honour of yerself. Is that it?"

"It's not a party. It's a wake. A celebration of your life. With friends. Whilst you're still here to enjoy it."

"Would you tell people go to the funeral parlour first?"

"You're not dead!" Matty said. "There would be no funeral parlour involved."

"And no funeral mass?"

"Optional."

"Oh, optional, is it? Hear that, Tommy? The mass is optional. I don't think Father Roche would go along with that."

"You are jokin," Matty said. "He'd love it."

"Where would ya hold the wake?" Lisa-Marie asked.

"You could hold it here."

"A buffet and that?"

"Yes, you can have a buffet."

"Free drinks?"

"Whatever ya like."

"But no presents?"

"Presents would be inappropriate."

"What's brought on this sort of talk from you, anyway?"

"I might have bowel cancer."

Lisa-Marie widened her eyes, parted her lips. "Fuckin hell, Matty." She lifted her breasts free of the counter, stepped back, hitched her knickers through her skirt. "I'll come."

*

The church was full. Matt Darcy helped me to the front row where we sat on our own, in the family pew.

Following his announcement of possible bowel cancer, it had taken Matty an age to answer Lisa-Marie's questions on when did he find out, and how it was diagnosed, and what tests he was yet to undergo. By the time he finished his pint, it was too late for him to go home and change.

If Rhiannon and the children had made it over, they would have been with me in the family pew. Matty wasn't family, but I wanted him there for fear I'd keel over like a mountain ram sick with liver fluke.

Sometime during the ceremony, Lisa-Marie Gavin made her way up into the shallow choir loft high in the rear of the church. She gave a solo rendition of 'Lady of Knock' to the back of the heads queuing for communion.

*

When the funeral mass was over, Father Roche stepped down off the altar and offered his condolences. "Thomas, Thomas, Thomas. She's with God now." He leaned over the pew front, smothered my hands with his. "Never really got over the loss of the baby, did she?"

I said, "And you never got over to christen the baby."

Matty laid a hand on my arm.

An embarrassed cough from Father Roche. He recovered quickly. "I didn't say it in my tribute on the altar, Thomas, but one could say Alma died of a broken heart."

I regretted my remark, but I didn't apologise.

"I'll see you at the graveside, Thomas." And the priest glided away.

Dessie Manghan sat in beside me. "What's wrong with Father Roche?"

"Thank you, Dessie," I said. "Taking care of the funeral. Last night, all the problems at the hospital, everything."

"Oh, not a worry, Tommy. I just wanted to ask." Dessie Manghan lowered his voice to a whisper so that Matty couldn't hear him. "Will Matty ride with you in the limousine?"

"If you don't mind, Dessie."

"Will you ask him to put the Wellingtons in a bag?"

"And go barefoot?"

"They're thick with muck."

"Matty has a lot going on at the moment, Dessie."

"Only, I've a wedding in town in a couple of hours."

"Right. I'll speak to him."

"Good man. The carpets are a holy nightmare to clean properly. Takes buckets of water and there's special stuff I have to use. You've to let it soak in, and then it's an age to dry out. Ya know how it is, Tommy. We'll bring the coffin out now. I've organised bearers, taken care of everything, so don't you be worrying about it at all. If you'd like to follow behind."

While Alma's coffin was carried out of the church, Lisa-Marie Gavin sang 'A Mother's Love's a Blessing' from the choir loft, because she sang that at every funeral for women Alma's age. It was inappropriate. Alma wasn't a mother.

*

It took two minutes to drive to the cemetery. Dessie Manghan led the procession, driving the hearse, Father Roche in the passenger seat. Buckley's son, Raymond, drove the limousine, Matty and I in the back.

We lowered Alma into a plot dug deep enough for the two of us. Matty had done a good job supervising the digging, the corners were square and sharp, the dimensions were perfect.

Lisa-Marie Gavin was right about the weather being good. The sun was gentle on the back of our bowed heads, and warm air lifted a sweet scent from the wreaths and bouquets.

As soon as Father Roche finished the Rite of Committal, all there made the sign of the cross, and Matty's grave-crew shovelled soil down on top of Alma's coffin.

I was like a bystander to events, tired and drowsy and numbed by the rattle of rolling stones on wood and the hollow thuds of damp soil.

After a few seconds, more men, dressed in suits and white shirts and black ties, took a turn with the shovels.

Matty caught my eye and intimated did I want to partake, my opportunity to contribute.

My breath wheezed in and out. I shook my head.

It didn't take long. Within minutes, two men were pressing down the freshly thrown soil with the heels of their well-polished shoes, dancing on Alma's grave.

I shook hands with more people, and the crowd dispersed, some visiting older graves. I was alone. Rhiannon should have been there. I scanned the graveyard.

Matty was out on the road, arguing with Dessie Manghan and Raymond Buckley.

By the time I got to the limousine, Manghan had driven off, returning the cleric to his church.

"I'm sorry, Matty. I can't let the Wellingtons into the car again. He'll kill me."

"Right, Raymond, that's it. I'll walk."

I wanted Matty with me. "Put them in the boot."

"For God's sake."

"Do it. Please."

Matty prised the Wellingtons off with his feet.

"Still have the legendary footwork, Matty," Raymond said.

Matty climbed into the limousine. "Enough a your cheek."

*

Matty was right about the wake at Buckley's. I was reminded of an old saying my mother used to repeat. 'If you want praise, die; if you want blame, marry'.

Scores of people told me what a wonderful woman Alma had been. Several mentioned how dedicated she'd been to the care of her own mother for so long. I met at least a dozen women who were in her class at school, most of whom claimed to have sat beside her. No-one mentioned the shilling-a-week rise for the laundry girls in the lace factory, which was a pity, I'd have liked to have heard that story. It would have been typical of an Alma I briefly knew.

Lisa-Marie was kept busy refilling the hot-water urn to keep people in tea and replenishing paper plates of sandwiches as she forced the food on people, the way elected hosts do at wakes. I was relieved to see there was enough.

Buckley was stacking a shelf behind the counter, tweaking bottles so that all the labels faced out.

I beckoned him to the end of the bar and retrieved his envelope from my pocket. "Mister Buckley, I need settle my bill." The slur in my voice surprised me. "What do I owe you?"

Buckley leaned over the counter. "Mister Cassidy." His arm held me steady. "As you well know, Alma helped me with my Vicky when you worked away in London."

I knew nothing of this.

"When the cancer came back for a second go, Alma was in every day until my Vicky died. And we all knew Alma was not in the best shape herself. Raymond used to call out for her in the morning, and she'd wait here until midnight. Three months she did that. Alma took control of all the medication, gave my Vicky her tablets, everything. I wouldn't have coped here without Alma. An angel down from heaven. You owe me nothing." Buckley squeezed my shoulder.

I would have struggled to read the contents of the envelope at the best of times, but tears didn't help. It wasn't a bill. I touched the silver-embossed cross on the front of the mass card. Inside, I could make out Father Roche's neat signature.

*

When her shift ended, Lisa-Marie strode over to me. She held my face in her hands, stretched on her toes, and kissed me on the lips. "Mind yourself, Tommy Cassidy. And give up them fags. I've a bull with lung worm who sounds healthier than you. A pity Rhiannon couldn't make it over."

I cried. I couldn't help it, couldn't control it. Huge tears filled my eyes, blurred my vision and ran between her fingers.

Lisa-Marie didn't pull away. "Ah, Tommy, I'm sorry for your trouble." She was referring to Alma, but Alma wasn't the reason I cried. She pressed my cheeks in a caring, affectionate way. "It's a sad day, Tommy. Ye were married a good while." She kissed me again, stared up into my crying eyes. "And come here. We'll watch after you. I'll put the doctor out to you tomorrow or the next day. He'll have a listen to that old chest. I'll be out to you as well. Make sure you're doin okay."

Chapter 43

"Mister Tommy, my father is died, actually." Zhoro Boguslav pointed at his mobile phone as if his father's corpse lay within its glass and plastic casing. Everyone now seemed to have a mobile phone. "My sister tell me. Last week I go there, but he didn't die. He now die, yesterday night, when I come back to Ireland. Fell from sick bed and it is goodnight Irene. Bloody bastard."

"I'm sorry."

"No need be sorry. Time he died, I think. But, please, I was told leave this at you. Please give it to Mister Ryan."

Zhoro Boguslav handed me a loop of hairy green twine, its ends joined with a square knot. The twine held a small yellow card smeared with greasy fingerprints, and a key. "It's key for excavator, actually. Give to him Monday morning so they can do stuff now. I get taxi to Knock. My sister book flight in three hour."

I gripped the key in my fist. "Have you any children, Zhoro?"

"Of course." Zhoro Boguslav relaxed his stance. "Four children, yes. Two in university at Jelgava. Study agriculture. Very proud. It's why I'm here, Mister Tommy. Pay fees."

"Good man."

"I bring you back another bottle of Rigas," he said. "I think you need. Catherine the Great, it make her better."

Matty had been right about Catherine the Great.

Before I could suck enough air into my lungs to tell Zhoro Boguslav that it was Matty who drank the last bottle of Rigas, he was gone.

*

The key lay draped against the brown neck of a bottle, angled askance like a metallic lure. The ridges of its cuts caught the curtained light of the kitchen window. I lifted it away from the glass and rubbed my thumb over its square bow. They had changed the design, no plastic head with branding embossed on its side in my day. It used to be a flat metal that would slip through a hole in your pocket in a step. I was forever losing excavator keys. "Going to tie it round yer cock and balls, Tom. Won't lose it then in a hurry." James Taylor often proposed unhelpful solutions to the lost-key problem. I let him nowhere near my cock and balls.

As I held the key in my palm, the rush of my heart pounded heat through my body. The surge of hot blood set a reel in my head. I gripped the edge of the table and called on my heart to settle. I needed to reign in my excitement.

I wheezed a breath through inflamed airways. I was dying. I had outlived Alma by almost half a year, but I'd not long left.

Zhoro Boguslav's misfortune had presented me with a window of opportunity. This could be better than what I had plotted.

I couldn't delay, needed to act right away.

Was I prepared to go through with it?

Was I *able* to go through with it?

Chapter 44

Sleep eluded me that night, my head restless with the implications of what I was about to do.

I left my bed full of self-doubt. My whole body craved drink, but I needed to stay sober and seize the opportunity, or forget about it altogether. It was that day, or not at all.

If it wasn't a Sunday, I'd have called the solicitor to reassure myself arrangements were in place.

I stood over the bottle with the twine necklace. The key was still there—of course it was—the dawn's light caught in its amber hue.

Could I remember how it worked? Did I have enough of everything to do a proper job? If I didn't do a proper job, I'd have to face Matty and John Kavanaugh. I wasn't able for either.

Was I ready?

I rotated the bottle, examined the fob. A stained yellow ticket, the colour of the excavator bodywork. The yellow held the letters steady. 'Property of MR J KAVANAUGH.'

I was ready.

*

At the place on the lane where the children's rest used to be, I said my first prayer in a long time. Not to God, but to Noleen Mae.

As I dragged my feet back inside, I waved my walking stick at the gander. If I had had the strength I would have thrown stones. "Gather the family and go," I told it. "And I won't tolerate any of your cursing."

It took an age to lug the containers outside from the bedroom. I had to pause several times to sit and pull breaths into myself. I wondered what Raymond Buckley must have thought when I phoned in the repeat orders, and whether he realised what the goods he carried in the boot of his car were capable of? He never commented. Glad of the work, I always assumed.

It took me until midday to get my 'chemicals' in place. My clothes stuck to my body and my feet bulged blue and crimson around the sandal straps. I needed to lie down but had no time. Sunday mass in town would be finishing, bringing people back into the village. And there was Matt Darcy, of course, who could have appeared at any time, pushing his bicycle, perhaps wearing new spectacles and carrying a feed of sausages. I needed to get the job done.

*

The climb onto the tracks of the excavator nearly defeated me. Raising a leg was arduous. In the end, I hooked the walking stick around a handrail and hoisted my weary body over the muddied metal.

I collapsed into the sprung seat like a sack of wet turf and sat there, coughing, for too many wasted minutes.

It smelled like Wembly in 2002: clean oil, the alluring overtone of industrial adhesive.

My rapid breath fogged the side window.

I checked off the pedals and levers and knobs and waited for my gasping to subside.

From my elevated position, I spotted the gander over the gable of the house. It stretched its neck and stared back at me, gave a nonchalant swing away of its beak, then stared again.

"Told you leave," I whispered.

It didn't budge. We stared our goodbyes before I gave a last look out over the village.

Rays of sunlight burst through gaps in the clouds and bounced off the lake like skimmed stones, gave it a glassiness that made it look like the end of the earth. Beside the lake lay fields of rural hues, an abandoned Bord na Móna bog with ditcher stripes still evident. Beyond that, the hill-strewn horizon and the Atlantic Ocean.

I pondered that landscape a million times during my life. Alma wasn't far behind. It was Alma that took to setting two chairs in the yard, speech rendered intrusive by the view.

The hillside to my land wept, its waters leaching from the ripped peaty layers, smearing the buff stones in dark streaks. Tanninned tears the colour of cold tea.

While I said my so-longs to Duncarrick, doubt returned to gnaw at my stomach and tighten my throat. I shrugged it off.

I fumbled the key into the ignition and twisted.

Nothing. The CAT 320D excavator sat quiet and still, the glasshouse of its cab stifling in the sun.

My throat throbbed. I formed fists to stop the tremble in my fingers, bowed my head, closed my eyes. The shame of another failure worked its way through me.

If Matty turned up, I'd be ridiculed.

Think.

I was exhausted.

Think.

Wembley Stadium. The busiest building site in the whole of London. Excavators, dumper trucks large enough to haul a house, concrete wagons—lines and lines of concrete wagons––cranes that circled above us, surveyors shouldering theodolites below us. And me, in the cab of a CAT 300.

The start-up procedure.

Think.

I wriggled my arse into the padding of the chair.

Battery-disconnect switch to 'ON'.

A confirmatory beep.

"What are you doing, Tom?" Alma's voice, as if she was in the cab. I had been expecting her.

Hydraulic lever to 'LOCKED' position.

"You have no idea what you're doing, have you, Tom?"

I twisted the key.

The engine grumbled at the disturbance, fired.

I fell back in the padded seat with relief, then sat up and scanned the village like a guilty sheep thief. I could see no-one.

Engage hydraulic controls and twist throttle knob.

The engine roared as power surged through the CAT.

My heart hammered against my rib cage. I felt giddy with elation.

The roar of the engine died to a whimper. I was losing power. What was wrong? I flexed my fingers in desperation, searched the cab for something to press, something to twist. What had I missed?

The automatic throttle. Ryan mentioned it when the excavator arrived. The power would be there when I needed it.

I gripped the levers on either side of my knees and squinted through the sunlight's glare. With an expectant breath, I pulled back a lever.

The cabin tilted as the front bucket lifted clear of the ground.

I burst into shocked laughter. My plan was working.

"What about Wembley, Tom?" Alma was back in my head, pretending not to be dead. "The young man. Did you kill the young man?"

I couldn't think about that. I set my swollen feet on the travel pedals and pressed.

The excavator lurched forward.

With movement came power. The engine's roar quickened my pulse, dried my mouth. Adrenaline flooded my body. I was too tense.

I swung the excavator's arm.

With a spray of sparks and a boom that must have been heard in town, the excavator bucket crashed into the side of the diesel bowser. The block platform buckled. The bowser toppled, crashing its heft into the side of the house and sending a crack up the lime-washed rendering from ground to guttering.

Slates slid from the roof, shattered on the bowser.

"Get out, Tom. Before you make things worse."

I manoeuvred the bucket over the bowser and dropped it down with a crunching jolt.

The cabin rocked. I slipped my footings.

I lifted the bucket and brought it down again. The excavator jerked in protest. Another lift and drop, embedding the bucket's teeth in the bowser casing. Diesel bled from the wound.

I swung the excavator arm around and scooped up the dumper truck in an unwieldy fashion. The dumper flexed but held. I hovered it over the collapsed bowser, and let it fall.

The dumper bounced and buckled and screeched to a halt against the roof of the house. It toppled the chimney, scattering bricks and slates over the rolled-stone apron. I dropped the excavator bucket down on top of the dumper.

A dumper tyre exploded as it pushed through the roof.

I reached the long arm over dumper and bowser, pulled back on the levers, pressed forward with the foot pedals.

The excavator reared like a startled stallion and trundled forward, crashing into the pile of twisted metal.

The arm pulled. The steel tracks slipped and screeched. The treads caught, and the excavator ascended in destructive determination.

A track lost grip. The cab lurched to the side, threw me from my seat.

I thudded against the decalled window. Red smeared the glass. I blinked to steady my vision. Blood filled an ear, deadening the roar of the engine.

Bending metal groaned in protest beneath the excavator's mass. I feared it would roll, topple from its precipice, crush me to death before I had completed my plan.

It rocked, balanced, then settled and became still.

A heady confusion of excitement and anticipation and dread overcame me. I gasped, greedy for air. "I've done it, Alma." I wiped sweat and blood from my eyes. "I've done it."

*

I'm not sure, but it must have taken me the best part of an hour to climb down from the cab. Time was lost to me. I grazed shins, bruised elbows, cut my hands, but I made it. I sat against the bank, careless of the dampness that penetrated my clothes. I breathed noisily, exhausted, and waited for the light-headed wooziness to subside.

Fretful bleats of Mulligan's sheep—the rams put out for tupping early in the autumn as is Mulligan's preference—tumbled down the slopes of Cloonta Beg towards me.

The sky was thick with bird voices, crows suspicious of my actions yet curious enough to swoop and hover.

I propped on my father's walking stick and surveyed my work.

The wound on my head dripped blood.

The towel bandage that collected serum from my leg slumped sodden over my sandal.

I spared a thought for Ryan Matthews and the predicament he would find himself in. He could not be held responsible for my actions. And I doubted very much that John Kavanaugh would come for him. But these were matters for which the time for contemplation had passed.

I heaved myself off the bank and shuffled over to my chemicals.

Chapter 45

"I let you down from the room because you said you'd take your tablets."

"I want no more of them."

"Take these, and I'll help you back up to the room."

"It's too many."

"Take them."

"I want to sleep."

"I'll remove some of the clocks."

"I don't take them all."

"What?"

"I don't swallow all you give me. The tablets."

"You said you wanted them."

"You said I wanted them."

"We agreed…I'll watch you from now on."

Chapter 46

I cleared debris from the seat and eased my sweating body down onto my chair.

The familiar yield of the cushion. I sighed, relieved to be seated.

Draughts brought the outside in. A caress of air, cool on my brow. A hint of the seasonal egg smell of autumnal turnover from the freshwater lake.

A shaft of sunlight shone through the hole in the roof, caught the dust stirring in the air currents like a cloud of tiny midges.

I barely recognised the ruin of my own home. The wall beside me bulged. A crack like a deep bolt of black lightning ran its height, the harbinger of a thunderous collapse. The grate of the fire overflowed with broken bricks and poppy-leaf delft from the table. A corner was missing from the granite mantle. Slates and stones and broken timbers, brittle and grey with age, littered the floor. A ceiling board, dull gold from the greasy stain of nicotine, lay ruptured on the floor.

A butterfly, as delicate as a baby girl, its pale-yellow underside veined and freckled, landed on a disturbed slate at the edge of the roof's opening. Its visit pleased me, but I wanted it to leave. Before the explosion.

The chemical fuse had been lit. I waited for the flames to catch, the chemicals to react, and the bowser to explode. The blast would destroy the machines, take my house, and take me.

The butterfly lifted, flittered away.

"The time is right, Alma," I said.

No response.

The solicitor should be in contact with Rhiannon soon.

I pulled cigarettes from my pocket.

Above my head, the rear axle of the dumper had penetrated the roof, opening up a hole you could slide a single bed through. A wheel hung buckled and busted at a peculiar angle.

I could make out the bucket of the dumper, but from where I sat I couldn't see John Kavanaugh's CAT 320D, just a blue autumn sky.

I drew on my cigarette and wondered would the roof support the weight of the machines until the bowser exploded, or would it all come crashing down on me before then.

Either way, this was it. The end. Like in one of Dexter McEvoy's books.

I was ready. Ready for the end.

*

"Tommy?" A woman's voice. A real voice. Not Alma's. Younger.

I emerged from my fugue, confused and disorientated in the flames and the smoke.

"Tommy!" The voice again, shouting, near the busted doorway, concern in its tone. "Tommy. What in the name a fuck?"

When I recognised it, my heart woke from its slumber, pounded in my chest. I tried to speak, warn Lisa-Marie Gavin. I grabbed at the air. Nothing.

The explosion. It must be close.

She was in danger. She needed to get away.

Lisa-Marie ducked her head beneath the fractured lintel. She was dressed in Sunday best. "Holy be to God." She hoisted the hem of her coat to her mouth and rushed towards me.

The bag she carried fell away, spilling groceries.

A length of broken roof batten caught her foot, skitted across the floor, sent her tumbling over the rubble.

I couldn't help her.

She was on her feet, beckoning. "Come on!"

I didn't want her there, but I panicked from loss when smoke hid her from me.

She burst through it. "Me fuckin knees are all cut, ya bastard. Move it!"

I tried to lift myself from the chair. There was neither strength in my legs nor breath in my lungs. I waved her back.

The smell of diesel and bleach on fire swept down around us like a toxic wreath. The explosion was imminent.

I croaked, "Leave."

"Come on so you, to fuck." Lisa-Marie lifted my arm over her shoulder and hauled me from the chair. "Fuckin hell, Tommy. You smell like a latrine."

We stumbled over debris as she dragged me across the kitchen.

At the bedroom door, I caught sight of Jesus peering from behind a circular holy host. He looked anticipative, expecting me to help him and Judas and all the other disciples.

"Wait," I managed to say, straightening. I freed my arm, pointed.

"Tommy, we'll burn–"

"Matty bought it. For Alma."

"The shaggin ornament?" Lisa-Marie relented, propped me against the table. "Fuckin Matty, the bitch. If I burn to death savin a statute of men eatin dinner, I'll kill you and Matty." She rushed to retrieve Alma's statue of the Last Supper by the Spaniard, Juan de Juanes.

Flames rushed down through the hole in the roof as if blasted from a furnace. The air was hot, hotter than in the boiler room of the Owencas Electricity Generating Station. I'd put Lisa-Marie's life at risk.

A chair ignited. Bottles beneath it exploded. Timbers twisted and contracted and spat and crackled. The roof folded in on itself, dropped, halted, sent a downpour of red cinders over the flaming chairs.

Lisa-Marie pressed the statue into my chest.

"Tells me the time," I said.

"Time to get the fuck out!"

It was then I first appreciated the pinched, bird-featured face of Judas, the raven nose like the pointed end of a pickaxe, the pursed mouth like a witch's navel. Judas reminded me of John Kavanaugh.

A carpet of flame defied the laws of gravity and rolled over our heads across the ceiling. It beat us to the door. Honeyed paint blistered and burst.

I searched for another route as a light bulb exploded, showered us in sparks and hot glass.

"We're going to fuckin roast, Tommy."

Lighted paint dripped around us.

The heat was in my hair, on my skin, in my throat.

Lisa-Marie screamed, "Shift!" and shoved me through the fall of flames.

The air outside was cool. I could smell the lake.

Wispy trails of smoke lifted from my smouldering jacket as we staggered over the rolled stone.

Lisa-Marie coughed. "Me bloody coat's a ruin."

I caught sight of the gander leading its flock away, and the first explosion sounded.

Lisa-Marie held onto me, dragging me from danger.

The house absorbed most of the blast, launching slates and timbers and rocks into the air.

Flying fragments pounded the ground around us.

The hiss of released pressure.

Another explosion, more furious than the first, shook the earth.

The rapid rush of hot air tumbled us to the ground.

I twisted and groaned and rolled over on top of Lisa-Marie.

A length of sheared metal drove into the back of my leg. I yelled in agony.

Hydraulic tubing bounced beside us. Hot rubble pelted us. A deadly, two-foot metal shard stuck upright in the stone near my arm, its row of yellow warning stickers scorched brown. Lumps of blackened steel and stones thudded and leapt and rolled around the yard.

The house and machines were one, mangled together in a burning mass of metal and masonry, the CAT wrapped in a blazing veil of flames.

An ignited spray of hydraulic fluid squirted from a fractured metal pipe, showering the dumper truck in a font of fire.

Dense, black clouds of acrid smoke rose over us, darkening the sky.

Lisa-Marie whispered, “What have you done, Tommy?”

I had no answer. The pain in my leg was excruciating.

The boom arm of the CAT stuck up through the flames like the leg of a partially cremated mechanical insect. Flames and smoke blurred the writing on its side and, in a way that surprised me, steadied the large three-dimensional black lettering shadowed in gold. ‘Kavanaugh Developments - Construction That Cares.’

Slowly, ever so slowly, the letters bubbled and peeled, and fell to ashes.

Lisa-Marie said, “I’ve a room spare beyont in the house.”

Chapter 47

I opened my eyes.

My surroundings were familiar, seemed unchanged since as far back as when Noleen Mae was born there. What is it that makes the appearance of a hospital room immediately recognisable?

Thunder roared outside. "God moving furniture." That's what Daddy used to say to frighten me. "Preparing a seat for you, he is."

Rain battered the large windows, the gusts so heavy I could have been at sea in a storm. When Dexter McEvoy read *Moby Dick*, we laughed as he stood and swayed his squat frame to imitate the typhoon battering Captain Ahab's whaler. Thunder, rain, and drugs made me feel as though I was in the story, on the boat, as unsteady and nauseous as if I was cowering in the forecastle praying for the storm to subside.

I was free from pain. Warm. Euphoric. My breathing was ragged, but the blockage was eased, my airway dilated by drugs.

The edge of a plastic mask pressed on the bridge of my nose. I inhaled clean oxygen.

A rail ran around my bed to confine me. Above my head, a bag of blood the colour of lamb's liver sagged from a pig-tail hook. Below the bag a blue and white unit with a small screen of green numbers was clamped to the stand's pole.

White tape held the cannulas of two tubes against the sallow skin of my arm. My fingernails looked abnormally clean.

A newspaper stirred. Matt Darcy peeked from behind it. Sticking plaster still held a spectacle lens in place. He had a clean bandage on his wrist.

His lips moved. It seemed as if seconds passed before his words reached me. "Readin through the death notices."

Was he looking for my name?

"Lookin for your name, I was."

I felt myself smile. My first smile in a long while.

"There's morphine dancing round yer brain cells," Matty said. "Twenty-milligram loadin dose at five milligrams per millilitre concentration. Two milligrams per hour continuous infusion. You've a button that can administer three milligram doses with a five-minute lockout. There's no four-hour limit, so be cautious. Make sure ya don't sign anythin official."

I smacked my lips, thirstily. "My plan?" The mask muffled my voice. I worked a hand up to my face, lifted the mask clear of my mouth and parked it on a cheek. Elasticated bands tugged at my ears.

"Oh, yer plan worked all right," Matty said. "They've put a halt to the quarry. Yer plan nearly put a halt to you, too."

Matty didn't understand, my plan had failed, I was still alive. I rubbed at my mouth, bristly above and below my dry lips.

"Look at this," Matty said. "You've only gone and turned yerself into a local celebrity." He held up the newspaper, read the headline. "It says, 'Inquiry into mishap at unauthorised quarry'." He folded the newspaper into quarters, squinted through the working lens and read on. "Lisa-Marie Gavin, thirty-nine, mother of local skating protégé, Julie Gavin, informed this paper that she thought Thomas Cassidy was put at risk of his life through unscrupulous exploitation by a corrupt and deceitful businessman. She said the same businessman has a handlebar moustache that would disgrace the face of any puck goat in the hills a County Kerry."

Matty was trying to cheer me.

"I made that bit up," he said. "About the moustache. And about the puck goat."

He didn't need to try to cheer me up. It was enough just to have him there.

Matty rose from his chair, leaned over the rail, clutched my arm. "Are you all right?" His face was a wrinkled mask of concern. Confirmation, if confirmation was needed, I was in a bad way. The tape-wrapping of his spectacle lens looked tattered and ridiculous.

I tried to nod. An ache bloomed behind my eyes. "Lisa..?" My voice was throaty. I dragged the mask back over my mouth, breathed the oxygen,

"Lisa-Marie is fine," he said. "Scratches, only. Tellin everyone you saved her life when ya took the metal stake in the leg. Making *you* out to be the bloody hero."

Lisa-Marie saved my life. Matty must have known that.

"I told her she's the hero. You're just an eejit. She has the statue I bought you and Alma. But the fella in the yellow dress lost his head when ye fell."

"Judas," I whispered. Words came easier with the mask on.

Matty straightened. "Why am I?"

"Yellow dress."

"Is that who he is?"

"Listen," I said.

Matty held up a hand to silence me. "I know all about it." He counted on the thin fingers of a hand as he spoke. "Ya lost a pint and a half a blood. There's a hole in yer leg I could get my boot into. And yer liver's banjaxed. But I warned you that would happen. Oh, and you've oedema. And type-one diabetes."

I nodded, waited for the pain in my head to flare.

"Ya might have type-two, I can't remember."

My eyes searched for water. The jug on the cabinet was empty.

"You'll be wonderin how I know all this?" Matty glanced at the door. "I'm good friends with the Senior Nurse. You know him. Rowan. We used to be close."

I smiled.

More of the tape had peeled away from the lens since I last saw Matty. Its sticky edges were lined black with captured dirt. He had the pirate look about him, again. A dishevelled pirate, without the long curls.

Matty caught me staring. "I want John Kavanaugh to pay for new glasses." His visible eye welled. "What about you?" He pulled back his head, sniffed into a hand. "You nearly died, Tommy."

But I didn't. Another failure.

His eyebrows furrowed, a wavering, conflicted smile that quivered with sadness. He ducked his head into his shoulders, turned away.

I wanted to tell him that everything was all right. I was going to die soon anyway, and I was grand with it. I relaxed my head back into the pillow, closed my eyes.

Shame is a curse. Shame is the worst of emotions. The unworthiness of it all, the inadequacy, the humiliation. Not feelings I could share, certainly not with Matt Darcy. That's what made shame so dangerous: you don't share it. You either run away from it, or take your revenge.

My eyes shot open. "Kavanaugh?"

Matty's visible eye had reddened. "Don't worry about Kavanaugh," he said. "Ryan Matthews went mad when he found out the paperwork was falsified. It scared Kavanagh off and Ryan's taken on the handlin of his affairs. There's a solicitor in Castlebar under investigation. I hear Ryan's tryin to get hold of the insurance money to pay for the work he's done. He'll be lucky if there is any insurance. But no-one blames Ryan."

I didn't blame Ryan. I was more concerned about Ryan blaming me.

"Sure everyone knows," Matty continued. "Ryan was duped as well."

Duped as well. As well as me. Everyone knows.

An itch nagged somewhere beneath the bandage that wrapped my leg.

"They're saying it was a faulty fuel bowser, but Inspector Michael Gilhooly is under the absurd impression there was evidence of an incendiary device. The man's only tryin to get himself in the papers if you ask me. He does still want to interview you though."

What was the worst Inspector Gilhooly could do? It was all too late.

"I cycled past the house on my way out. Must be a million euros of warped metal."

Almost the same price as the Rolls-Royce Phantom.

Matty bent closer. "But listen." His eye became sombre. I didn't want him to cry again. "I think I should tell ya that Nurse Rowan told me everything. I got a full prognosis. It's not good news."

So much for patient confidentiality.

"Reassuringly, Rowan also told me cancer's treatable if discovered early."

My eyes widened.

"Me," Matty said. "I mean me. I'm the one with cancer. Bowel cancer. Confirmed. Results came through." A wistful smile.

Matty would need looking after.

"Anyhow," Matty said. "That's me. You, you've just an incurable breathing disorder. Chronic obstructive pulmonary disease. C.O.P.D. Late stages. So ya might as well have cancer."

"Treatment," I said, my voice hollow and echoey. I wasn't sure if Matty could hear me from beneath the plastic.

"Nothing they can do for you. Sorry to break it to ya while you're laid up and all."

"You."

Matty drew back. "Yes. I'm startin treatment. Soon, maybe."

I wanted to tell him that he needed to take all the help offered, get well.

"I'll be all right," he said, as if he knew what I was thinking.

A disturbance in the corridor. Senior Nurse Rowan was trying to explain the rule that patients were only allowed two visitors at a time, and under no circumstances could a dog be allowed onto the wards. The boom of a familiar voice, "He'll see us."

"Ryan told me he was comin in to see ya," Matty said.

Heat flooded my face. I wanted to hide behind the mask.

Ryan Matthews sailed into the room like a mighty galleon, his belly swinging in the swollen mainsail of his tartan shirt. Zhoro Boguslav was with him, following like a pilot boat in pointless pursuit. I couldn't see the dog but heard the rapid pad of canine footsteps on the plastic-tiled floor.

I braced myself for the onslaught.

"Tommy! Bogsey insisted on comin in with me. Matty said it would be all right." Ryan Matthews steered around his huge frame and grinned. "Thank you, Rowan. We'll find him from here."

Matty winked his visible eye and sat down.

Ryan Matthews was as wide as the end of the bed. "I understand yer fecked, Tommy. We've come in to say goodbye."

Zhoro lifted a plastic SuperValu bag onto the bed. A chink of glasses. "My country is like Ireland, Mister Tommy. Not afraid of death. We celebrate the life, actually. Even to my miserable father, me and my brothers find something for celebration. Now I'm here already, and it's very good thing."

Ryan Matthews was grinning the head off himself. "We're only back from the airport."

Zhoro reached inside the bag and pulled out a conical black bottle. It looked out of place in a hospital. "I ask you about the clocks, Mister Tommy."

"That's right, Tommy." Ryan's smile became a thunderous laugh. "Jesus, yeah. There's a million bloody clocks buried up in the bloomin field. I thought Bogsey here had discovered the clock-nest monster." A pause. "See what I did there, Matty? There's a lake near Inverness, over in Scotland–"

"I have you, Ryan." Matty stood. "But it's a reach." He took hold of the Rigas Black Balsam. "Have ye glasses?"

A spasm in my throat reminded me of the damage there. I restrained the cough. While the three of them shared out tumblers for drinks, I reached for the morphine button. A bleep sounded from the unit on the stand.

All three men stopped and stared.

"The P.C.A." Matty said.

Blank looks.

"Patient Controlled Analgesia. Twenty-milligram loadin dose, two milligrams per hour continuous infusion. He has a button that can administer–."

"Can I interrupt?"

Ryan Matthews and Zhoro Boguslav turned and stepped apart.

Garda Inspector Michael Gilhooly strode into the gap.

Matty hid the bottle of Rigas Black Balsam like a naughty schoolboy caught stealing from the sweet shelf in Buckley's grocery store.

"Thomas Cassidy?" Gilhooly said, though he knew bloody well it was me. He fixed those eyes of his on me and announced, "I'd like to speak with Mister Cassidy in private."

My three visitors and the dog shuffled towards the door.

His tone still ominous, Gilhooly said, "I'll catch up with you another day, Mister Matthews." He eyed Zhoro Boguslav suspiciously as he spoke.

"We'll wait, we will?" Ryan said.

"I wouldn't linger. Mister Cassidy and I have a lot to discuss. Visiting will be over by the time I've finished."

Matty halted his departure. "He can barely talk," he said. "He's on analgesics. Twenty-milligram loadin dose–"

Gilhooly cut him off with a raised gloved hand. "I know all about it. Now fuck off."

"Right," Matty said. "Go easy, so."

When we were alone, Gilhooly said, "Curiouser and fucking curiouser."

Alice, the young girl in the wonderland. I remembered the line from one of Dexter McEvoy's books. Gilhooly had thrown in the swearing to intimidate.

"I'm just off the phone to Missus Rhiannon Kavanaugh." Thunder, louder than before, clapped up against the sash windows. Gilhooly had dragged the storm after him. "She told me about the unwanted pregnancy."

Chapter 48

It was so hot the tarmac made the air above it shimmer. On straight sections of road, bent light made it look as if we were driving into the sea, travelling in the wrong direction altogether.

The windows were open to blow away the smell of recent lovemaking. Smoke wriggled from my cigarette to be caught in the currents and whipped from the car.

Rhiannon shouted to be heard above the roar of turbulence. "If these four appear on stage together tonight, it'll be a minor miracle."

"Do they still hate each other?"

"From all accounts."

I laughed. "It'll be fine. Sláinte are back together for the money."

"You're so right." Rhiannon relaxed back into her chair, tapped her hands on her bare knees. "Tolerate each other for one night, surely." Her hair flagged in the draughts, casting curls around her head.

I said, "It's a long drive to Dublin to find out they don't bother in the end."

"Jesus, that'd be mad."

"Looking forward to it?"

"Very much," she yelled. "That Stephen Moor. I think he looks like a sweaty, bearded potato."

"Hold on," I said, laughing. "He also sings like an angel."

"God, yeah." She raised her arms, swayed her head, and sang. "To sit watch you dance. The most me I can be. My purest devotion. Oh, woman of Knocknagree."

"I didn't realise *you* sang like an angel," I said.

"I belong on the stage," she laughed.

"The most me I can be? Does that even make sense?"

"Doesn't have to when Stephen Moor sings it." Rhiannon held her hair back from her face with long fingers. She was smiling. Beautiful smiling. "How about we go to London tonight? Let's not wait. Get the ferry after the show and keep going till we reach London Bridge?"

"I don't think so."

"You, Tommy Cassidy, make me the most me that I can be."

I was hoping to wait until after the concert, but I needed to talk to her. Without shouting. I wound the handle. "Close that window?" I said.

She glanced at me, perturbed, but worked the winder around. She combed her hair with fingertips in the sun visor's tiny mirror.

"I'm not going to London, Rhiannon."

"Why wouldn't you go to London?"

It was important to be honest with her. "If you want to go, you'll have to go on your own."

She paused before she spoke. "What are you sayin?"

"You're set on England, a life in London. I understand that, but I can't go."

"Why not?"

It was a waste of time me trying to explain. "We'll have tonight, then maybe look at things again."

"Look at what things?"

This wasn't how I intended the conversation to go. "I just think, maybe..."

"Maybe fuckin what?"

"Maybe it's best we call a halt?" It came out as a question, a pathetic, non-committal question. My back was shedding sweat.

"Call a halt? Jesus! Are you dumpin me?"

"Dumping? No. No, there's no dumping. We're on a night out. I just think that…Our hearts are set on different things, Rhiannon."

"Is it the gossip in town?"

"What gossip?"

"That you're too old for me."

"Who's saying that?"

"Have I done somethin wrong?"

"You've done nothing wrong."

"Is there someone else?"

"No. Nothing like that." I wound down my window a fraction to let the tension escape. "There's nothing like that."

I hadn't anticipated this reaction. I didn't know what I had anticipated. I lit another cigarette and tried to backpedal. "Look, let's enjoy the show. I paid enough for the tickets."

"Fuck the show. Why're you dumpin me?"

"I'm...It won't work. Me and you, it won't work. London's all you've spoken about since we've been together, and I have plans here, with the farm. I'm just about getting it straight and I could make a go of it. Take people on, buy more land, get a real business going. Expand it. London isn't part of my plans. And you've made it clear that farming isn't part of yours."

"It's not. You're right. There's no way I'm staying here to raise fuckin sheep."

"Don't I know that? It's bloody hard work."

"But there's a complication."

"What complication?"

She pushed back into her seat, slapped the visor closed as though no longer able to look at herself.

"Rhiannon, what's wrong?"

She turned her head, stared out at the bushes rushing by, and said in a whisper, "I didn't want to tell you like this."

"What's the complication?"

"Jesus, this is fucked." She still couldn't face me.

"Rhiannon?"

"I'm carrying your child. Our child. I'm carrying our baby."

If we *were* driving towards the sea, we had just sailed off the edge of the cliff. My insides were in freefall. I wanted to throw up. The road shifted in front of me.

"Tommy!"

I blinked. We were travelling too fast. In the middle of the road. A Bord na Móna peat wagon bore down on us. Its inside wing mirror chopped lumps out of the roadside hedge.

I swerved the Austin back.

Rhiannon had her arms wrapped over her head.

"It's all right."

"You nearly just bloody killed us all," she screamed. "What in hell is wrong with you?"

I slowed the car down. "I'm sorry, I…"

I swear the heart in me was up in my mouth. She was right. I had nearly killed us all. Not us, not Rhiannon and me, *Us all.* It was no longer just Rhiannon and I in the car. "How?" I said. "How did you get–"

"Men ask some fuckin questions."

"You better not be saying this just to get back at me."

She scoffed. "Eight weeks…I reckon on it being our first time."

"Which first time? At the river?"

"How many first times were there? Yes, at the river."

"And it's eight weeks?"

"Yeah. I'd say."

It was no time for a baby. I had plans made, and a baby with Rhiannon was not part of them. The farm was expensive. Children were expensive.

We went too far that time at the river. We lost control. And now we were paying the price.

We said nothing to each other for long minutes. Rhiannon tilted back her head. I think she had her eyes closed.

When is a good time for a baby? It was an inconvenience, but a baby wasn't something you could turn away from the door when it presented itself, not something you tell to go away until you were ready for it.

I drove several miles in a fugue. I didn't remember the turns in the road, the rises and dips. We might have passed through some traffic lights, a small townland, over a railway crossing. When I emerged, I struggled to work out where on earth we were, and where the hell we were going. I wriggled against the restrictive cling of my damp shirt on my back. "When were you going to tell me?" I said.

"What odds?" She stared down into the footwell. "Tonight, maybe. After the concert. Who knows? I might've told you on the boat on our way to London. Starin out to sea, under the stars."

Was she mocking me?

"We need to decide," I said. "What we're going to do about it."

The briefest of pauses. "Meaning what?"

"I don't want you to do anything you don't want to do, but we've a decision to make."

"Yeah, go on." She tugged on the seatbelt to give herself room to shift in her seat and face me. "What is it you're suggesting?"

I found her derisive tone infuriating. This was not the way I envisaged things working out. I said it anyway. "You and me and the farm in Duncarrick." I warmed to the idea as soon as the words came out of my mouth. "And the baby." That's how I said it, not the most romantic, not the most enticing.

Rhiannon was silent. Maybe that was what she wanted, too. She shuffled in her seat, stared out the window, and weighed my proposal for what seemed like an eternity. "That's a fuckin turnaround," she said at last.

"What is?"

"Dumpin me one minute, now this."

"I wasn't…For Christ's sake, Rhiannon. We've little choice. We can't ruin everything now. Look at our options."

She pursed her lips, shook her head. "No. I won't. I can't do that." It didn't sound like Rhiannon's voice. All life had been strained out of it. "I don't want–"

"Rhiannon. Think for once."

Her head lifted. "Stop the car."

"What?"

"Stop the fuckin car!"

"Don't be stupid."

"I'm not going to the concert. I'm going no further with–"

"I paid out good money. You're going."

"I couldn't give a shite." The vigour was back in her voice.

"We're going to the show. We'll enjoy it, and then we'll discuss a plan." I was getting it all wrong. I hated confrontation.

Rhiannon turned to look at me. Her lip curled in a snarl I'd not seen since the night in Buckley's with the bucks watching the football. "You and me and the fuckin farm?" she said. "Here? With a baby?"

My stomach cramped. I didn't know what to say. I took a deep draw on the cigarette, hoped the nicotine hit would inspire me. "Could be worse." It sounded so bloody lame.

"There's no way I'm stayin here," she said. "And there's no way I'm havin this baby."

It was my turn to ask. "What is it *you're* suggesting?"

"I'm not suggesting anything. It's what's going to happen."

"Rhiannon."

"I'm going to England. You can do the decent thing and help pay for it, but I'm not ready for children."

I flicked the cigarette out the window, rummaged one-handed for another.

I nearly laughed out loud at our circumstance. There we were, both our futures in the balance, me sweating and smoking like a damp fire, Rhiannon brooding like an angry ewe with a troublesome pregnancy, and us on our way to a concert by Irish folk band, Sláinte. She wouldn't go through with a termination. I was sure of that.

I punched the cigarette lighter deep into its socket.

Doubts about the long-term viability of Rhiannon and me together flooded my thoughts. She was not the woman for the life I had planned. The burn of our relationship was too intense to last— Christ, it wouldn't be long before I burnt out, myself—but I couldn't see any other way. Rhiannon could change. I could, perhaps, change. We'd work something out. There was a baby, and we had to accommodate it.

I steeled myself. "If you go ahead with your plan, Rhiannon, it will be the end of you and me." I hid my uncertainty with a nonchalant light of the cigarette, the heat of the lighter's red coil hot against my sweating face.

She plucked the cigarette from my lips, sucked hard on it.

"Rhiannon."

She blew out the smoke as a child would. It billowed greyly against the windscreen.

"You shouldn't be at that," I said.

"So you weren't bein genuine?"

"I'm not sure what–"

"You don't know what you want, do you, Tommy? You've not a clue. Half an hour ago we were ridin the hole off each other. A minute ago you were ending us. Next thing you're suggestin we stay together for the baby."

"Rhiannon–"

"Now you're usin the baby as an excuse to dump me."

"Rhiannon, I don't want to dump you."

"Right now, Tommy Cassidy, it's impossible for you to fuck far enough off."

I gripped the steering wheel so hard, I squeezed the blood from my knuckles and, I'd near swear to Christ, resin from the Bakelite.

Chapter 49

The last thing I wanted to listen to was Michael Gilhooly's inspectorial appraisal of my relationship with Rhiannon.

He moved alongside so that he could stand over me, gripped the rail with damp gloves, and hovered his peak-capped head in over the bed. The sloe-coloured eyes bore into me with their familiar sour scrutiny.

I flapped a hand at him.

"What is it?"

I beckoned him closer. "I admit it."

"You admit what?"

"Explosion."

He straightened, tilted his head a fraction, stared.

I took a long blink, hoped my deflection worked, and hoped too that when I re-opened my eyes, Gilhooly would be gone.

He said, "We'll come back to the use of unregistered explosive material in a public place in due course. When we do, we'll also address the small matter of arson and gratuitous criminal damage to property. You're not the first mad fire-starting fucker I've had to deal with, Thomas. I'd love to go around blowing a few things up, myself, but I can't. And if I can't, you can't either. But sure enough to say, it was you're little escapade that got me thinking. It's what put calling Missus Kavanaugh into my mind."

Gilhooly was still there when my eyelids lifted.

"Why would you, Thomas…" He spoke deliberately, jutted his chin. "…go to all that effort to destroy John Kavanaugh's machines, and your house, and a bowser full of diesel, and then sit yourself in underneath it, waiting for it to go up?"

I pressed my P.C.A. button. No bleep.

"What awful shame, or terrible guilt, caused you to try and do away with yourself like that?" He broke off from his smug posturing, glanced at the morphine pump. "Yoke in your hand drives that machine, does it? Nurse mentioned the C.O.P.D."

If the opportunity presented itself, I would have a word with Nurse Rowan about the disclosure of my medical records.

Gilhooly said, "It's a cruel bastard. An uncle of mine down in Kerry died of it last year. Choked to death alone in the house. Near the end, he told me it felt like he was drowning in his own boiling lung juice."

A rush of rain crashed against the hospital window. A series of huge electrical discharges filled the casement. Their flashes lit up the room like a strong bulb with a faulty filament.

I counted for the thunder to measure the storm's approach. A reflex, a habit since the days that Mammy and I hid beneath thin blankets and hoped the blessed candle in the window would chase the lightning away from the kitchen. If Mammy was there, she'd chase the inspector. I missed Mammy.

Gilhooly leaned in. "Missus Kavanaugh told me you turned up drunk outside her flat in London. Said you made threats against Alma."

I pressed. The beep sounded.

He looked up. "It's true then?"

I thought back to that dreadful night in Camden, the night cold, the natives colder. My heart shrank.

"According to a Mister…" He delved two fingers beneath the flap of his chest pocket, withdrew a scrap of paper. He unfolded it, squinted. "I sometimes struggle to read my own fucking– Alan Hughes. According to Mister Alan Hughes, you *did* make threats. He's a neighbour of Missus Kavanaugh's. Lives in the flat below. Number thirteen. I phoned him as well. Seems a pleasant-enough chap."

I couldn't remember making any threats, but I remembered I was drunk. Drunk and emotional. I could have said anything.

Gilhooly consulted his paper. "'We will be better off without her.' That, allegedly, is what you said. We. Will. Be. Better. Off. Without. Alma. You claimed you had a plan. You claimed to have had a plan to get rid of your wife, Thomas."

I shook my head, winced at the pain of it.

"You think the whole thing ridiculous?" Gilhooly said. "What's ridiculous is the amount of paperwork it'll take to get

Mister Hughes over here to testify. But if the toxicology report raises concerns, I'll do it. It's what I do. It's why I joined up. To catch the bad fuckers. The bad and the mad. Which one are you, Thomas? I know from experience you have a temper."

My bandaged leg itched. My body sweat. I gasped at the oxygen.

The plastic chamber of the mask amplified my agitated breaths.

"Mister Hughes had a lot to say for himself," Gilhooly said. "Told me everything you shouted up to Missus Kavanaugh."

Hughes could have told him anything.

"According to Mister Hughes, you woke up the whole bloody block shouting. He reckons you said, 'I'm in love with you, my darling.'" Gilhooly smirked. "Love and darling? And you married to Missus Kavanaugh's sister at the time? That sounds bloody complicated."

There was no point in trying to explain.

"But there was this pregnancy." He smirked, in the way I imagined a spider might smirk when it detects a tremor in its web. "Missus Kavanaugh told me how you paid for her to go to England for a termination. You got her pregnant and then, according to her, you dumped her."

I could feel the increased pulse of my heart in the tender tissue of my inflamed throat.

"She would have been Rhiannon Harkin at the time, of course. How old would she be? Eighteen? Nineteen? Not what I'd want for my daughter," he said. "What about you?"

Gilhooly consulted his paper. "I've a witness that says you declared to the whole of Camden that you planned to get rid of Alma."

His head was over me again, his eyes burning into me. "So, what I really want to know, Thomas." There were dark bristles on one underside of his jaw, remnants from a hurried shave. "Is, did you kill your wife?"

Chapter 50

"I've enough."

"A few more."

"I want no more."

"You must."

"I can't."

"Swallow them down."

I swallowed. My head was a fuzz. "Why?" I gazed around me, listless and lethargic. "Why we doing this?"

Alma was emphatic. "We know why."

I barely recognised the surroundings of my own neglected kitchen. "Can I have a cigarette?"

"No cigarettes."

"They're poison."

"Yes, they are."

"The tablets," I said. "Not the cigarettes."

"That's enough talk."

She shook tablets from the bag into her hand, stared me in the face, challenged me to defy her.

"You jealous, Alma?"

"I said that's enough of the talk."

"That's it isn't it? Jealousy."

"You're feisty today, Tom."

"Jealous of Rhiannon and of John?"

"Do I need to increase your dose?"

I held a hand in front of my face, turned my head. "No more."

"Let me see you swallow these, and I'll help you up to bed."

"Could you not bear see them do well?"

"We'll talk about this another time."

"I can't remember why we're doing this."

"Oh, I have my reasons," Alma said. "I know everything that went on, Tom."

"Money? Was it? Money and success? And children?"

"Yes," she said. "Everything, Tom. All that and more. Whereas you've succeeded at nothing."

She was right, of course, I hadn't.

"I'm tired." I was fumbling, sunk in a cloud of confusion. "Must get up." Even with a fistful of new tablets inside me, I knew I needed to move. A cough kicked its way out. I wiped at my mouth with an arm.

"Come on," she said. "Back up to the room."

"Look…Everything's..."

"Why won't you die, Tom?"

"A ruin." I tugged at my collar in a futile attempt to stop my body from overheating.

I was an easy lift, skin and bone. "Come on."

"Don't, Alma." I scanned the room, wide-eyed and mouth gaping, for an escape route. It was my home, and I was trying to breakout.

She squeezed my arm. "You'll do as I say."

"Please, Alma." I wasn't sure she was Alma, anymore.

"Listen to me."

"Don't pull." Muscles tensed, I summoned my strength, shrugged her away. "Leave–" My flailing arms hit her a blow in the chest.

She stumbled, caught her foot on my chair, fell towards the fire.

I made an awkward grab for her, afraid she'd land in the flames, afraid I'd tumble into the flames after her.

The sickening thud of her head on the granite edge wrenched at my dulled nerves. "Alma."

She was still.

I dropped to my knees beside her. "Alma?"

Blood on the hearth.

I was scared to touch her.

A stain on the granite seeped from beneath her head, through her hair, growing like a bloated dark spectre from a drug-induced dream.

I rolled her over.

Her eyes were sunk back into the cavity of their sockets.

"I didn't mean..." I looked around the kitchen, searching for...I didn't know. "Alma. Can you hear me?"

The seizure started slowly. She grunted, twisted, curled onto a side. Her tongue stuck out between her lips. Her arms and legs juddered. A wet stain spread through her skirt, making the black material blacker.

I stared, rigid with fear, not knowing what to do.

Her arms and legs flexed and straightened. A slipper fell from a foot. She croaked, froth on her cheek, jaws clenching and unclenching. Blood from her tongue coloured her teeth redly.

"Alma?"

She didn't hear me.

Louder. "Alma!"

The ticks of a thousand clocks filled my head. I pressed my hands to my ears and rocked, helpless with regret. "No, Alma." A crushing, to and fro, self-loathing regret.

She became still. Pale and vulnerable and still.

"Alma?"

I placed an ear to her mouth.

Her chest fell a fraction, then rose again.

I rolled the hearthrug, made a pillow of it.

*

I coughed all the way along the lane, wheezing, staggering, falling.

I regained my feet, looked about me like a lost man.

Light off the lake dazzled. A bank post, warped to the whims of the wind, had slipped its wire and leaned ready to topple. Cloonta Beg, its sloping fields crisscrossed with stone walls, loomed large over me.

I turned and stumbled towards the light. I dashed into the middle of the lake road, threw my arms into the air.

The lorry's brakes screeched in startled fury. The engine growled and spewed its oily heat over me as if I'd stilled its rattling bulk with a punch to the guts.

Chapter 51

The weather drew Inspector Michael Gilhooly to the hospital window. He set his feet square and stood looking out at the storm. "I suppose murdering your wife with a blow to the head wouldn't be the sort of thing you'd readily admit to."

Alma died in my arms on the way to the hospital. Ryan Matthews drove us. It was him I flagged down on the lake road. He was delivering topsoil to a job in town. He carried Alma from the house, and after he shoved me up into the cab, he lifted her up onto my lap. I think that blood leaked from the back of her head and stained the seat, but I could have imagined that. I couldn't remember, the details were vague.

God dragged a heavy chair across the sky, a sturdy leather-and-oak judging by the sound. My chair.

Gilhooly waited for the rumble to subside. "I used to think," he said, "that the old love triangle tragedy only belonged in books and films. I've never dealt with one. Don't get me wrong. Domestic disputes? Fuck domestic disputes, I've done more than my fair share of them. I've stepped between two men fighting over a woman, two women fighting over a man, even two women fighting over another woman. But there's been no fatality involved. No dead body. In all my twenty-one years in the force. Never."

His chin was raised, there was a controlled sway to his stance, his gloved hands were linked behind his back. It was as if his mind's eye was looking out at a hall of new Gardai recruits, hundreds of open-mouthed youngsters hanging on his every word.

"But you know," he said, "I only have to scan back through the files for a few minutes to find that such calamities are commonplace. They're at it all the time in bloody Leitrim. Dublin? Well, what'd you expect from the Dubs? Five cases. *Five* domestic murders in the last nine months. Don't ask me about Donegal. Just don't ask."

The lightning came. A blinding white ribbon of it flashed in the window and threw Inspector Michael Gilhooly into negative. Heavy thunder pealed on high. The storm was overhead.

I found myself wishing the bolt had struck him dead.

Gilhooly turned from the window and approached the bed like a fox stalking chickens. "A case in Wexford two and a half years ago. A woman killed her husband with a pitchfork in the neck because he couldn't make her pregnant and give her a child. She was having an illicit affair with his more fertile brother at the time."

What started him on this?

He leaned in over the bed. "A fellow in County Louth drove a tractor into his barren wife, impaling her on the hay bale fork. Was seen carrying her back across the field to the hayshed hanging from the bastarding spike. Made out she fell off the stack and impaled herself.

"Another fellow, a doctor in Limerick, overdosed his brother with anti-depressants so that he could move in with the sister-in-law. A doctor overdosing the brother, by God."

If I was stronger, I would have shouted for him to stop.

"You didn't have surviving children with Alma, did you, Thomas?" He said it as though that was now a crime. "Rhiannon Kavanaugh mentioned it to me on the telephone. Said it bothered you. Said you blamed your wife for losing the baby. Said you held Alma responsible. Noleen Mae. Nice name."

I pressed the button.

"One bleep for yes," Gilhooly said. "And two bleeps for no." He turned to the pump machine, flicked the plastic compartment that held the syringe of morphine with a gloved finger. "Better than any lie detector, this."

I didn't want to die in prison.

"When I did my poking around, Thomas, I spoke to a few people in the village and in town. Their stories were pretty consistent. Your wife was very ill after she lost the baby, but she was recovering. Apparently, she spent several months attending the sick wife of Buckley the publican. Your wife was getting back to her old self is what I've been told. Until you returned from London. People then describe a deterioration, before she disappeared altogether. Not seen out for months before she landed up in hospital. Dead."

It was all speculation. Loose talk. Rumour. He had no proof.

"So, Thomas. I have questions that need answering. Are Rhiannon Kavanaugh's concerns founded in reality or just her way at getting back at you? God knows, she had bloody reason to be angry after what you did to her. And what will the toxicology report reveal? Was Alma Cassidy illegally and deliberately overdosed in a sustained attempt to cause her harm? Are you, Thomas, like the doctor in Limerick, guilty of carrying out that overdosing? And if you are, where did you get access to sufficient quantities of the drugs? And what in hell drove you to sit in your chair waiting for a bowser full of diesel to explode next to you?"

He was interrupted by Senior Nurse Rowan tapping a knuckle on the open door. "Syringe change, Thomas. Okay if I come in?" He walked in anyway, carrying a fresh jug of drinking water. He put a drop in a beaker, held my head as he removed the mask and let me drink. He talked as he worked. "Thomas needs his rest, Inspector. We're well past visiting hours, and I'm sure you can come in another day. Can I get to the machine, please?"

Gilhooly backed away from the bed.

"How you feeling?" Nurse Rowan said.

I blinked.

"Worn out I bet. Too many visitors aren't good. You need your rest. Matt Darcy's been at your bedside since I last changed this. I know you two are close, so I allowed it. Hasn't changed has he? Still full of questions. But not as many questions as Inspector Gilhooly, no doubt." Nurse Rowan flipped open the cartridge, pressed buttons to silence the alarm, replaced the syringe. He checked the cannulas in my arm. "You're all set for a few more hours." He turned to face

Gilhooly. "I'm about to go off-shift, Inspector. Can I escort you out?"

Gilhooly stepped towards the bed. "It's not looking good for you, Thomas."

I was unsure if he meant my illness or the murder charge.

"I'd advise you to arrange a solicitor."

My solicitor was busy. I would not be distracting her from her task.

"I'll be back tomorrow. In the meantime, be sure not to die on me."

Nurse Rowan creased his brow. "Inspector?"

Gilhooly paused on the way out. A spider's grin. "I'll pray for you, Thomas."

Prey for me, more like. I would not allow that to happen.

Nurse Rowan leaned across me, patted the ends of my pillows. "You look pale, Thomas." He laid the back of his hand against my forehead. "You all right?"

I managed the slightest of nods.

"Seen the eyes on that fella?" Nurse Rowan was trying to calm me. "Thomas, listen. I'm in again in the morning. Let me know if you need me do anything. The solicitor, for example. Get some rest, now."

I gave Senior Nurse Rowan sufficient time to leave the hospital.

The corridor was quiet.

I reached for the pump. The machine buzzed as soon as I flipped open the enclosure paddle. I extracted the syringe, pressed random buttons to shut down the alarm.

The buzzer continued to sound. I thought of Alma, the episode in the visitors' room, alarms in the corridor, nurses running. I had to act fast.

I pressed the plunger on the full syringe. Don't rush.

A distant voice in the corridor. "Check on Mister Cassidy, please."

Further away. "I'm at this, Philomena."

Press.

"Make Mister Cassidy your priority, please."

Ease it in.

"I've the one pair of hands, only."

Push.

"Now, please. Can't you hear the alarm?"

I didn't intend to be available for the interview tomorrow.

"A few more staff on rota wouldn't go amiss."

My breathing eased as the morphine kicked in. Was breathing easier or had it, somehow, become unnecessary?

I thought about Matt Darcy, and Ryan Matthews, and Zhoro Boguslav, and the bottle of Rigas Black Balsam. My living wake. Matt Darcy had arranged it. Inspector Michael Gilhooly had fouled it up.

Lightning flashed in the window.

The storm was receding. I counted its withdrawal. One, two.

Press.

Thoughts of Alma. Three, four.

Footsteps, close. "I'm seeing to it, Philomena."

I thought of Noleen, my baby girl. She'd be four or five now. I couldn't remember which.

Five. Thoughts of Rhiannon. Sweet Rhiannon.

A breathy voice at the door. "Holy be to God." A yell. "Philomena! Come quick!"

Six. Six miles away and counting.

"You shouldn't be in here, Miss."

"Tommy?" Rhiannon's voice, as if in a dream.

"Miss, step clear of the doorway!"

I didn't hear the thunder.

Chapter 52

For long, drawn-out moments, I am not myself. I can't feel me. It's as if I'm within myself, looking out through the windows of my eyes, dashing around inside my head to catch noises that enter my ears.

I am the least me I can be.

I only inhabit me.

I am dead or dying, and the disconnect is strangely settling.

"Oh, thanks be to fuck, Tommy."

I listen, yet I am sure the woman I hear is only a part player in the images and thoughts of the slumber I've just emerged from. A character from the storybook of my suspended consciousness. My storybook. The one I can read in my sleep.

I look out at her. What I see pleases me.

"How do you feel? I was warned you might never stir again." Her voice has changed since London, the syllables having settled into their native stresses and pitches. The warmth of it brings pleasure.

I feel a little more me.

"I need to talk to you." She shuffles closer in her seat.

Rhiannon always needed to talk.

I work my cannula'ed hand up to my face to find my mask gone. I summon my strength, send a word from my mouth. "What?" That's all I can manage.

"What 'what'? What day of the week is it? What am I doin here?" Rhiannon stands. The bedrail rattles as she pushes against it. "Hello to you, too." She tilts her head, gazes down at me. Her face is all contrasts: black hair, fair skin, dark violet eyes, red lips. She looks like a film star.

I'm comforted by the sadness in her eyes and the smile on her lips.

"To come home was the least I could do," she says. "Heard you were in bother. Felt a little responsible, so I did. That bastard Hughes, my friendly neighbourhood thug, nearly got you locked up." She lifts her face to the window. "I nearly got you locked up."

It seems a lifetime since the visit from Inspector Gilhooly and my failed episode with the morphine. I'm convinced there is nothing I am able to do right.

She purses her lips, steels herself. "I was here, Tommy. When they caught you."

Cool sunlight floods the hospital room.

"You were tryin to do yourself in. Scared the shite out of the whole bloody place."

The top window sash has been lowered a tiny fraction. An invasive breeze whistles in the smell of damp, dying leaves.

Rhiannon's hair is held off her face by two clasps of blacks and golds and siennas. A confusion of autumnal colour.

"Were you really tryin to kill yourself, Tommy?"

I say nothing. Talk is impossible.

"Finish what Alma started, was that it?" She reaches, runs a finger across my forehead to align my sleep-hair fringe. "It's grand," she whispers. "No-one can see me."

I savour her touch.

"I opened Alma's bloody letter," she says. "Remember I told you she sent me a letter?"

A slow blink is all I can do.

"It was a shocker, Tommy. The bitch was set to kill you. Did you not realise?"

It was no more than I deserved.

"She said as much in the letter. It's all in there. How she talked you into gatherin the tablets. How she convinced you to start takin them. She said there was nothin you wouldn't do for her, that she had you on a leash. A leash of guilt is how she described it. I thought, what the fuck is she on about? I couldn't believe what I was readin. She was mad you didn't stay in London. She wanted proper rid of you, Tommy."

I know all this.

"When you called to tell me about Alma's funeral, you sounded dreadful on the phone. That phone call came back to me when I read the letter. No wonder you sounded so bad. You reminded me of how Mammy sounded before she died."

What was she suggesting?

"When I heard what Hughes said to Inspector Gilhooly, I thought Gilhooly needed to see what she wrote."

Rhiannon had shown Gilhooly the letter. On another day I might have found Gilhooly's incursion disturbing.

"Why didn't you do somethin, Tommy?"

I have no reply.

"Listen, though. I need to tell you. The letter held some other news that I didn't pass on to the feckin inspector." She hesitates, as though asking for permission to continue.

I stare my consent.

Rhiannon leans back her head, checks the doorway, bends her body over me. "Alma found out," she whispers.

I watch her through the eye-windows, waiting.

"About us. You and me. In Buckley's. Your wedding."

The wedding night. The alcove. Alma knew.

I have no reaction. It's too late for regrets.

"Alma became close to Buckley's wife." Rhiannon talks rapidly, anxious to get this over with. "Nursed her when she was ill, or something. While you were in London. Typical of Saint Alma to be a bloody street angel." A glance at the door. "Apparently, Buckley's wife heard us the night of the wedding."

I am not capable of a response, but I am amused by my indifference.

"That was probably my fault." She widens her eyes, stretches her red lips. "The noise I was at. Sorry. She came downstairs and bloody saw you. Us. Both of us. In the alcove."

Rhiannon's cheeks colour, but only faintly.

"Can you imagine?" She coughs to clear her throat. "Anyhow, she told Alma all about it. Too embarrassed to confront us, apparently. But obviously not too embarrassed to make sure she informed Alma."

I search for regret in Rhiannon's eyes. I come away empty-handed.

"Missus Buckley was lying on her death bed and told Alma everything. Virtually the last feckin thing that came out of her mouth before the cancer took her off to work in that great public house in the sky. What do ya think of that?"

I think nothing of it. I have no remorse left. In the chamber of my head, I file it away under 'No Longer Matters'.

"Wait a fuckin minute," Rhiannon said. "Jesus Christ. Do ya think Alma had anything to do with Missus Buckley's tablets? She could be a fuckin mass murderer for all we know. Mammy, Missus Buckley, then you. Saint Alma, the mass murderer." Rhiannon laughs away the suggestion. "Remember," she says. "I was the lad who warned you about Alma. Didn't I warn you? Never thought she'd try to kill off the whole town, but." She smiles. "Ah, Jesus, I shouldn't be laughin. I'm sorry. But this is so fucked up. The whole thing. Fucked up to hell. My own sister writin letters to me about how she knows all about how I shagged her husband on the night of her weddin. And how she had set about overdosing you with tablets in revenge. How fucked up is that?"

She rattles the bedrail, looks away. When she turns back there are tears. "You fucked it up, Tommy. You. Letting me leave. The baby. Why didn't you come with me? No wonder I ended up fuckin marrying John fuckin Kavanaugh? It was your blasted fault, Tommy."

Most things are my fault. She is right, I should have talked her out of going to England and kept her here with the baby.

"I loved you, Tommy Cassidy." She rubs an eye with the heel of a hand, leaves a dark smudge on her cheek. "Probably always loved you."

She catches me staring out at her. "Sorry." She turns, wipes her face, blows her nose into the tissue. "I'm sorry," she says and regrips the bedrail. The used tissue bulges from her tight fist.

It's me who should be sorry, not Rhiannon.

"Nothin makes any sense no more."

If it was a story in a book, it would have to make sense. Dexter McEvoy told me that. "In storybooks, everything must make sense. In real life, nothing has to make sense." Something like that, he said.

"Listen, Tommy." She fights more tears. "I'm away back to London in the morning. I could only take a week, or the fuckin Post Office will have a hernia or something. I've got to go back." The tears come, despite the bravado. "Your solicitor has been in touch. Told me about the money." A rapid wipe at both cheeks. "But there's somethin else. She told me to tell you. It's about the land. Your land. She thinks she can challenge the sale of your land to John."

I'm filled with a warmth that cannot be explained by the sunlight from the window. I'm hollowed, drained and ready to die, but the relief makes everything seem worth it.

"The solicitor said..."

I want to sit up. I want to tell Rhiannon all about Noleen. I blink my eyes closed and imagine Rhiannon as the irresponsible loving aunt who'd buy Noleen too many sweets, advise on what vegetables to dislike, teach her improper words, how to tease the boys. But I cannot sit up, cannot talk. I breathe easy, relax. The mattress seeps up around me, as if to envelop my remains.

"The solicitor told me," Rhiannon says. "She said you left it all to me and the children." Bulbous tears with light-grey trails descend her pale cheeks. "No-one's ever...I don't know what to say, Tommy."

I stir my head: nothing. There is nothing she has to say.

The tissue is released from its crushing, opened out, pressed to her face. "I don't know what to do..." Her shoulders hitch as she sobs.

I recall the touch of her shoulders.

"I should have met you when you came to London."

I close my eyes.

"I would've seen how bad you were."

This is nonsense. She is in danger of spoiling everything, just as I did all those years ago.

"There's something more, Tommy. Something you should know before...Before it's too late."

I try to work another smile into my face, to reassure her, to let her know that everything is all right, that she doesn't have to say anything. The effort is too great.

"That night in Buckley's," she says. "You and me. I've no regrets about that night."

I drift away, come back.

"And it couldn't matter less who saw us." Rhiannon liked to talk, one of the things I loved about her, but her voice was fading in and out.

"Because, Tommy. That was the night me and you made Ronan. My eldest son."

It takes a while to absorb and process.

"Our eldest son. Ronan is yours, Tommy. It's right that you know. I want you to know. He's eighteen this year. A man."

Pride. That's what I feel. A smile comes. I smile with pride. Is this what achievement feels like?

"He's good to his mother, and he has your eyes. People say he looks like the actor, Montgomery Clift, but I know he looks like you. The image." Her giggle sounds like celestial music. "Seems I only have to be in the same feckin room as you for me to get pregnant."

She leans away from the bed, disappears from view.

A panic flares. I dart to the windows of my head, search for her.

She returns, wipes tears from her face. "I'm going on," she sobs. "I'm sorry. I'll be quiet." The bedrail squeaks as she collapses it flat. She scrapes her chair closer, takes my hand in hers. "Do you mind?"

Of course I don't mind.

"I won't fall pregnant holdin yer hand, will I?"

I have a son. His name is Ronan.

"I'm here, Tommy. I'll wait with you."

And she does.

Until the end.

Acknowledgements

My sincere thanks to those who made suggestions and commented on early drafts, in particular: Joan Carey, Jem Lough, Lorraine Morrell, Chris Carey, Chris Devane, Emma Roach and Ellen Lessner.

Also by Dennis Carey

Printed in Great Britain
by Amazon

54475662R00158